# the archipelago game

# the archipelago game

a novel

**DOMINIC MARTELL**

db
DUNN BOOKS

Copyright © 2023 by Dominic Martell

All rights reserved.

For information, including permission to reproduce this book or any portions contained therein, please visit www.dunnbooks.com.

Published by Dunn Books. First edition December 2023

This title is also available as a Dunn Books ebook.

This book is a work of fiction. Any references to historical events, real people, or real places, are used fictitiously. Other names, characters, places and events are products of the author's imagination. Any resemblance to actual events, places, or people living or dead—is pure coincidence.

Dunn Books and its logo are registered trademarks of Adam Dunn, Inc.

Library of Congress cataloguing-in-publication data is on file with the U.S. Copyright Office.

HARDCOVER: ISBN 979-8-35094-127-2
PAPERBACK: ISBN 978-1-951938-20-8
EBOOK: ISBN 978-1-951938-21-5

Book design by Archie Ferguson
Maps design by Joe LeMonnier

Manufactured in the United States of America

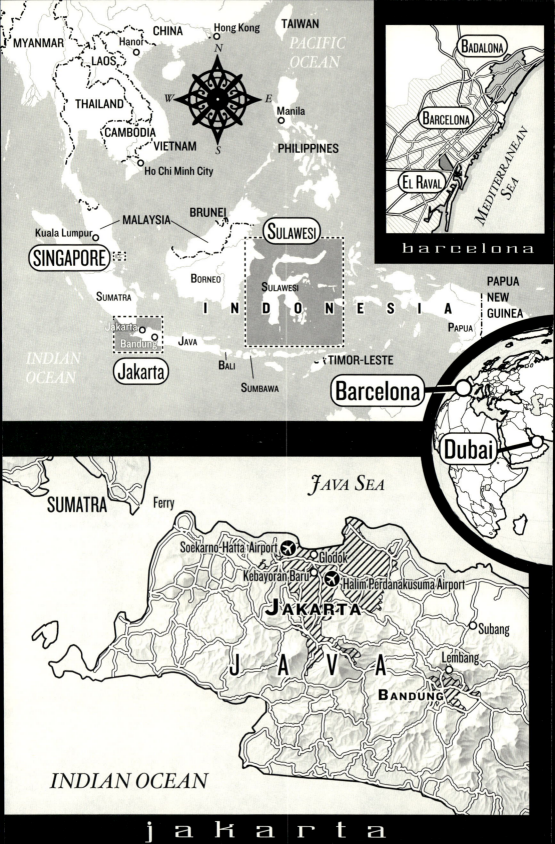

the

archipelago

game

# 1

Heaven is Badalona, thinks Pascual, on a bright spring morning with the sea sparkling down at the end of the street under a sun that has just cleared the horizon. He hauls the chalkboard with the day's menu choices out onto the sidewalk and positions it, then stands in the doorway of the bar for a moment with his hands on his hips, contemplating his contentment.

Nobody could ever claim that Badalona was heaven, but according to Pascual's lights the converse rings true. He has learned to cherish the little parcels of bliss that come his way in a life that against all expectations, and arguably quite undeservedly, has wound up a reasonably happy one. Bliss is a sea breeze in his face with a busy day ahead, dispensing coffee and spirits here in a working-class town on a grubby stretch of seashore. He turns and goes inside.

Powering up the big six-spout Italian espresso machine, Pascual feels like an engineer preparing to take a steamer out into the roads. As it hisses gently he takes the inverted chairs from the tables and sets them on the floor, scans for any dirt old Prats might have missed while sweeping up the night before, sets cups on saucers in a line on the zinc countertop, preparing for the rush.

Bliss is a slightly seedy neighborhood bar just opened in the morning, waiting for the first customer, waiting for the hum of talk and the clink of crockery, waiting for whatever spectacle another day will bring. Heaven is where you are, thinks Pascual, leaning on the bar surveying his domain, at least until it's not.

■■■■

When Anna walks into the bar Pascual knows instantly why she is there. The sight of her freezes him in his steps, and he stands for a moment, *café amb llet* in hand, watching heaven recede in the rearview mirror and thinking it was nice while it lasted. He smiles at her and resumes his trajectory to deliver the coffee. Here it is, thinks Pascual, the inevitable. He has always known it could come at any time but lately has allowed himself to lapse into complacent denial.

Anna must have been a pretty child; as a young woman she was alluring in a petite and gypsyish way. In middle age she has become a gnome, gray locks straggling from beneath a velvet turban, a sash at the tiny waist bunching somebody's castoff silk dress. The eyes are still there, dominating the little moon-face more than ever, dark and intense. She looks like a witch, a sorceress, an *hechicera*. "You don't answer your phone," she says, hiking herself up onto a barstool, settling herself like a queen on her throne, adjusting her scarves.

Pascual shrugs. "Sometimes I forget to turn it on."

"Never mind. It's good to be prodded out of my routine. I haven't been to Badalona in years. So this is where you've gone to earth," she says, looking around, returning the stares. "I wouldn't have predicted it. Can you make me an infusion? *Camamilla?*"

"Of course." Pascual fetches the chamomile tea and then attends to a flurry of other orders. When he finally has a moment, he drifts back to Anna and says, "So who was it? A big burly *yanqui* in a trench coat and fedora, or did they send somebody less conspicuous?"

Anna blinks at him over the rim of her cup. "It was a *yanqui*, but he wasn't particularly big. He had good Castilian, with a Mexican accent. No more conspicuous than your average tourist lost in the Raval. He seemed to have trouble believing I was the right person to talk to."

Pascual laughs gently. "He was probably expecting the usual delinquent. There is significant overlap between intelligence agencies and the underworld."

"I confess he caught me off guard with that nonsense about your cousin in New York. I'm afraid it took me a moment to remember the correct response. I never really believed you were serious about all this. Mysterious strangers and secret passwords, *què bestiesa.*"

"It seems to have worked. They have no record of my whereabouts, but here you are, with a message from them, no doubt."

"Yes. They are anxious to talk to you." Anna pulls a business card out of her sleeve and slides it across the bar to Pascual. "Be here at two o'clock this afternoon. He said to tell you, that's an order, not a request."

Pascual looks at the card: *Import Export Barcino* with an address on the Via Augusta in the sprawling city just across the river. "I have to work this afternoon."

"I did not get the impression he will be swayed by that. He said there were conditions attached to their protection, and the first one is, when they want you, you show up."

Pascual stows the card in his pocket. "Well. It's nice to be wanted. I'll try to be there."

■ ■ ■ ■

"Who's the little number in the fortune-teller getup?" The man behind the desk is American, pale and severely groomed. He is lean and fit, somewhere in his forties, graying, with eyes the color of a cold winter sea. He introduced himself as Gardner, which is almost certainly not his real name. "I thought she was going to ask to read my palm."

"She's a feminist scholar, a respected academic and author of a comprehensive history of rape as a political and military tactic. I hope you were polite to her." Pascual tries to keep his expression blank, watching the superior smile fade from the American's face. Through the window behind the desk he can just see the tops of the trees on the Via Augusta, a short way above the Diagonal, where the street begins to climb in a graceful curve, following the contours of the land and the old Roman road that gave it its name.

Frowning now, Gardner says, "No disrespect intended. I assume you chose her as your cutout because there is no traceable association between you."

"We have been friends for years, based on chance encounters in bars and on the street."

"Why are you still here? Lester Gray could be living in New York, perfectly legally. When we go to the trouble of providing someone with a new identity, they are usually grateful enough to make an effort to embrace it."

"Oh, I'm happy to have the passport. I just don't want to live in exile. And I certainly don't want to die there. Badalona's perfect. Nobody I know ever sets foot there except my wife. She grew up there and still has one connection, an old widow who lets us meet in secret, like Romeo and Juliet, in her house. I've got a place to lay my head, a job that pays me in cash under the table, and I only have to cross the railroad tracks to get to the beach. What more could a man ask?"

Gardner smiles, but the effect is not amiable. "Well, I hope the old widow keeps her mouth shut. We went to a lot of trouble to sell the idea you're on the run, far away. Thanks to some cyber manipulations on the part of our computer wizards, there's evidence Pascual March has been spreading money around in Brazil and Argentina."

"Ah. My wife and son have been telling people they think I'm in France."

"Well, confusion is good. The whole point was to convince people your wife and son have no idea where you are. Now, let's talk about your end of the deal. We have a job for you."

"I was afraid of that. Am I going to be Pascual Rose again?"

"You never stopped being Pascual Rose, did you?"

"I gave it my best shot. What's he supposed to be doing now?"

"What he always does. Engaging in speculative financial operations. Setting up holding companies, purchasing assets, making deals."

"How can he possibly still be in that business? He's got to be on every watch list there is. He ought to be in jail."

Gardner's expression is amused. "He has never been indicted for anything. The companies he controls are perfectly legitimate enterprises. He is listed as the beneficial owner, in compliance with all regulatory requirements. There are no cases pending against him, no warrants out."

"It's well known that he and Pascual March are the same person. And March is a fugitive, you tell me."

"March aka Rose seems to have left Spain and gone to Latin America, but he's not a fugitive. Nobody's looking for him. All the cases in which he was suspected of theft or money laundering have been resolved without any charges being brought."

Gardner delivers this deadpan, but Pascual fails to suppress a smile, admiring the formula that covers the stitch-up. "Well, that's a relief." He sighs, resigned. "So, what about this job?"

Gardner leans forward and reaches for a laptop on the desk. He taps at the keyboard, waits a few seconds and says, looking at the screen, "I've got Rose here. Ready to go?"

A voice from the laptop says, "Let's do it," and Gardner swivels it around to face Pascual. On the screen is another man behind a desk, this one older, approaching sixty perhaps, gray and bald and a little heavy, in shirtsleeves with a tie. At Gardner's muttered instruction Pascual adjusts the position of the laptop until his own face appears centered in the smaller window in the corner. "Mr. Rose," says the man on the screen.

"Whom do I have the pleasure of speaking to?" Pascual tries not to make it sound too snide.

"My name is Phillips. This little operation falls under my remit. It's a pleasure to meet you. I've heard a lot about you."

"That's not very reassuring," Pascual says.

"Oh, don't worry. I wouldn't say you're well known, exactly. You have a certain reputation in select circles, let's say."

"Well. Tell me about this little operation."

"Actually it's a fairly big operation. And as always, it has to be paid for. That's why we need you. You're the money man. You control a network of companies with a complicated ownership structure that makes it difficult to follow the money."

"Actually, I don't control anything. Not without the documents and the passwords."

"Don't worry, we'll get them to you."

"I see. And my job is to launder the money that's going to bankroll somebody's private army?"

On the screen Phillips makes a vague gesture. "Launder is such an ugly word. You'll channel operational funds to the right places, yes. Discreetly and perfectly legally. And if somebody does manage to trace the money back to you, you're a dead end. You're just a financial hustler based in Dubai with a shady reputation and no official connection to the agency. You're deniable."

"A professional scapegoat."

"If that's how you want to look at it. But you'll be compensated for your trouble and any risk you may run. All you have to do is play dumb, collect your fee, and go home."

"There's a fee, is there?"

"Of course there's a fee. How else can we insure your performance? We certainly don't believe in your loyalty. Your relationship with the agency has always been purely transactional, wouldn't you say?"

"That's certainly true." Pascual hesitates. "There's usually a stick to go with the carrot, in my experience."

Phillips's lips tighten in a grim smile. "Well, I wouldn't call it a stick. If you don't come through, we just stop protecting you, that's all. We'd have to cancel your passport, and if Pascual what's-his-name ever wants to get back on the grid again, I think he'd find things might start to catch up with him."

Pascual shakes his head in admiration. "No doubt. So, this job. Does it involve travel?"

"Of course." Phillips assumes a serious expression. "Have you ever been to Singapore?"

# 2

"Singapore." Pascual is beginning to feel a familiar mixture of dread and anticipation. "I'll have to learn Chinese."

"I think they all speak English out there. The Brits used to run it, you know."

"I know. Raffles and all that. Why Singapore?"

"Because that's where your contacts are, the people who are going to transfer the funds to your financial empire so you can pass them on to where we need them."

"And it can't be done remotely? You can't fake it all like you faked my spending spree in South America?"

Phillips looks irked. "What, you're having such a good time there in Barcelona, or wherever it is, that you'll pass up a free trip to Singapore? Number one, we're not faking anything. These are going to be real transactions. You're going to need to open bank accounts in Singapore, and that has to be done in person. And number two, the point is to sell Pascual Rose as the source of these funds if anyone ever asks. We want people to be able to testify that you came to Singapore and cut the deals. Any genuine investor would actually make the trip out there to talk to people, take advice, meet with potential staff, and so forth. You'll do all that, and there will be a record of it. That's your role. That's what makes you valuable to us."

Pascual chews on this for a moment, scowling. "How valuable can I be? You've stepped in more than once to keep me out of the newspapers and out of jail. At this point, surely Pascual Rose has to be tainted as a CIA stooge."

"All that's nothing but rumors. As far as anyone can prove, you're just another speculator on the international markets. Your identity is unshakable but your loyalties are vague. We don't care what people think as long as they can't prove anything."

Pascual shrugs. "So, who am I cutting these deals with?"

The irritation on Phillips's face eases. "You'll be thoroughly briefed. You'll need your American passport. You will get to Dubai as Lester Gray and switch over to being Pascual Rose there, in case anyone gets curious about your movements."

"You mentioned a fee. Can I ask how much it is?"

On the laptop screen Phillips nods once. "Of course. Given the amount of money you'll be handling and the time commitment required, we think a million dollars is a fair payment. The money will be deposited in any account you designate to us when you complete the job. You'll have to pay taxes on it, of course."

Pascual strives to look thoughtful. "A million," he says finally.

"What, it's not enough?"

What Pascual is thinking is that a million is a nice round figure, easy to remember, easy to promise, not obviously linked to any realistic assessment of amount handled or time committed. If you want to get a man's attention and have given little thought to actually funding the budget item, one million dollars is a figure that easily leaps to mind. "I don't know if it's enough. I don't know what the going rate for laundering someone else's money is these days. I do know that it's easy to promise somebody a million dollars when there's no contract involved, nothing in writing, no way to enforce payment. I guess I'm expected to take it on faith that the money will be there when I'm finished."

"Not at all," says Phillips. "We certainly wouldn't expect you to work without a contract. We've already drawn one up. Of course, it doesn't mention money laundering, which by the way is a highly inaccurate and misleading description of what we're asking you to do. It's a contract for consulting services rendered to a hedge fund domiciled in the Cayman Islands by one Lester Gray. Gardner there has a copy for you to look at."

On cue, Gardner slides several sheets of paper stapled together across the desk to Pascual. At the top of the first sheet Pascual reads *Consulting Agreement between BXD Ltd. and Lester Gray Consulting*. Pascual flicks through the four pages of the contract, his eye glazing as he skims over a thicket of legalese.

"It's boilerplate," says Gardner. "Most of it's there just to look good. If anyone ever gets curious and wants to see the expense reports and detailed invoices you're supposed to provide, we'll cook them up."

Pascual spots a key phrase: *the lump sum of one million USD, payable on completion of services*. "Completion of services as determined by whom?" he says.

"By us," says Phillips on the screen. "But look, we're not

going to be difficult. It's not in our interest to screw you. You're too useful, and you could make too much noise if you're unhappy."

Pascual gives that an indulgent smile. "What court do I sue you in if you don't come up with the money?"

There is a brief silence, and Gardner says to the screen. "Maybe it's time to show him the earnest money."

"Show him," says Phillips.

Gardner reaches into a desk drawer and comes out with a legal-sized envelope. He hands it to Pascual. "We figured you were not likely to have opened a bank account for Lester Gray. So we have to pay you your retainer this way."

The envelope is not sealed, the flap merely tucked inside. Pascual opens it and pulls out an inch-thick stack of one-hundred-dollar bills. He riffles the stack, shakes his head once and looks at Gardner. "How much is this?"

"That's ten thousand dollars. That should be enough to pique your interest. And get you to Dubai."

Pascual puts the stack of bills back into the envelope and sits holding it for a moment. He sighs. "That will be just fine, thanks." He taps the contract. "Do I sign this thing?"

"Right there on the dotted line," says Gardner. "Make sure you sign it the same way you did Lester's passport." He proffers a pen.

Pascual signs and shoves the contract away. "What happens now?"

Phillips says, "Short term, you need to get to Dubai the day after tomorrow. I'll meet you there and brief you. Now swing me back so I can see Gardner again, will you?"

Pascual complies and watches as the two spooks wrap up the proceedings. Gardner stabs at the laptop and turns to Pascual. "So. Everything clear?"

"Oh, yes. I've always appreciated the way the agency goes out of its way to make everything clear to all involved."

Gardner is apparently more inured to sarcasm than Phillips; he actually grins. "You're familiar with the expression 'on a need-to-know basis'?"

"It rings a bell faintly."

"Great. Then all you need to know is that Lester Gray has a reservation on the Emirates flight to Dubai the day after tomorrow. Booked on a BXD company credit card. We're paying Lester's way."

"Do I have a place to stay in Dubai?"

"Of course. That's Pascual Rose's base of operations, remember? You've got a pretty nice crib there. We'll make sure it's vacant when you get there."

"You let other people use my place in Dubai? I don't recall giving you permission."

Gardner gives Pascual's little joke the brief grin it rates. "It's an agency property that's available to anyone who needs it on legitimate agency business. We put people up there for short stays, a few times a year. But it's officially owned by you. When you get to Dubai, have the taxi driver take you to Planet Properties. That's a real estate office not too far from the airport. Ask for Mr. Gasparian. He'll give you the address along with the keys. He'll want to see your passport. He's expecting Lester Gray."

"I'll try not to disappoint him."

Gardner produces a cell phone from a drawer and slides it across the desk. "Here's Pascual Rose's phone. Phillips's number is listed in Contacts. Use this phone exclusively. Leave any others you have at home. You'll find the password on that sticker on the back. It's got top-of-the-line encryption and malware detection. You won't have to worry about being eavesdropped or hacked."

"You can guarantee that these days, with Pegasus and whatnot on the prowl?"

"The known vulnerabilities have been fixed. Of course, there could be new variants. But anyone who wants to implant Pegasus or some other zero-click attack on your phone needs to know your number. Don't give it out to just anyone. *De acuerdo?*"

To Pascual the accent sounds more Yank than Mexican. He shrugs. "Whatever you say."

■ ■ ■ ■

"It seems to me I've heard this one before," says Sara. She takes a sip of wine and sets the glass down. "Those spies are aways promising you a million dollars, aren't they?"

"Well, it happened once, yes."

"And it didn't turn out very well, as I recall."

"No."

"So what makes you think this time will be different?"

"Besides the ten thousand dollars?"

"That's a lot less than a million. It seems to me they just bought you at a very steep discount."

"That's quite possible." Pascual considers while he surveys

the spread on the table before him, olives and *gambas* and *pa amb tomàquet*. From the kitchen come soft clattering noises as the widow Quintana goes about her business. Pascual plucks an olive from the plate. "I know the passport's real. It got me back from Virginia after my little vacation there."

"I told you not to go."

"That was a condition of the arrangement, and the arrangement is to protect you and Rafael. They give me a new identity, Pascual March disappears, and in return I do jobs for them."

"But Pascual March hasn't disappeared. He's working at a bar here in Badalona."

"Prats knows me as Pascual Ferrer, if he ever thinks about my last name. He was so happy to find someone who would work cheap and off the books, he's not going to ask questions. It was the only way I could see to live near you and Rafa. In any event, it's over. I told him today I'm quitting."

"And what happens when you're done with this job the Americans want you to do?"

"Then it will be time to find a more permanent solution. Whatever solution we come up with, money will help. I think the million will be as real as the passport. And even if money doesn't mean much to me, it would be nice to have some to pass along to my wife and son. This is a chance to make up for twenty-five years of fecklessness. And a wealthy Lester Gray will find it a lot easier to pamper his Spanish mistress than a poor one."

Sara regards him with narrowed eyes, head canted slightly.

"Don't let your male ego lead you astray."

Pascual has to laugh at that. "I've been led astray by worse things."

# 3

Pascual considers himself an old Mideast hand, but Dubai is like nothing he has ever seen.

Many years ago, as a useful idiot employed by a Soviet-backed Palestinian terror gang, Pascual did time in a training camp in the bleakest part of Yemen, a sun-blasted moonscape. Later he lived for some time in Damascus, a sophisticated city and ancient center of civilization harried and scourged by five separate bodies of thoroughly modern secret police. Neither of those prepared him for the awestruck daze he finds himself in, slumped in the back of a taxi speeding down a twelve-lane superhighway through a corridor of skyscrapers, phallic spires from a fever dream piercing the desert sky.

If there is an old Dubai, Pascual has failed to catch sight of it; the Dubai he is racing through is thirty miles of explosive sprawl stretching southwest along the shore of the Persian Gulf. Mr. Gasparian of Planet Properties was unctuous and cooperative, delivering address, keys and access cards. Pascual Rose's bachelor pad is in a quarter called Al-Barsha twenty miles down, hypermodern and sterile, only a few shops at street level beneath the sleek ten- and twenty-story high-rises. The address Pascual gave the taxi driver is merely the name of a building in a numbered street.

Inside the glassed-in lobby, nobody questions him; a doorman hustles his luggage to an elevator and leans in to spare him the labor of pressing the button for the twelfth floor. The key works, the flat is clean and stocked with food and drink, and two hours after exiting the Emirates flight from Barcelona, Pascual is standing on a balcony with a scotch in his hand, looking at what oil money and globalized finance have wrought and wondering what the hell he is doing here.

Phillips answers his call on the second ring. "I'll be right over."

In person Phillips is larger than Pascual expected, middle-aged weight on a big frame, in a lightweight sport jacket, carrying an attaché case. His handshake is aggressive. "Welcome to Dubai. Ever been here before?"

"Never."

Phillips leads the way to the table in the dining area; he is obviously familiar with the place. He places the attaché case on the table and sits, waving Pascual to a chair. "Well, take a couple of days, relax a little. Get over the jet lag and get used to being Pascual Rose. Can I have some of whatever that is you're drinking?"

Pascual brings the bottle and another glass, with ice. Phillips pours himself a couple of thick fingers. "OK, forget Lester Gray. He's gone off to see the friend he's here to visit. That's why there won't be any record of a hotel stay if the question ever comes up. Meanwhile, you're gonna spread a little wealth around with your credit cards and make your reservations for Singapore."

"That sounds like it could be fun."

"I would hope so." Phillips raises his glass in a toast and drinks. "You want a rundown on the vice situation here, I can give it to you. You can have a pretty good time if you've got the money, but you have to be careful."

Pascual gives him a blank look. "I'm too old for that kind of fun. And I'm not sure my wife would approve."

"Oh, well. The wife." Phillips manages to convey that he gets the joke. He sets down his glass, pops the latches on the case and opens it. "So, you know the drill. You're the one who set up this whole financial empire, right?" He slides a manila envelope across the desk toward Pascual.

Pascual frowns at it. "I managed to follow instructions well enough to set up several fraudulent financial entities in various tax havens, yes. Knowing the drill would be stretching it."

"Well, the people in Singapore will help you."

"And who are they, exactly? What's their angle?"

"The main contact you'll be working with is a guy named Dexter Fang."

"Fang? As in tooth?"

"That's right. I don't think there's anything sinister about it. It's a common Chinese name."

"Like Dexter."

"A lot of Chinese people in Singapore and Hong Kong use English first names when they're dealing with Westerners.

Dexter's actually from Indonesia. You may be aware there are a lot of people of Chinese descent there. He has an Indonesian name, too, but in Singapore he goes by Dexter."

"So who's Dexter? A banker?"

"Not exactly. He runs a single family office."

"What's that?"

"It's a wealth management vehicle, a privately held company set up to handle the assets of a family group. Singapore has a lot of them. Very popular with rich Chinese families, both from the mainland and the diaspora. Dexter's an experienced money manager. He'll advise you on setting up your Singapore operation so you can start to collect the proceeds of the deals you'll swing out there. You in turn will arrange for these funds to be available to us, via a range of financial vehicles that Dexter will discuss with you. The structures you'll set up will be legitimate financial entities for the purpose of administering funds the agency uses in its operations in Asia."

Pascual reaches for the envelope. "So what do we have here?" He opens the envelope and spills the contents onto the desktop. Out slides a passport with a dark red cover with the words *UNJONI EWROPEA MALTA PASSAPORT* embossed in gold on it. Pascual opens it and sees himself staring glumly out of a photo next to the name ROSE, PASCUAL. He is all too familiar with this character and tosses the passport aside. Next is a United Arab Emirates residence permit for Pascual Rose with text in Arabic and English and the same photo. "I know you can buy a Maltese passport. Are these for sale, too, or is it a forgery?"

"Neither one. We have pretty good relations with Emirati

intelligence, and they were kind enough to provide this for us."

Pascual examines a wallet with an array of cards in the pockets: two credit cards, both platinum, a UAE driver's license, a card for international health insurance coverage with a British company, a membership card for an athletic club in Dubai, all in the name of Pascual Rose. "Is the health insurance for real?"

"It's for real. You break a leg in Singapore, you'll be covered."

"That's a relief." Pascual pulls a sheet of paper out of the envelope. "And this?"

"That's a list of the companies you own, with bank account numbers, passwords, and so forth. Online accounts where you'll find company documentation and statements. The things you need to know to function as Pascual Rose. So there's homework. You'll need to familiarize yourself with your holdings and know where to go to find the documents they'll want in Singapore. By the way, you have about three million dollars in the Cyprus bank account for your Maltese company."

Pascual's eyebrows rise. "That will buy a few nice dinners, I imagine."

"That's to purchase a property Fang will offer you for sale. That provides the pretext for your visit to Singapore. You're going out there to buy property, and anybody who checks will see a perfectly genuine transaction. And then you'll have a place in Singapore just like you do in Dubai. Don't bother to take possession of the title and the keys. We'll just discreetly pick them up from Fang at some point. And just in case you get any wild ideas, we're monitoring the account, and we'll cancel any withdrawal or any transaction that does not involve Fang."

"Please. I'm smarter than that."

"I hope so. Finally, when everything is up and running to our satisfaction, you will fly back here and contact me again. We'll discuss arrangements for paying your fee, and you'll hand over all documentation, passwords and so forth for the structures you've set up. Then you'll be locked out of everything. We don't really want you running the show long term."

"Of course not. Perish the thought."

Phillips eases off a little and says, "When you've made your travel arrangements, let Dexter know. You've got his contact information there on the sheet. He's expecting you. He'll probably arrange to have you met at the airport. You should make your own hotel reservation. Put it on one of the cards and treat yourself. You could stay at the Marina Bay Sands if you want. That's the one you see in all the photos, the spectacular building that looks like a surfboard laid across the tops of the supporting towers."

"Ah. Yes, I think I've seen the pictures. But if the idea is to be awed by the building, I'd look for another hotel that offers a good view of it."

Phillips rolls his eyes. "Whatever you want. So. Any questions?"

Pascual muses, sifting through documents with his fingertips. "Just one."

"What's that?"

"Who do I call when things go belly-up?"

"Nothing's going to go belly-up. It's a simple series of procedures, entirely legal, as I told you."

Pascual stacks the documents, squares the edges, clasps his hands. "Humor me. I've done this before. I know how it goes. The only reason I'm not in prison is that somebody from the agency always shows up to bribe or threaten or sweet-talk the right people and spring me out of jail. For once I'd like to be ready in advance. Who's my Get out of Jail card?"

"Fang and his people are there to help you. If anything goes wrong, they'll handle it."

"And they're hip deep in it from the start. It's their ball game. Who's there to bail me out if the thing blows up? What's plan B? Can I call you at three o'clock in the morning?"

"The number you called me at here will be disabled as soon as you fly out. Delete it from your contacts."

"So who's my emergency contact? Does Fang know how to get in touch with you?"

"Fang doesn't know I exist."

"Terrific. Look, it's not that I don't trust your pal Fang. But I've done this enough to know that there's a million ways things can go wrong. And if that happens, I want *you* to know about it, and fast. If I can't get in touch with the guy who sends me out there, I don't go out there."

Phillips sighs. "You can't contact me directly. Officially and for the record, we have never met and never will. If you need emergency help in Singapore, something Fang and his people can't handle, there are assets there you can contact, and they'll get a message to me. But it would be a last resort, for emergencies only."

"Wonderful. Who do I call?"

Phillips frowns, reaching for his phone. "Let me get back to you on that. I'll have to see what we've got out there."

Pascual shakes his head. "So you were just going to leave me dangling if something went wrong? I'm glad I asked."

"Nothing's going to go wrong. I'm telling you, Fang and his people are first-rate. They'll handle whatever comes up."

"The crew of the *Titanic* was first-rate. It still would have been good to have a few more lifeboats."

"There are no icebergs in the Strait of Malacca," says Phillips, smirking.

"There are sharks," says Pascual. "And if the ship goes down, I want to be rowing for shore, not swimming."

# 4

Pascual anticipated a visually dramatic approach to Singapore, sweeping in over the Strait of Malacca, the vastness of Asia spreading to the horizon. Sadly, he neglected to specify a window seat, and he has had to content himself with following the track of the jetliner on the screen in front of him, stuck in the middle of the cabin. After seven hours, it has ceased to amuse.

He exchanged texts with Dexter Fang last night, and the last message he received said *You will be met at the gate.* Pascual is expecting the standard flunky in coat and tie, holding up a sign with his name, and he spots him as he emerges from the tunnel: Chinese, diminutive, middle-aged, morosely surveying the trickle of arriving passengers. But the name on the placard is not his, Pascual sees as he draws near, and he is startled by the woman who steps toward him and says, "Mr. Rose?"

She is a different proposition altogether: tall, of indeterminate ethnicity but unmistakably female in a sleek fawn jacket and skirt, wavy dark hair gathered behind her head. Most arresting of all, she is smiling at him and extending her hand. "Welcome to Singapore."

"Thank you." Her grip is firm, her smile brilliant, her eyes as black as night. A delicate whiff of scent comes with the smile. Pascual realizes he is gaping at her. "I'm sorry, I wasn't sure who to look for."

"I'm Renata Taggart, Mr. Fang's assistant. I'm here to help you with the arrival procedures."

Pascual rouses himself. "Oh, that's very kind."

She steers him gently by the elbow away from the gate. "Was the flight all right?"

"Pretty much as expected. Long."

"Is this your first time in Singapore?" On top of the perfect caramel skin and the cascade of mahogany hair, the voice is silky and cultivated, with an accent Pascual cannot quite put his finger on. Not British, not quite American, a deracinated, supranational English, elegant enough.

Pascual makes an effort to watch where he is going. "First time in Asia. East Asia, anyway. I've spent some time in the Middle East."

"Well, we will try to make sure you enjoy your visit."

This is a good start, thinks Pascual. Her coloring could be Mediterranean, but something in the face says farther east. Persian? Indian? A complicated gene pool, probably, and a favorable one. To his surprise she has ushered him to a shuttle cart of the kind he has always associated with the elderly and infirm, and she is evidently expecting him to mount it. A smiling Asian youth stows his bag at the rear and slides behind the wheel. Pascual climbs aboard and Renata Taggart sits beside him. "I'm going to take you to a lounge where you can relax while I see to your luggage."

The cart purrs into action and Pascual tries to enjoy the ride. The airport is opulent, filled with potted greenery. Tinkling piano music is just audible over the hollow murmur of crowds in large spaces. Pascual is tongue-tied and feels he is cutting a poor figure. "You're working overtime tonight," he says finally. "I'm sorry you have to devote your evening to this."

"All part of the job. Mr. Fang would have been here himself, but he's engaged elsewhere tonight. I'll get you settled, and we'll make arrangements for tomorrow."

"Wonderful. I have a reservation at the Mandarin Oriental."

"Actually, I've taken the liberty of cancelling your reservation there. Mr. Fang has instructed me to put you up at one of his properties near Holland Village."

"Oh? And where's that?"

"A few miles on the other side of the central area. Just beyond the Botanic Gardens. He's got a bungalow there. I think you'll find it's just as comfortable as the Mandarin Oriental."

"I'm sure it will be fine." A bungalow sounds tame by comparison with the swanky hotel bar Pascual was looking forward to, but it occurs to him that there may be compensations if Ms. Taggart's instructions will stretch to a nightcap in the living room.

The lounge where he is deposited is darkly paneled, softly carpeted, warmly lit. It contains its own passport control station, where Renata assists Pascual in submitting his electronic arrival card and contending with a bored immigration officer who duly admits him to Singapore for ninety days. Pascual surrenders his baggage check to Renata and watches her in wonder as she glides out of the room. She reappears a few minutes later, talking on her phone, along with a porter wheeling his luggage on a cart. She ends the call and says, "Just a quick customs procedure and we should be good to go. I've called the driver and he's bringing the car round."

The customs check is perfunctory and they proceed to an exit. It is only when Pascual steps out of the air-conditioning into the Singapore night that he realizes he has arrived. The air is heavy and warm, bearing a smell like nothing he has experienced before, something rich and organic. Renata smiles. "Yes, we are in the tropics. Singapore couldn't function without air-conditioning."

"Very different from the Middle East. It smells like . . . I don't know, a garden. A jungle maybe."

Renata looks amused. "I must be used to it. All I can smell is automobile exhaust."

Pascual looks away, fearing he sounded fatuous. After a moment Renata says, "Not much jungle left, I'm afraid. But gardens, yes, lots of those. Here's Archie with the car."

■ ■ ■ ■

An hour later Pascual is standing bemused in the midst one of those gardens, stupefied by sensory overload and temporal dislocation. Palm fronds wave above him, dark against the urban glow, and if there is any car exhaust to be detected it is overwhelmed by the scent of the orchids, bougainvillea and hibiscus he can just make out around him in the dark. A glimmer of water beyond the honeysuckle hints at a swimming pool. He turns to survey the back of Dexter Fang's little bungalow rising above him, with its balustraded galleries and tile roof, discreetly floodlit.

The ride from the airport took him on fast roads through the center of Singapore, with a close view of a glittering skyline as hallucinatory as Dubai's, past endless ranks of high-rises and finally into quiet streets with glimpses of lighted windows through foliage. By the time Archie pulled up in the forecourt and Renata Taggart handed him over to the elderly couple who run the house, the small talk had died, and Pascual was feeling once again like the peasant admitted to the manor house, hoping his feet are clean and suppressing an urge to tug at his forelock. After agreeing on plans for the morning, Renata Taggart took her leave with cool professionalism while conferring one of her blinding smiles.

Careful, Pascual thinks. There is no space in this undertaking for even idle flirtation, and you will need your wits about you. He rouses himself and walks back up onto the terrace and through the French doors into the house. The soft lamplight shows the solid teak furniture, the silk tapestries, the pottery, the jade, the flowers, all to great advantage. He wanders into a larger room and stands for a moment orienting himself; which way to the stairs?

"Would you care for something to drink before you retire?"

Startled, Pascual turns to see Mr. Tan the butler in a doorway. Pascual barely noticed him when introduced, distracted as he was by the opulence of the setting. Now he sees a Chinese man of slight build and advanced age, though still trim and erect, his hair still black, in a white shirt and black trousers. The question was spoken in an English that displayed only the slightest accent.

Pascual just blinks at him for a moment before answering. "Yes, thank you. That would be nice. Uh . . ."

"Whisky? Cognac? A cocktail? Or something without alcohol?"

"Oh, definitely with alcohol, I think." Pascual flashes what he hopes is a disarming smile. "Cognac, if you've got some handy."

Mr. Tan nods and retreats through the doorway. Pascual looks around and decides that he is not likely to soil this gold brocade sofa too badly if he sits on it. He is pretending to study an intricately carved ivory vase on a table at his elbow when the butler reappears with a glass of shining amber on a tray. Pascual takes it and says, "Thank you, that's very kind."

"Not at all," says Tan. "It's what I'm paid to do."

Pascual thinks he detects a glint of humor in the man's eye. "Thanks anyway," he says. "Say, tell me something."

Tan halts, eyebrows raised. "Yes?"

"Mr. Fang lives elsewhere, is that correct?"

"That's correct."

"How many of these little bungalows does he own?"

"Mr. Fang has several residences. When he is in Singapore he usually stays in his flat in Marina Bay."

"And when he's not here, he's where, in Indonesia?"

"Sometimes, yes. He travels a great deal."

Tan's face has settled into an expressionless mask, and Pascual senses he is reaching the limits of discretion. "Well," he says. "I look forward to meeting him."

Tan sketches a little bow. "I'm sure the feeling is mutual."

Pascual nurses his cognac, looking around the immaculate room and thinking about people who have so much money that their guest houses could be museums. This is the company you are keeping, thinks Pascual. And they in turn are keeping strange company, at a nexus of money and covert power.

Be wary, Pascual thinks.

# 5

"Think of it this way," says Dexter Fang. "You're the cash machine. And we're the fellows in the armored car that comes around to replenish it." Fang grins, swiveling back and forth in his chair. To Pascual it looks as if he is perched on the edge of a precipice; the wall just behind him is floor-to-ceiling glass, beyond which is a forty-story drop and a stomach-fluttering view of central Singapore, a thicket of skyscrapers and between them glimpses of the sea, ships riding at anchor far out in the roads.

"That should make me very popular," says Pascual. He is showered, shaved and outfitted in one of his Dubai purchases, an off-the-rack tropical linen suit. All he lacks is the pith helmet. Following a lavish but solitary breakfast served with mute efficiency by the Tan *ménage*, he was whisked to this citadel of finance in the Mercedes, the taciturn Archie at the wheel. Rested and fed, he is ready to take instruction on his role. "Will I be responsible for dispensing the cash?"

Fang shakes his head. He is fiftyish, plump, cheerful, a man who enjoys life. He wears a light blue linen suit and a tie that verges on the frivolous with a flowery design. "Not according to what I've been told. You must understand, I'm just cooperating with certain . . . parties with whom I've had business relationships in the past and who have requested my assistance. From what I know of these parties, my assumption is that they require a discreet method of directing funds to places where they are needed." Fang delivers all this in impeccable English, lightly accented with the slight lilt of the native Chinese speaker well educated in British English.

Pascual wonders briefly what's in it for Fang. Possibly a cut of the action. In any event, there is nothing surprising about connections between titans of finance and intelligence agencies, particularly in regions not easily accessible to congressional oversight. "They do seem to value discretion."

Fang flashes the grin. "Yes. I was told you would contact me regarding some investments you wish to make in Singapore. You want to acquire some real property in the region, for speculative purposes, and I have a few I would be happy to dispose of. That's the public part of the trip. I think we could call that the cover story. In addition, you wish to establish a permanent presence in Singapore with an eye to future activities. I believe that is the real interest of our mutual friends. They will of course guide those activities. My understanding is that all you need to do is set up your Singapore subsidiaries and designate a resident director and company secretary for each one. They'll carry out the day-to-day business of the subsidiary."

"And you'll provide me with the names."

"Of course. Or to be more exact, I have been provided with

the names."

Pascual nods. "Solid citizens and wise stewards of my wealth, I'm sure."

Fang hurries on. "Once we've taken care of all the paperwork, your role will be finished, at least for the time being. My understanding is that you will be willing to return in the future if more entities become necessary." He finishes with raised eyebrows, waiting for a response.

"Sure." Pascual shrugs, though his heart sinks a little at the idea. "So what's involved in setting up these subsidiaries?"

"Lots of red tape, of course. Renata will help you with that. Can you just remind me how many entities we're talking about? What exactly are you bringing to the table?"

Pascual unzips a leather portfolio and fishes out a sheet of paper. "My principal companies are these." He leans forward to lay the paper on Fang's desk. "Regenta Holdings Ltd., a BVI corporation. Mostly a vehicle for property companies with Brazilian real estate. Liaison Ltd., a Maltese corporation, another holding company, with subsidiaries in the logistics business, shipping and trucking. And a Luxembourg public limited company called Serapis, which has holdings in a variety of European banks." Pascual is reciting memorized descriptions; he set the companies up himself on a previous excursion into the world of obscurantist finance but has had no hand in anything that has been done with them since. "I would be happy to take advice on the most suitable way to make our mutual friends happy."

"Well." Fang looks pleased; after glancing at the paper he pushes it away. "You'll need Singapore subsidiaries to open bank accounts. Once you have the companies in place, they'll be able to issue invoices for services such as consulting, training, design, and the like, take loans or receive venture capital. In fairly short order, provided there's no hitch with the paperwork, you'll start to see money flowing into your accounts. At that point, your role will be completed. The director and company secretary you have designated will take care of everything from then on. That's the secret of good company administration, isn't it? Hire good people, delegate, and sit back and relax." Fang beams.

He's enjoying this, Pascual thinks. Moonlighting for intelligence agencies would provide a little spice in the life of a man who has everything. "How long is it all likely to take?"

"That depends on the completeness of your documentation, the workload at the registry office, things like that. Figure in opening the bank accounts, miscellaneous hoops to jump through, you'll be busy off and on for a few days. I can lend you Archie with the car. And I'm taking you to dinner tonight, at a little place I think you'll like. As for the red tape, Renata will assist you. She's done it quite a lot and is familiar with the procedures." Fang reaches for a button on a console on the desktop. "Things always go smoothly when Renata's in charge. She has a wonderful knack of getting people to do things for her."

Pascual smiles. "That I can believe."

∎ ∎ ∎ ∎

"Normally you would have to go through a professional corporate services firm," says Renata, jabbing deftly at the keyboard of a laptop. "But since we have staff who are experienced in this process, we can fill that role for you. It should only take a day or two, if there's no problem with the documents or the company name. When all that's done you can think about opening corporate bank accounts. That's another story all by itself."

Pascual nods, content merely to stare. Today she is in green, the forest color setting off the flawless tawny complexion delightfully, the mass of hair piled artfully on top of her head. Her desk is considerably messier than Fang's, but behind her is the same soaring view. Pascual digs in the portfolio. "I've got some documents here, and I can direct you to my online accounts for anything that might be missing."

Renata riffles through the papers he hands her. "All right, let's see. Certificate of registration of the parent company, documentation of the address of the company and the directors. . . . For what, three companies? Very good." Renata shoves the papers to one side and clasps her hands on the desk, frowning a little, a picture of complete professional competence in a distracting physical package. "I understand Dexter has some candidates in mind for the local representative of the company and directors of the subsidiary. I'll delegate someone to walk you through the paperwork this morning. This afternoon I understand you're to go and look at a number of properties around Singapore."

"Ah, yes. The main point of the trip."

Renata's frown eases. "I could delegate that, too, but I think I will take advantage of the opportunity to get out of the office and conduct the tour myself, if you have no objection."

Pascual is aware that the thrill he feels is utterly puerile. You are sixty years old, and a pretty face still has the power to do this to you, he thinks. "No objection whatever. I would be very grateful. I know your time is valuable."

"All part of the job. Shall we meet here at say, one o'clock?"

■ ■ ■ ■

"For three million dollars, there's a limited range of properties we can offer you," says Renata, steering one-handed along a tree-lined six-lane highway. "I'm afraid a bungalow is a little out of your reach."

Pascual tears his eyes away from the road, still discomfited by being on the left side of the car with no steering wheel in front of him. His eyes land on Renata's legs working the pedals, but he does not allow them to linger. "I'm not surprised. The word bungalow seems to be used a little differently around here from most places."

"Yes. Here it's short for Good Class Bungalow. That's a planning designation. It means a house of no more than two stories on a plot of at least 1,400 square meters. That's quite a large plot by Singapore standards. And ordinarily only native Singaporeans can get a license to buy one. As a foreigner the best you can do is probably a penthouse. We've got a couple of nice ones I'll show you, though for three million they won't be at the best address." Renata flashes him a brief smile by way of apology.

"That's all right. I wouldn't want to lower the tone in your better neighborhoods."

Pascual senses that she is trying to decide how seriously to take that. After a moment she says, "To be perfectly frank, Mr. Rose, if you have money, you can live anywhere you want.

Old Singapore money will always look down on new money. But they'll cash your check."

Pascual grins at this. "So fill me in, if you don't mind. Is Mr. Fang old money or new?"

"Mr. Fang? I'd say old money, but not Singapore old money. He's from Indonesia. His father sent him here in 1998, after the anti-Chinese riots, to set up the family office. A lot of people have done that, from all over Southeast Asia. Singapore's stable, with a good legal system, which is more than you can say for some of those countries. A lot of money is coming in now from China, too. The Chinese have gotten rich, but the party still has absolute power, and if the party wants to, it can crush you." She shoots Pascual a quick smile. "Sorry, excuse the political commentary. Anyway, Mr. Fang's done his best to become an anglophile Singapore Chinese. But most of his wealth is still in Indonesia."

■■■■

Pascual watches high-end real estate flash by as Renata takes a curve. "Well, I'm not rich enough to make anyone want to crush me, I hope. But I'm looking forward to seeing what three million bucks will get me."

■■■■

"The view," says Renata. "This is what three million will get you."

Pascual is not sure which view she means, whether the one out over rooftops and greenery to the distant Singapore Strait, or the one nearer at hand, a thousand square feet of luxury apartment occupying the top floor of a twenty-four-story building in

Novena, a neighborhood not terribly far inland from the spectacular bay, and as far as Pascual is concerned, with or without the view it will do quite nicely. "Sold," he says, turning to the view that interests him most.

"What, without seeing any of the other properties?" Renata is blinking at Pascual in disbelief.

Pascual is briefly tempted to level with her, to tell her it's all a charade anyway. He settles for the pose of a man with enough money to be careless with it. "I don't have to see any more. I like this one."

"Very well." Renata looks disappointed, and Pascual realizes that whisking clients around town in a fast car probably beats an afternoon in the office any day. Renata manages a smile and says, "You are a man who makes decisions quickly, I can tell."

Pascual wheels to survey his domain, hands in his pockets and a smile on his face. "Oh, yes. Some have even called me impulsive. It's gotten me in trouble a few times, I have to say."

"So, a productive first day," says Dexter Fang. "I think that's worth a toast."

Pascual has no objection. He hoists the glass into which the sommelier has just poured a pale golden, delicately effervescent wine out of a bottle tenderly swaddled in white linen and smiles across the table at his host. On Fang's right, Renata does the same. Beyond the glass wall is a breathtaking light show, central Singapore at night, geometric fantasies and a spectrum from cool blues to furnace orange reflected in the bay. Nearer at hand is an equally splendid view of a spread of dishes bearing crab with salted mullet roe, smoked bonito, razor clams and risotto with black truffles, with Anjou pigeon or roasted turbot to follow.

Glasses are clinked and the wine goes down smoothly. "So," says Fang. "Step number one is completed. I think you've made an excellent choice with the Thomson Road property. We should be able to get everything signed tomorrow for the sale. And then we'll move on to discussing your new Singapore subsidiaries."

"I look forward to it." Pascual is delighted with the luxurious penthouse he casually acquired this afternoon, but what he has been mostly looking forward to is this little welcome dinner, held in a private dining room of one of Singapore's toniest restaurants, with Renata in attendance. She has let her hair down, literally and figuratively, and is toying with her wineglass while looking splendid and regarding her two companions with queenly detachment.

"I congratulate you on your purchase," Fang says. "You know, I could have some furniture delivered and you could move in in a day or two if you want. I could even find you some domestic help."

Pascual laughs. "If it's all right with you, I'll stay in that cozy little bungalow you have me in now. Mr. and Mrs. Tan are taking good care of me."

"Ah, yes. They're wonderful, aren't they? They actually came with the house. I purchased it a few years ago from an electronics tycoon who was downsizing to a villa on Sentosa Island. He sold on condition the Tans had a position there for life. That is quite unusual, as servants tend to come and go. They are a classic Singapore story, humble origins, rose through hard work, made sure their children did better. They are the masters of the house. When my family comes to stay, they are under orders to mind their P's and Q's around the Tans."

"Where does your family usually live?"

"Oh, we're all over the map these days. The family home is actually in Jakarta, and my wife lives there most of the time. She only comes to Singapore for shopping sprees. I've got a son at university in the UK and a daughter in boarding school in

Switzerland. When they're not in school they like to party with their friends here. Me, I jump back and forth between here and Jakarta. I've got business interests all over Java and a few things on other islands as well. So I get a lot of use out of the jet."

Pascual cannot match the jet, but he knows he has a role to play, and he gropes for something suitably impressive. "I'm still dependent on the airlines, alas. But at this point I can keep an eye on things remotely for the most part, and these days a lot of my travel is just wanderlust. I've got homes in Malta and Dubai, and friends and connections all over Europe."

Fang puts on an inquiring expression. "And your original nationality is what, if you don't mind my asking? I've been trying to pin down your accent."

"The accent is Brooklyn, mostly. That's where I spent my adolescence. But I'm Spanish, originally, Catalan to be precise, and I lived in Paris for a few years. My ancestry and my loyalties are mixed."

Fang smiles. "Like our Renata here."

Pascual is pleased to have an excuse to look at her. She raises her eyebrows at Fang and turns a cool gaze on Pascual. "I am a Singapore mongrel," she says. "A product of British imperialism, no doubt a few sordid histories of men going native at lonely outposts. Scottish, English, Malay, Bengali, God knows what else on my father's side, English, Dutch, Javanese on my mother's. Raised a good Anglican girl right here in Singapore."

Pascual just admires her for a moment before saying, "Well. I would not attach the word sordid to anything that could produce such an impressive result." He knows he is laying it on thick, but one benefit of his advanced age is that she cannot possibly suspect him of making a pass.

Fang is amused. "I must tell you, Mr. Rose, sadly our Renata is spoken for. As you can imagine, there has been no shortage of suitors. And I believe there is now an official fiancé, isn't there, Renata?"

Her chin rises a degree or two. "He would like to think so. There has been no formal agreement."

Fang laughs. "You are not to be pressured, are you? Forgive me. I've been peeking at the society pages again. There was a lovely photo of the two of you in the *Straits Times* last week. What's his name again?"

She hesitates a beat before saying, "His name is Rohan Fernandes."

"And he would be with us tonight but for the press of work," Dexter says to Pascual. "He is one of Singapore's most eligible bachelors. From a prominent family, making a brilliant career in the law."

"The better to support me in the style to which I am accustomed," says Renata deadpan, making Dexter laugh.

"The style you richly deserve," says Pascual. He raises his glass to her and is gratified when she graces him with a smile.

*Club owner jailed, fined: The operator of an entertainment club in Singapore has been convicted under the Prevention of Human Trafficking Act for exploiting three women hired as dancers from India. . . .*

Pascual has read this one before. Wherever there are vulnerable young women with poor prospects, there are men on the prowl for them. He reaches for his cognac and sips, pausing for a moment after he sets the snifter down to admire his surroundings again. In the lamplight the statuary gleams; the house is quiet. Mr. Tan has brought Pascual's nightcap and glided away. Pleasantly tipsy, Pascual shakes his head in wonder and scrolls down on his phone, scanning the Singapore news.

*Editor found guilty of criminal defamation for accusing Cabinet of corruption.* This surprises Pascual; he was vaguely aware that political freedoms in Singapore were not quite what they were elsewhere in the advanced regions of the world, but throwing people in jail for criticizing the government puts Singapore in a class with less admirable places.

*Three years in jail, six strokes of the cane for man accused of molesting children.* The cane may be another sign of lingering barbarism, but the sentence strikes Pascual as too light. Make it ten or twenty, he thinks, and scrolls on.

*Regulatory squeeze wipes out billions in market value of Chinese companies. Disappearing Chinese tycoons prompt speculation. Chinese money moving to Singapore in wake of crackdown.* Here is a trend Pascual was only vaguely aware of. If China does not want its billionaires, it appears that Singapore will be happy to take them.

*Singapore Fintech sector on the rise. Monetary Authority of Singapore probes firms connected to Malaysia's 1MDB scandal. Singapore to host ASEAN summit. Singapore and Indonesia discuss bilateral cooperation and regional security.* Pascual reads about Southeast Asian finance and geopolitics until he loses focus and begins to doze. He shuts down the phone, drains the glass and rises to his feet, a little unsteadily. He knows he has drunk too much.

Tomorrow he will be onstage again, and he does not want to muff his lines.

▪ ▪ ▪ ▪

"I apologize for the delay, Mr. Rose. Thanks for waiting." The woman who lowers herself onto the chair across the table from Pascual is Chinese, not far past forty, impeccably dressed, with sleek black hair severely disciplined into a bun and the no-nonsense manner of a regimental sergeant-major going over duty rosters. Half an hour ago she introduced herself to Pascual as Mrs. Li before disappearing with the documents he handed her.

Pascual waves a hand, lazily. He has been admiring the usual upper-floor view, across the harbor and out over the Strait where something that must be Indonesia lies in the hazy distance. "Please. No worries. I understand there are procedures to follow. Boxes to check and figures to verify."

"Yes. Though the figures don't seem to be the problem here."

"Oh? There's a problem?" Pascual tries to feign surprise.

"I'm afraid so." Mrs. Li folds her hands on the tabletop and frowns at Pascual. "As you know, financial institutions must comply with a number of regulations designed to prevent illicit activity. Here in Singapore we take these things very seriously. And we find . . . how shall I put this? That when entered in our system, your name sets off certain alarms."

Pascual has been prepared for this; he assumes the expression of a man confronted with old and tiresome slanders but prepared to be indulgent. "Ah. No doubt I have been flagged as a suspicious character because of some accusations that were made in connection with an affair in Istanbul a couple of years ago. In that case my identity was stolen. In any event, my understanding is that the money in question was recovered, and no charges were ever brought."

"Be that as it may, you are listed on the Regulatory Enforcement List as having been named in official documentation by a law enforcement body. In addition you are cited for Reputation Risk Exposure, having been reported in the media as being involved in financial crime. And, according to certain reports, terrorism."

Pascual plays this for all it is worth, a deeply wounded expression settling slowly onto his features. "I am pained to hear this. As I said, I have never been charged with a financial crime. As for the allegations of terrorism, they relate to political activities in which I was involved as a youth. I have repudiated the views I held at that time, and cooperated fully with the agencies charged with investigating my actions. Again, I was never charged with a crime."

This is all true enough, though it was only a series of arguably cynical bargains that kept Pascual from being charged with any number of crimes. He assumes a chastened expression. "I was young and stupid. I have done my best to stay within the confines of the law ever since."

This, he realizes immediately, is not as solid a claim to probity as it might be, but it is too late to amend it. Mrs. Li gives it the skeptical look it deserves. "Well. Be that as it may, I'm afraid we cannot process your application for an account with us. In our judgment, if we were to allow you to open an account we would attract scrutiny from the Monetary Authority of Singapore. They are the principal regulatory agency in this field, and we take pains to follow their guidelines." She flashes a very brief smile. "Of course, you are free to approach other financial institutions if you wish. You may find one that is less discriminating than we are."

Pascual would be irked by her superciliousness if he did not thoroughly approve her judgment. He returns the smile as he rises. "Thank you for your frankness. I believe I will take my business elsewhere. I'm confident that an unbiased examination will find nothing to object to in my record."

"I wish you luck," Mrs. Li says, and her nod and smile are thoroughly gracious.

■■■■

"Don't worry," says Dexter Fang. "There are other banks." Fang seems unconcerned, swiveling back and forth on his chair. "Renata deals with these people all the time." He tosses things over to her with a look.

Renata is skeptical, Pascual can see. She says, "I'd bet he'll meet with the same response wherever he goes. Banks have gotten very careful about this stuff."

Fang gives it some thought, swiveling to look out at the view. He turns back and says, "You probably just didn't offer them enough money. What were you prepared to deposit?"

"Fifty thousand dollars. That's what's left in the Cyprus account after paying for the penthouse."

"That's pocket change. Let's up it to half a million. I'll shift some funds from one of my Delaware corporations to your bank in Cyprus. Let's call it a loan. Or whatever you want, a consulting contract maybe. Renata can help you with the paperwork. Once the money's transferred, make that your initial deposit. That will get the bank's attention. The prospect of a big deposit can overcome a lot of scruples. I can probably come up with a million for you. That should get you in the door at two different banks. And then we'll be off and running. OK?"

Pascual is speechless, watching high finance in operation. Renata and Fang trade a look and Renata nods. "OK." To Pascual she says, "I'll need the information for that account. Account number and SWIFT number. We should be able to get it done this afternoon."

"Just tell me where to sign," says Pascual.

# T

"So let's just go through your documents quickly, Mr. Rose, if we could." The conference room where this bank has chosen to receive Pascual offers no views except for the pretty young woman in charge of the laptop, who Pascual suspects is the brains of the operation. The senior member of this tag team, a middle-aged man with jowls, keeps looking to her for silent confirmation by way of barely perceptible nods.

"I believe you'll find everything there," says Pascual, nodding at the stack of papers he has just shoved across the table.

"Very good. Let's see, identification documents for directors and major shareholders, description of the company's business activity, bank statements for existing account, Certificate of Good Standing with apostille. Now, proof of established connection to Singapore?"

"I have just purchased an apartment here. You'll find the title there."

"Ah, I see. Very good. And . . . ah, yes. The initial deposit. Yes, I think that will be quite satisfactory." The man looks to the young lady, who takes her time riffling through the documents, frowns once at the laptop, and finally nods. The man beams.

Pascual returns the smile. "Now, what about the onboarding process? Know Your Customer and all that? When is that likely to be completed?"

The man squares his shoulders and sits up a little straighter. "There will be no problem with that, Mr. Rose. We have already done our due diligence. We will be pleased to host your company's account. I will leave you with Miss Chan here. She will guide you through the registration process."

"Wonderful," says Pascual. "I can't tell you how pleased I am."

■ ■ ■ ■

"Take me somewhere where I can look at the sea," says Pascual, settling onto the back seat of the Mercedes. Archie is looking at him expectantly over his shoulder. "Close up, I mean, not from thirty stories up."

Archie gives it a moment's thought, nods and puts the car in gear. "Maybe along Marine Parade."

"Take me there," says Pascual grandly and settles back to enjoy the ride. Singapore streets are an endless visual distraction with their jumble of modern construction thrusting up through a crust of colonial-era arcades and tile roofs, with palms, flowering trees and miscellaneous greenery everywhere. Archie steers through a few patches of sluggish traffic and then fights free of the congested center and onto a multi-lane highway that rapidly takes them eastward, toward the airport. After a few miles he exits the highway and rolls a short way along a service road to a parking lot. He pulls into a slot and points. "There's the sea."

Through a screen of trees Pascual can see it, a metallic blue under the sun. "Let's take a walk," he says.

Archie shoots him a look. "Sir? You don't want me to wait with the car?"

"No, I'd enjoy the company. You can educate me a little."

Archie looks unconvinced. "OK, whatever you say."

They get out of the Mercedes and walk through a strip of parkland to a broad expanse of grass that reaches to the edge of the water. An astonishing number of ships are riding at anchor offshore, dozens of them. Pascual stands with his hands in his pockets contemplating the utter surreality of the last few days of his life. Last week he was drawing *cañas* in a bar in Badalona.

And if you want to make it back to Badalona, Pascual tells himself, you need to step very carefully here.

Pascual has had enough dealings with intelligence agencies in his life to know that what you see is never what you get. Ever since this little jaunt to Singapore was first proposed, Pascual has been trying to figure out why the agency would send a man who was almost guaranteed to set off alarms to make arrangements for shady financial transactions.

Sloppiness is never to be ruled out where government work is concerned; it is just conceivable that the people at Langley are counting on Pascual's never-indicted status and regulatory laxity to move a few million dollars before anyone gets wise. But other things are equally possible, and Pascual wants to be ready for them. He turns to Archie, whose gaze has been wandering back toward the Mercedes parked a hundred yards behind them. "Tell me something."

"Sir?" Archie has been driving Pascual around for two days without Pascual taking much notice of him. Now Pascual sees a Chinese man in middle age, still lean and spry, with a mop of hair flopping casually on his forehead and slightly comical big black-framed glasses with flip-up sun lenses. Archie's English is fluent and sounds as if it might have been learned somewhere in North America rather than Britain.

Pascual throws a glance back toward the parking lot. "Is that silver Toyota still with us?"

Archie just stares at him for a moment, frozen, and then smiles. "You're very good, sir. Yes. He just pulled into the lot, at the other end."

Pascual nods. "Actually, I'm not especially good. I noticed you before I noticed anything else. You were paying more attention to the mirror than you would for normal driving. So I started looking, too."

"The traffic in the center gave him away. He had to take some risks to stay close to us, and it was impossible not to notice."

"How long has he been with us?"

"Since I picked you up this morning. Yesterday it was a different one. A black BMW."

"Yesterday, too, huh?" Pascual frowns. "So who is it?"

Archie scowls out to sea. "I thought you would be more likely to know, sir."

Pascual shrugs. "I could make some guesses. But yours are probably as good as mine. If somebody's following us, it could be because they're interested in me, or because they're interested in your boss."

Archie nods. "He's a wealthy man. And a foreigner. And the authorities here like to keep a close watch on foreigners, and the people they associate with."

"But it could also be me they're interested in. In which case, who alerted them to my arrival?"

"That's a good question."

For a moment they stand looking out to sea in silence. A couple of miles offshore, a freighter is moving slowly through the anchored fleet toward the entrance to the harbor. Pascual says, "I assume you've told Mr. Fang about this?"

"Of course."

"And what did he say?"

"With apologies, sir, he said you had a certain reputation and the Singapore authorities had probably taken note of your arrival. They are reputed to be very good and to keep a close watch on who enters the country."

"That seems believable. Tell you what. Can you drop me somewhere where I could stroll for a while and then get a good lunch? It's just the sort of thing I might have you do if I were happily unaware I was being followed, and it would be interesting to see what happens."

Archie kicks at the grass a few times and says, "I agree that it would be interesting. But Mr. Fang said one other thing when I told him about the surveillance."

"What's that?"

"He said don't do anything stupid."

Pascual has to laugh. "I will try to take that to heart."

■ ■ ■ ■

When his phone warbles, Pascual puts his fork down and picks up the phone. "Yeah."

"Nobody behind me now," says Archie in his ear. "It's you they're interested in."

"OK, good to know, thanks."

"Where are you?"

"Boat Quay."

"OK. Then they're on foot just like you, and probably close."

"Unless they gave up and went home. I'm just having lunch. I don't think that's illegal."

"Don't bet on it. They'll want to know if you're meeting somebody, where you're going after lunch. Which, by the way, Mr. Fang needs me this afternoon. Can you get back to the office by yourself?"

"If the taxi drivers speak any kind of English, sure."

"They do. Mr. Fang will be free by five, and he'll want to hear about this."

"I'll give him a full report."

"OK. Have a nice lunch and go to a movie or something."

"I know, don't do anything stupid. Thanks."

Pascual puts down the phone and scans the shaded riverside terrace where he is getting outside a pleasant lunch of braised duck, having opted for that over the *Pork Visceral (Intestines)* listed on the menu. Boat Quay with its promenade lined with restaurants appealed to Pascual immediately, and not just for its culinary diversity. The main point of dawdling indecisively up and down the quay was to give him a chance to exercise his rudimentary skills in spotting a tail.

A toss-up, he thinks, looking again at the Chinese man who has been nursing a beer and peering at his phone on a stool at a high table outside the bar two storefronts down the way. If the Chinese all look alike to his untrained Western eye, they do not all dress alike, and Pascual is certain he spotted that vintage bowling shirt with red stripes on black at least twice as he reversed direction repeatedly along the quay. Maybe just a fellow idler, but he has been nursing that beer throughout Pascual's lunch.

Pascual finishes his meal, pays, and steps back onto the walkway. He assumes a look of touristic interest and begins to drift in the direction of the bar. He comes to rest in front of it, marveling at the decorative touches on the façade, the graceful figures in plaster relief, the Palladian windows with their shutters. He pokes at his phone, activates the camera. He makes eye contact with the man in the bowling shirt and smiles at him. The man grins back. Pascual takes a step back and raises the phone to take a picture, but instead of focusing on the upper stories he frames the entrance where the man sits.

The grin vanishes and the man abruptly slides off the stool and turns his back on Pascual. He steps quickly into the dark interior of the bar. Pascual snaps a shot of the ornate façade and resumes walking. Fifty yards along there is a gap between terraces, giving access to the river. Pascual sits on a bench and pretends to look at his phone. The man in the bowling shirt steps back out of the bar, looking up and down the way, talking rapidly into the phone at his ear.

▪ ▪ ▪ ▪

"I caught a cab at Collyer Quay. I don't know if anybody followed it. Nobody stuck out, but I could have missed them." Pascual shrugs.

For a moment nobody says anything. Dexter Fang swivels slowly back and forth behind his desk and Renata Taggart sits frowning faintly at Pascual. Fang says, "If they're professionals, they would have had more than the one fellow. They would have had a team. That's who he was alerting after you spotted him. Somebody else would have picked you up."

A look passes between Fang and Renata, expressionless on both sides. Renata says, "Perhaps we should consult Mr. Campbell."

Fang grimaces. "I think not, actually."

Pascual says, "Who is Mr. Campbell?"

"My security chief. Ex-copper from Melbourne, and then in corporate security for BHP Billiton. He manages everything from night watchmen to cybersecurity for me. But he doesn't know anything about the operation you're here for. He's been told you're a prospective investor, that's all. And I hesitate to widen the circle."

Pascual says, "So. Local law enforcement, or counterintelligence maybe, alerted to the arrival of a reputed international criminal? Singapore has a reputation for running a very tight ship."

"The reputation is deserved. And your reputation just might be bad enough to trigger some reaction."

"Who tipped them off?"

Renata says, "Your arrival card, at the airport. That's all it would take. They'd see you're staying in one of Dexter's properties and pick you up there."

"And are they going to step in? Thwart my evil designs by preventing me from opening bank accounts?"

Fang smiles. "Not if they want to see what you do with the accounts."

Pascual nods slowly, looking out at clouds massing over the Strait. "I see."

Fang clasps his hands over his ample stomach, eyes narrowed. He looks at Pascual and says, "I think you proceed with your dealmaking, and we wait to see what happens."

Pascual tries to read his expression for a few seconds before looking away. Nice for you, Pascual thinks, that whatever happens is likely to happen to me.

# 8

Pascual is gratified to see that he was right: from the bar at the Mandarin Oriental, the view of the Marina Bay Sands hotel is spectacular.

With another free evening on his hands and neither Dexter nor the ravishing Renata showing the slightest interest in after-hours socializing, Pascual asked Archie to drop him here, opting for a night on the town rather than another quiet evening being ministered to by the taciturn Mr. Tan. This is an aspect of international skullduggery he recalls from his days underground in Europe: crushing boredom.

At least in his present incarnation as a globe-hopping scoundrel he can afford a better class of tavern to skulk in. In addition to the view, the bar offers a solid granite bar top, soft lighting and artistically crafted cocktails at prices to make an oil sheikh wince. Pascual has no need to wince, possessing a credit card backed ultimately, he calculates, by the full faith and credit of the United States government, meaning American taxpayers are on the hook for his luxury cocktails. He is nearing the bottom of his second one, this one tasting of gin and seaweed, and he knows he has entered the danger zone in which the only threat to his happiness is the conviction that a third drink will make him even happier.

One more and you won't be able to find the restroom, much less spot a tail, thinks Pascual. As far as he can tell, he was not followed here; as far as he can tell, none of the mixed crowd of Australian expats, French tourists, Japanese salarymen, Chinese capitalists, ethnically indeterminate beautiful people and miscellaneous riffraff, with whom over the past hour he has exchanged nods, greetings, idle chat and brief random eye contact, is at all interested in him. Everyone is in pairs or groups; there are no suspicious loners peering at him from behind a column or lurking further down the bar, pretending to read the labels on the bottles.

But if they are professionals, thinks Pascual, as far as you can tell is not very far. He signals to the bartender and reaches for his wallet. If the evening is to serve any purpose beyond killing time, he needs to be reasonably sober for the duration. A stroll along the bay and a nighttime taxi ride might be instructive, but only if he is capable of paying attention. Pascual settles his bill, nods a friendly farewell to the elderly British couple whose account of their vacation-blighting medical travails he suffered in patience, and heads for the exit.

The opposition appears out of nowhere as he approaches the elevators. He was vaguely aware of loiterers on the concourse; hotels are made to loiter in. Pascual becomes more sharply aware of them as they converge on him, two of them, making straight for him like barracuda closing on a wounded grouper. They are Chinese, dressed in black, and focused on him. The younger one is more formidable-looking, with an athletic build. The other is older and looks permanently irritable, the type of man who elbows you when you jostle him on the bus. Their aspect shouts copper a mile away. "Mr. Rose?" says the one in the lead.

The smart thing would be to deny it and press on blithely for the elevators, but Pascual fails to think of that in time. "Yes?"

The one on Pascual's right produces a leather holder and flips it open, revealing a badge of some sort and a photo ID with Chinese and English writing. "Immigration and Checkpoints Authority. May we have a word?" His tone is courteous, his accent stronger than Fang's.

Pascual has halted, bracketed by the two men. "Immigration? Is there a problem? I thought everything was checked at the airport."

"Just a formality, sir. A few questions." The one speaking is past forty, but his partner is twenty years younger and stone-faced, a hard case. "We will need you to come with us."

Pascual does not like the sound of this. "Hold on. If you've got questions, I'll answer them right here. What is it you want to know?"

"We would like some information about your association with Mr. Dexter Fang."

"Ah. Well. I'd be very happy to tell you anything you want to know. Why can't we just sit down over there?" Pascual nods in the direction of a couple of vacant chairs.

"We will need you to accompany us, sir. In order to conduct the interview properly. It is required."

So far the conversation has been conducted quietly, free of tension, three men talking business on a hotel concourse. But that *required* sounded authoritative to Pascual. "Am I under arrest?"

"Not at this time, sir. But if you refuse to come with us, a warrant will be issued and you will be subject to deportation."

Pascual blinks a few times, thinking about reporters thrown in jail, strokes of the cane, the occasional hanging. A tight ship indeed. "How long is this likely to take?" he says.

"Not very long, if you are cooperative, sir. We don't have far to go."

Pascual makes a snap judgment: Singapore is known for severity but not for disappearing arrestees. Most likely this conversation is inevitable, and it might as well happen now. "Very well," he says. "Lead the way."

■ ■ ■ ■

Fifteen minutes later, Pascual is wishing he had chosen to devote his life to that third drink. His captors, as he has just begun to think of them, have brought him on the back seat of a Hyundai sedan, the younger man at the wheel, through nearly deserted streets in the city center onto a highway that is carrying them west, away from any plausible location for a government office. Pascual slides his phone out of the inside pocket of his jacket. He taps on Dexter Fang's number and puts the phone to his ear.

"Mr. Rose," says Dexter, sounding slightly surprised. "What can I do for you?"

"Hello, Dexter. I just wanted to let you know, I'm in a car

with two fellows who claim to be from the immigration authority, and they're taking me in for a talk. I don't know where exactly. I just wanted to make sure somebody knows what's going on."

After a brief silence Dexter says, "Let me talk to them."

"Hang on." Pascual hands the phone to the man in the passenger seat. "Mr. Dexter Fang wants to talk to you."

The man takes the phone and puts it to his ear. A conversation in Chinese ensues. The man hands Pascual's phone back to him. Pascual raises it and says, "Are you still there?"

"Still here," says Dexter. "He says they're taking you to an ICA facility in Bukit Merah. I didn't know they had one there, but it's probably legitimate. I'm a little surprised they're doing this at ten o'clock at night, but then their methods are inscrutable to me. In any event I think there's nothing I can do. Just answer their questions and stick to the cover story, all right?"

"All right." Pascual signs off and stows the phone. Exiting the highway, they slow at a traffic light, turn away from the sea and go slightly uphill into parkland, trees black against the glowing skyline. Erupting from the trees is a thick column supporting cables stretching overhead, cable cars moving slowly along it. A short drive brings them to the entrance to a parking lot.

Pascual looks in vain for anything resembling an office building as the Hyundai rolls to the far corner of the sparsely populated lot. Beyond the back fence is darkness under a stand of trees. The driver pulls into a slot facing the trees, douses the lights and turns off the engine. The two Chinese turn to look at Pascual. Pascual can barely make them out in the light from distant lamps.

"All right, what's the story?" says Pascual, reaching for his phone again. His alarm has returned full force, his heart pounding. "And don't give me any more bullshit about immigration."

"So we lied to you, Mr. Rose. Sorry. You would not come with us if we only asked. There is someone who wants to talk to you."

"And he can't talk in a public place?"

"That would not be good." He nods at Pascual's phone. "If you want to call Mr. Fang again, please do. But don't call the police. Nothing will happen to you if you are patient. You will please wait here."

Simultaneously the two men open their doors and get out of the car. They stroll a few feet away and stand behind the car, the older man talking into his phone. Pascual sits holding his phone and trying to anticipate. Is this Langley, reaching out in typical heavy-handed fashion to tap him on the shoulder and remind him who's boss? Pascual's captors begin to walk off toward the entrance to the parking lot, at a leisurely pace.

Pascual steps out of the car into the sultry evening. He stands for a moment listening to the dull roar of traffic from the highway. He scans the half dozen widely spaced cars parked in the lot. His eyes rise to the cable cars silhouetted against the glowing sky. He reviews the odd sequence of events of the last half hour, and suddenly things become clear.

You have been set up, Pascual thinks.

He moves rapidly toward the fence. It is a standard chicken-wire fence with three strands of sagging barbed wire along the top, not impossible to get over in an emergency if you are willing to risk some minor damage to trousers and skin, but this giant tree trunk interrupting the fence looks like a better bet; you can just squeeze through the gap between the fence post and the sloping trunk.

Pascual stumbles over tree roots and thrashes into brush; he turns to look back just as the first police car turns in at the entrance to the lot.

■ ■ ■ ■

"The whole thing was a fake. The point of the exercise was to get me to sit there patiently waiting while the police rolled up. I'm guessing the trunk of the car was full of drugs or something."

The look on Dexter Fang's face is just slightly incredulous. He sits on the edge of the armchair, leaning forward, elbows on knees and hands clasped, the pose of a therapist watching a patient having an episode.

The evening's exertions have left Pascual drained and uncomfortably sticky, and he is rapidly being overcome by fatigue, aided by the cognac which appeared magically courtesy of Mr. Tan a couple of minutes after his arrival back at the bungalow. Behind Fang, Archie is perched on the arm of a sofa, frowning at his cell phone, no doubt still irked at being called out to rescue Pascual, who got through to Fang on his phone from the cable car station at the top of a considerable hill after blundering onto a trail in his flight from the car park.

Fang and Archie exchange a look. "He's right," says Archie. "That's how they operate. Framing him for a drug deal would put an end to any chance of his operating in Singapore, even if he beat the charge."

"Who?" says Pascual. "That's how who operates?"

Archie shrugs and turns away. Fang says, "The opposition. Whoever doesn't want . . . our mutual friends to succeed in financing their operations."

Pascual has a distinct impression that Archie's reference was more specific than that. He also has an impression that for a chauffeur Archie is awfully casual about lounging on the boss's furniture, but just as Pascual turns his attention to Archie, Fang stands up and says, "Well. We're not going to solve this tonight. But obviously we have to take it very seriously. I think we can forget about the financial authorities. This is somebody much more . . . formidable."

Pascual says, "Is it time to bring in your security guy, what's his name?"

"Campbell? I'm not sure."

Archie's head comes up sharply and he delivers a short monologue in Chinese. Fang nods and mutters a response, then turns to Pascual. "Archie has a point. Campbell's concerned with the security of the Fang family office. What we're doing is something apart from that, and the fewer the people who know about it, the better. However." He turns to Archie. "You might consult him on the surveillance issue, these people who are tailing you. That's the sort of thing Campbell's there for. You wouldn't have to give him the background. Just see if he can spot them, advise on how to evade them, whatever."

Archie looks dubious. "You'll have to give the order. Campbell doesn't approve of me."

"I don't blame him." Fang laughs, and again Archie switches

to Chinese. Fang nods and makes a placating gesture before turning back to Pascual. "All right. Maybe we should move you. I'll give that some thought. For the moment, why don't you just stay out of sight? Hang out here and relax."

Pascual has an idea or two of his own, but he nods. "I can do that."

"Fine. I'll contact you tomorrow and we'll figure out where to go from here." Fang looks into the shadows and Pascual becomes aware that Mr. Tan is hovering in a corner. "Make sure everything's locked up tight."

Tan nods. "As always, Mr. Fang."

# 9

"More coffee, sir?"

If Mr. Tan is responsible for the late-night boozing, it is his wife who sees to it that Pascual is resuscitated in the morning. Breakfast is served in a sunlit conservatory with French doors opening onto the terrace and the sumptuous colors of the garden beyond it. Mrs. Tan is petite, still black-haired like her husband, but with a face that shows the years. Also like her husband, she moves with a soft tread.

"Yes, thank you." Pascual looks up from his phone. The coffee comes from a porcelain pot ornamented with landscapes in pastel colors and gold leaf trim, no doubt an antique. The perfect brew complements the perfect croissants and the delectable slices of melon and mango. Pascual smiles to show his appreciation, but it brings no reaction from Mrs. Tan, who merely wafts back to the kitchen. Since landing *chez* Fang, Pascual has felt uncomfortably unable to decide whether he is a houseguest or a hotel resident. He would feel less terrified of breaking something if the latter. He doctors his coffee and returns to his phone.

"Good morning." Mr. Tan's greeting startles Pascual; how the hell does he do it, appearing out of nowhere like that? Today the old man is wearing a short-sleeved shirt, untucked, the uniform of the older Chinese male in Singapore. "Everything to your satisfaction?"

"Oh, yes, very good, thanks." Pascual sets down the phone. "All quiet on the western front? No sign of hostiles?"

Mr. Tan pulls out a chair and sits across from Pascual. "You won't see them," he says. "Not the people who tricked you last night."

Pascual stares at him. "Do you know who they are?"

"I could guess, but it would be idle. But they clearly have resources."

This has the ring of authority, and Pascual wonders how Tan attained it. "Do you think they're watching the house? I was hoping to arrange a meeting in the city today, but only if it can be kept private."

Tan considers for a moment. "It's not impossible they're watching. But I think you could manage to depart without being observed. I am acquainted with the houseman at the property behind ours, which gives onto Cornwall Gardens. The properties are separated by a wall, but with some cooperation from my friend and the ladder from the garden shed, I think it would be easy for you to scale the wall and meet a taxi in Cornwall Gardens."

Pascual sits shaking his head in wonder. "I'll need a little time to make my arrangements first. I'll let you know when I need to leave."

"Very good, sir."

"I am much obliged, Mr. Tan."

The old man shoves away from the table. "All part of the service, sir."

▪ ▪ ▪ ▪

*B. BALASUBRAMANIAN & CO. ADVOCATES & SOLICITORS SINGAPORE.* Pascual stares at the screen, wondering if what he is about to do is wisely seeking counsel or giving in to panic. This is the name Phillips gave him in Dubai, the man to call when things go belly-up.

He scans the website for Balasubramanian and Company, wondering if the CIA has lawyers at their beck and call in every port and how an Indian solicitor in Singapore gets his name on the roster. The website features the usual mission statement, contact information and map with office location, along with testimonials from satisfied clients. *Experienced and excellent lawyer, trustworthy and compassionate. Thanks to God for Mr. Balasubramanian. . . . I would like to thank you for your firm and knowledgeable support. You are an authentic and professional lawyer. God bless you. . . .*

Below the testimonials are boxes to click on for *CALL NOW* and *GET DIRECTIONS*, and a single sentence at the bottom of the page: *A good lawyer makes you believe the truth but it takes a great lawyer to make you believe in a lie.*

You sound like my kind of lawyer, thinks Pascual, and taps on *CALL NOW.*

▪ ▪ ▪ ▪

"I was alerted to the fact that you might call," says Basil Balasubramanian. "But I'm not quite sure what it is you require." The accent is South Asian, the man himself dark-complexioned, portly and bearded in a serious blue suit. The window behind him shows the featureless façade of a parking garage. The lack of a sea view is compensated by the efficient air-conditioning. Pascual arrived in a mild sweat after a short walk from the multi-story mall on New Bridge Road where he had the taxi drop him to cover his tracks. The building is a squat four stories of commercial space, shops at street level, with ten or so floors of condos tacked on above, convenient to the State Courts in Havelock Square. If the building is undistinguished, the lawyer's office is amply ornamented by a luxurious carpet of intricate oriental design, a massive teak desk, and, in an anteroom, a secretary of striking dark-eyed subcontinental beauty.

"I'm not, either," says Pascual. "I was sent here to help launder some money, but somebody's determined to stop me."

Balasubramanian's eyes have gone wide. "To launder some money? Please, Mr. Rose. I can't have anything to do with such things. They are strictly illegal."

Pascual raises his hands, appeasing. "Excuse my frankness. Let's use a less inflammatory term. I was sent here to aid the agency that gave me your name in transferring some funds from a source to a recipient, disguising their provenance. I am assuming that if the agency gave me your name you are not easily shocked by things like that. Perhaps you could start by clarifying your relationship to this agency."

The lawyer nods. "Quite right, perfectly reasonable. Though I'm surprised that wasn't made clear to you by the people who sent you."

"They don't dispense information very willingly."

"No, I suppose not." The look on Balasubramanian's face goes just slightly coy. "Well. I have been . . . retained, you could say, by the agency for some years now, and asked to do occasional small tasks for them in the legal realm, as well as to provide information from time to time."

"So. You're what they call a CIA asset."

For a moment Pascual thinks Balasubramanian is about to protest. Then the man's frown eases and he says, "I suppose I am."

"They've got them everywhere. Now, I'm hoping you can get in touch with a man called Phillips, who sent me out here. It's probably not his real name. He's the one who gave me your name."

"I don't know anyone named Phillips. But my contacts will know what to do. What is the message?"

"Tell them the opposition has reared its ugly head." Pascual sketches his adventure of the previous night.

Balasubramanian gapes at him. "Extraordinary. I saw it in the news this morning. In the Seah Im car park, wasn't it? The Central Narcotics Bureau received a tip regarding a drug sale that was to take place. They found a car abandoned there, with five kilograms of heroin in the boot."

Pascual laughs, weakly, seeing himself placidly waiting on the back seat as the police cars raced toward him. "They missed me by a minute or two. I'd have had some explaining to do. They still hang drug dealers here, don't they?"

"They do. Why would anyone try to implicate you?"

"To stop me from doing what I was sent here to do."

"And how did they find out about that?"

"That's a very good question. You might pose it to your contacts."

Balasubramanian is beginning to look positively enthused. "I see. Very well. I will pass this along."

Pascual stands. "Whoever it is, it's somebody who can afford to waste five kilograms of heroin. That puts them in the premier league, I think."

■■■■

Pascual's phone goes off as he is digesting his lunch on a mercifully shaded bench in a patch of parkland on the side of a steep hill and wondering how to kill the rest of the afternoon. He answers to hear Dexter Fang's voice. "Where are you?"

"Somewhere in Chinatown, I think. Not too far from South Bridge Road."

"I thought you were going to lie low at the bungalow today."

"Mr. Tan helped me get away from the house unobserved. I had errands to run."

"So he told me. Well, if you haven't been kidnapped or assassinated, you have probably escaped detection. Can you find your way to my office? I have decided that we should have a talk with Mr. Campbell. Take a taxi if it's too far to walk. I think there's a taxi stand on South Bridge Road."

Pascual judges that if it is not too far to walk, it is definitely too hot. His phone shows him where the taxi stand is, and in twenty minutes he is sitting at a long table in a conference room in Fang's office suite with arresting views of the Singapore Strait in one direction and of Renata Taggart in another. At the head of the table sits a man in a gray suit that matches his close-cropped gray hair. Pascual has dealt with ex-coppers before and knows an old head-knocker dressed up in a suit when he sees one. "Mr. Campbell has been fully informed," says Fang, sitting next to Renata opposite Pascual. "He is aware that you are here to establish some financial entities in cooperation with me, in the service of our mutual friends, and that the operation has been compromised somehow. He is going to help us decide how that happened and what we should do next."

Pascual looks from Fang to Campbell and back again. "Does Mr. Campbell know who our mutual friends are?"

Fang looks slightly abashed. "Ah. . . . Yes, he does."

Campbell clears his throat and says, "It wasn't Mr. Fang that told me. You might say your reputation preceded you. All it took was a little research. Your ties to those people aren't exactly a secret." The accent is broad Australian, the voice a little rough around the edges.

"No. I suppose not. Actually I've been wondering why I was sent here."

Fang says, "I think I can answer that. I spoke with my, er, contact this morning to report what happened last night, and he did not seem surprised. He said it appeared you had, and I quote, 'served your purpose,' and the operation was to be put on hold until further notice. He said I need have no further dealings with you."

There is a brief silence. Campbell smiles a wicked smile and says, "You've been fired, mate."

# 10

Pascual frowns. "And yet here I am."

Fang says, "Yes. Well, I thought it only fair to keep you informed."

"I appreciate that. And are our mutual friends aware Mr. Campbell has been informed?"

Fang says, "No." He sends a nervous look toward Campbell and says, "Actually, I have made a unilateral decision. We are going to proceed, with Mr. Campbell's advice, with the financial operations you were sent here to facilitate."

Pascual works on this for a moment. "But those operations were for the benefit of the CIA. And they've told you to cease and desist. What am I missing?"

"Well, strictly speaking I was not told to cease and desist. I was told I need have no further dealings with you. But your part of the operation is only half completed. Renata, where do we stand with Mr. Rose's affairs?"

Renata has no need for notes; without hesitating she says, "All the Singapore subsidiaries have been registered. One bank account has been opened. Presumably the same bank will be happy to host accounts for the other companies. I think all that can be accomplished in the next few days."

Dexter turns back to Pascual. "But it can't be accomplished without you. To return to my analogy, we have not yet finished installing the cash machine. When my contact said that the operation was to be put on hold, I interpreted that to mean that the fellows who are to fill it with cash will not be doing so immediately. But as long as you are here, I think we should finish constructing the machine. If you leave now, it will be very difficult to resume the operation later. However, I'm aware that you are the one who bears all the risk. So I would not blame you if you chose to catch the next flight out."

Pascual suppresses an urge to say thank you very much and sprint for the door. "I was promised payment on completion of the job. So I'm inclined to complete it, unless told otherwise."

"Perhaps this would be a good time to consult with the people who sent you."

"That is already underway," says Pascual. "I'd be curious to know if they're on speaking terms with your contact. I am obviously a completely disposable asset. I would be a lot happier if I knew who I could blame if I wind up in front of a judge. You apparently know that. Would you care to let me in on the secret?"

Fang's face settles into a frown. "I'm afraid I can't. The importance of security was impressed on me. Need to know, you know."

"Yes. All right, I can live with that. As long as you, and the people above you, are clear on the fact that I have no institutional loyalty. That's the downside of hiring mercenaries. You might pass that up to our mutual friends."

"I can do that." Fang turns to Campbell. "So, Mr. Campbell. In light of what occurred last night, what do you advise?"

Campbell clears his throat. "Well. The first question would be who has an interest in torpedoing your operation. Any guesses?"

■ ■ ■ ■

Fang says, "Ideas? One or two. But I was not entrusted with the full story of this exercise. I was merely given instructions as to the setting up of these companies that will be used to finance this undertaking, and Mr. Rose's role in that. Who the antagonist might be, I can only guess. In any event, the big question would be, how did they get wind of this operation?"

Fang's gaze comes to rest on Pascual, who says, "Any number of ways. Beginning with the arrival procedures at the airport, as Renata suggested the other day. As Mr. Campbell said, I am somewhat notorious, and anyone with a big intelligence presence here would notice when I entered the country. Or when I made my first application to open a subsidiary here."

Fang frowns at him. "All right, they'd notice. Why are they so anxious to put you out of action?"

"Because they know what I'm here for. I'm a known CIA asset. Which to my mind makes me a poor choice for this job, but here I am. Take it up with our mutual friends."

Campbell says, "My next question would be where they picked you up. And how they knew what car to look for. It's actually not a trivial matter to identify a subject's vehicles when you're planning surveillance."

The silence is broken when Renata says, with a shocked look on her face, "Dear God. It's my fault."

Everyone stares at her for a moment. "What happened?" says Fang.

She slumps a little on her chair. "I fell for a stupid ruse. Somebody who said he was from the tenants' car park at your residence called to confirm how many cars you have registered with them. He said they were updating their list. I completely failed to confirm his identity, completely failed to exercise the most elementary skepticism. I handed over the license numbers like an idiot. I'm sorry."

There is a moment of painful silence, and then Fang says, "Well, I'm sure he was very convincing. We can check with the garage. Perhaps it was legitimate." He is not pleased, but like any red-blooded male he is inclined to forgiveness where attractive females are concerned. He wheels to face Campbell. "If not, that's how they did it. They set up surveillance on the car park and started tracking Archie when he came out. They knew if Mr. Rose was staying in one of my properties he'd be likely to use one of my cars."

Campbell's expression says he will take that provisionally. He looks at Renata. "Can you give me the number that call came from?"

She hesitates. "I'll have to go back and look at the log on my office phone. I'll get it to you later today."

"And when did this call come in?"

Renata, clearly flustered, exhales and closes her eyes. "When was it?" She opens them and says, "Two, no, three days ago. Tuesday afternoon."

Campbell turns to Fang and says, "My next question would be whether this new driver of yours is completely to be trusted. It's not too late to run a full background check on him, you know."

Fang says, "I told you, he's an old boyhood chum and I'd trust him with my life. But go ahead and vet him, by all means, if that would make you happier."

"I've got old chums I wouldn't trust to hold my beer," says Campbell, smiling. "Just send me his particulars, will you?" His smile fades. "They've got a lot of resources. It's not easy to maintain surveillance on that scale, especially in a dense city. Not to mention investing five pounds of heroin in a frame-up." He levels his gaze at Pascual. "Are you quite sure you want to go on with this?"

Pascual is fairly sure he doesn't, but he is also fairly sure that there will be no million dollars at the end of the rainbow if he bails out now. "What else am I doing with my life?" he says, trying to sound cavalier.

"Well, obviously, from this point on we have to prioritize your security. I'd find a new place for you to stay, to begin with."

Pascual suffers a fleeting pang thinking of sunlit breakfasts and fine cognac, but he nods in agreement. "Whatever you say. I don't need to be chauffeured everywhere, either. Blending in with the populace a little might be a good idea."

"Unless it makes you more vulnerable. I don't know that

you're safer hanging onto a strap on a bus than you are in the back seat of a Mercedes."

Fang says, "The best thing might be to spirit you away to one of my vacant properties. Or your new penthouse, maybe. I can have it furnished by the end of the day."

Renata says, "The purchase will have been recorded. If they can look at immigration controls and company registrations, they'll be able to look at property records as well. And if they know he's associated with you, your vacant properties won't be any safer."

"Good point. Where do we stash him, then?"

A few seconds go by in silence. Fang reaches for his phone and says, "Mr. Tan will have some ideas." He swipes at the phone and in a moment is engrossed in a conversation in Chinese.

Campbell stands and says, "I'll let you make your arrangements. Do get that number to me, will you, Ms. Taggart?" He makes for the door.

Pascual stands and goes to look out through the wall of glass at the spectacle of central Singapore from forty stories up. A step sounds behind him. "I suppose you're the one I should really apologize to," Renata says quietly. He turns to see her looking troubled. "I'm horrified to think what might have happened to you." In her distress she is for the first time just a fallible human, almost a peer.

"Please," he says. "You were victimized by professionals. You're not the first."

He strives for a reassuring look but those extraordinary eyes flee his. "Mr. Fang told me there might be . . . security concerns with this project. I suppose I didn't take them seriously enough."

"Chalk it up to experience." Pascual has been working on the assumption that Renata is fully clued in as to the nature of the operation; now he wonders just how far she has been briefed.

"Excellent," says Fang, stowing his phone. "Mr. Tan says there is a very good bolt hole for Mr. Rose. In Chinatown."

■■■

"Tell her I'm sure I will be very comfortable here," says Pascual. He smiles and bows toward the ancient wrinkled Chinese woman who is wringing her hands in the doorway of the room.

The room is a tiny chamber under the eaves of a house just off Neil Road, in a district full of traditional shophouses with their shuttered windows above arcaded walkways, evoking the old Singapore. Pascual was driven here by Mr. Tan after a rendezvous in the parking garage of Fang's office tower. There is just enough room for a cot, a chair, a wash stand. A small window gives onto a tiny walled yard at the rear of the building. Pascual's suitcase sits on the floor in a corner, delivered by Mr. Tan.

Mr. Tan speaks briefly to the woman and she backs out of the room after flashing Pascual a final smile. "If you need an interpreter," says Tan, "Kenny here can help you." He nods at the youth lounging at the head of the stairs. The boy is maybe sixteen, the tips of his black hair tinted blond, wearing a basketball jersey for a team Pascual has never heard of and voluminous blue shorts.

"Eh boss, anything you need," he says in the singsong Singapore English. "Just ask me, okay?"

With an amused look Mr. Tan says, "Kenny is a bit of an *ah beng*, but he is reliable, I think."

"*Ah beng?*"

"I think you might translate that as 'anti-social youth,' or perhaps 'juvenile delinquent.'"

Kenny laughs. "Juvenile delinquent? Your head, *lah*." He says to Pascual, "What you want, just tell my auntie, she will tell me and I get it for you, boss." He trots down the stairs.

Pascual turns to Mr. Tan. "Thank you again. You seem to be the man with all the answers."

"I am the man with the connections, let's say. Here's a key. You can come and go by the back door, through the courtyard. Your hostess is Mrs. Eng. She asked if you would require meals. I said you would arrange that with her if you wanted. She has enough English to do that."

Pascual takes the key. "I hope she is being compensated. I would be happy to pay whatever she asks."

"Mr. Fang will take care of that." Tan smiles. "I will make sure of that. But if you could spare the time to exchange a few words with her now and then, just a smile, perhaps a small gift when you leave, that would be the best compensation she could receive. She has been very lonely since she lost her son. This was his room."

"I will do that." Pascual sticks out his hand. "Thank you, Mr. Tan. Again I am obliged to you."

"Not at all, sir. I wish you luck." The old man holds Pascual's grip for a moment after shaking hands. "I have a feeling you may need it."

# 11

"I have spoken with the people who sent you here," says Basil Balasubramanian when Pascual answers his phone. "Or with their local representative, to be precise. The conversation was quite illuminating."

"I'm all ears," says Pascual. He is sitting in the little rear courtyard of his bolt hole, watching his hostess pluck a chicken and nodding agreeably at her nonstop and completely unintelligible commentary. "What does this representative have to say?"

"I think I would prefer to discuss the matter in person. Why don't you come by my office? There are always security concerns with telephones, and I prefer talking face to face."

This is the best idea Pascual has heard this morning; he has been cooling his heels and waiting for instructions from Fang, who has promised a plan of action before the end of the day. "Give me a few minutes. I don't think I'm very far away."

In the event it takes Pascual a laborious hour to find his way back to the lawyer's office, guided by his phone. He thinks it unlikely that he could still be under surveillance, but he takes the precaution of using the mall on New Bridge Road again to filter out pursuit, ducking in and out of stairwells. He arrives enervated by the heat and once again embarrassed to present himself to the winsome secretary in such a condition but grateful for the lawyer's air-conditioning. "Mad dogs and Englishmen," says Balasubramanian as Pascual collapses onto the chair opposite him. "Nobody warned you about the heat?" Today the lawyer is resplendent in a lavender shirt with a dark gold tie, a cream-colored suit jacket draped over a chair to one side. His cologne wafts to Pascual on the cooling draft.

"It's not quite midday, I believe," says Pascual. "Anyway, I'm not English. I'm a pan-Mediterranean. We like the heat."

The lawyer raises his hands. "My mistake."

"So what's the story?"

Balasubramanian's grin fades. "I'm afraid I have bad news for you." He leans forward, elbows on the desk, hands clasped, frowning, a principal about to explain to a parent why their child is being expelled. "The story is that you are a bad apple and a disreputable character, with no connection to the agency. If anyone asks about you, you are to be disavowed."

Pascual's chill is suddenly due to more than the air-conditioning. That was fast, he thinks. "You don't say."

The lawyer nods once, slowly. "I'm afraid so. I was told that you have on several occasions passed yourself off as having some connection to the agency, but that this is only a fiction. You are apparently quite notorious in some circles as a former political extremist who now dabbles in dubious financial transactions."

Pascual's expression hardens. "This comes from the people at Langley?"

"Via our local man, yes." Balasubramanian's eyes narrow. "He said they were quite emphatic that you were not to be trusted."

Pascual finds nothing to say for a long moment, meeting the lawyer's gaze and feeling the anger building. "They don't want to pay me," he says.

Balasubramanian inclines his head slightly. "I should imagine they don't."

"I want to talk to this local man," says Pascual. "Call him up."

"I'm afraid it's not as simple as that. When we communicate, there are some security precautions involved. There's a cutout procedure."

"Fine. Set up a meeting, set up a call. I want to talk to him." Pascual, invigorated by his anger, pushes back his chair and stands up. "They promised me a million dollars. I've done what they asked, provoked the opposition, narrowly escaped being framed for something that in Singapore could get me hanged, and now they're trying to stiff me. Do me one favor and put me in touch with this guy. They owe me that much. They owe me an explanation. Can you do that?"

The lawyer's eyes have narrowed again. After a moment he says, "I will see what I can do."

■■■■

*There are always security concerns with telephones,* Pascual can hear Balasubramanian saying, and he wonders why it has taken him this long to grasp that elementary fact. He has had enough experience with compromised technology to know better. In a food court deep in the bowels of another gigantic mall in New Bridge Road he lunches on steamed pork ribs while thinking over everything that has brought him to this point.

It did not seem strange that Phillips would issue him a phone as part of his cover story, but now it occurs to Pascual that if anyone has an interest in monitoring his conversations and tracking his movements, it would be the people who sent him out here to fail. Give him a competently bugged phone, assure him it can't be hacked, and sit back and watch and listen. When the opposition outs him, pretend you never heard of him.

As a strategy to draw the opponent's fire, it has its merits. Pascual is aware that this may be paranoia. He is also aware that paranoia is a survival strategy in the intelligence business. He has been lulled half to sleep by his luxurious reception in Singapore, and it is time to wake up.

Pascual stares at his phone for a moment, wondering if someone somewhere is staring back. He knows that a cell phone can be tracked even when it is turned off if the right kind of spyware or secret transmitter chip or God knows what new technological magic is implanted; the intricacies are beyond him. Removing the battery is also beyond him. He contents himself with turning the thing off pending further consideration. He wipes his lips with a paper napkin, disposes of his trash, and heads for the exit.

When he lets himself into the tiny rear yard of his hideout, the smell of stewing chicken almost makes him regret his hasty lunch. Mrs. Eng beams at him and beckons him into the kitchen. Pascual manages to ward off a second lunch and climbs the narrow stairs to his room, where he stuffs his dormant phone superstitiously under a pillow. Pascual thinks hard for a moment: Did he ever call Mr. Tan on the phone he was given? No; there should be no record in the cloud, the ether or wherever these things are stored that Pascual Rose ever contacted the house manager at Dexter Fang's bungalow. Hence there is no reason to believe anyone interested in Pascual's communications will be monitoring Mr. Tan's phone.

Returning to the kitchen, he approaches his hostess and manages to convey in a sort of pidgin with gestures that he wants to speak to Mr. Tan but has lost his phone. Somewhat to his surprise, she ducks into the next room and produces one. He manages to convey to Mrs. Eng that she should ring up Mr. Tan for him. She punches at the phone, listens, says something in Chinese and hands the phone to him.

"Mr. Tan," says Pascual. "I am going to impose on you again, I'm afraid. I need you to get a message to Dexter Fang."

■ ■ ■ ■

"I am astonished," says Fang. "Why would they disavow you?"

"Because that's what I'm here for," says Pascual. "I think I was sent here to fail."

Fang looks disconcerted, possibly because of the assertion or possibly because he does not ordinarily frequent down-market places like this coffee-and-sandwich nook on a mezzanine several floors below his office suite. Pascual discovered it while poking about during an idle hour two days before; tucked out of sight of security cameras but with a view of the elevators, it allowed Pascual to be sure he was not under observation while waiting for Fang to follow Mr. Tan's directions to the rendezvous. Piped-in music and the ambient noise of big spaces cover their conversation.

"Why would they send you here to fail?" says Fang, frowning at his paper cup full of coffee as if he had never seen such an object before.

"Because they wanted to see what they're up against. I'm a sort of tethered goat, staked out here to see how serious the opposition is."

Fang takes an experimental sip of coffee and grimaces. "Who is this lawyer, exactly?"

"He's the man I was told to contact if I ran into problems. He is going to try to set up a meeting with the local man, but I'm not optimistic. It sounds as if they're throwing me under the bus, and I think they're going to refuse to pay me."

"Surely not. That would be quite unjust."

"You're new to the intelligence business if you think it has anything to do with justice. I've been at a disadvantage here from the start. I don't even know who sent me. I have no recourse, nobody to complain to, nobody to support me if things go wrong, nobody to hold to account. That makes me a perfect patsy, the ideal scapegoat. I need somebody in the agency to hear my side of the story. If the lawyer doesn't come through for me, will you intervene? Just put me in touch with your contact. That's all I ask."

Fang smiles, and for a moment Pascual thinks he finds the situation funny, but then he realizes that it is merely Fang's way of masking discomfort. Fang shakes his head. "I can't do that, Mr. Rose. I was sworn to secrecy."

Pascual sits for a moment tight-lipped, suppressing a flare of anger. "Then I'm done," he says. "I'll fly out tomorrow and they can go directly to plan B. That's obviously what they want. And if they stiff me, our agreement is dead. They won't owe me protection, and I won't owe them silence. You can tell them that."

Fang's smile is gone, and he leans a little closer to be heard over an outburst of chatter from an arriving party of customers. "Don't do anything hasty. There must be some communication mix-up, or maybe some security reason why this lawyer was given that story. I will be your advocate. I can testify that you've done everything according to instructions and that you deserve to be paid. Don't do anything until I have a chance to inquire through my channels."

Pascual watches the pretty Chinese girls at the counter, thinking hard. "All right," he says. "But tell them I'm on strike till I get some guarantees."

Pascual is finally getting a taste of the chicken, stewed with ginger, scallions and other unidentifiable vegetable matter, when there is a knock at the door in the courtyard. Mrs. Eng hastens to open, and Kenny comes in from the alley. He exchanges a few words in Chinese with the old lady and comes into the kitchen, holding out a cell phone. "Eh, I got you the phone *liao*. Very cheap, fifty dollars only. Plus fifteen for SIM card, plus one hundred for ID. No one can trace it to you."

"ID? I thought you were getting me a burner."

"In Singapore don't have burner phone like in US. You need ID to activate. No problem *lah*. I pay my friend one hundred dollar to use his ID. If anyone trace the phone they will trace to him. And they won't find him *lah*. His ID got no good address."

Best not to ask too many questions, Pascual decides. "I see. So, you spent, let's see, a hundred and sixty-five dollars. That was Singapore dollars?"

"Ah, the phone and SIM card, Singapore dollar. But my friend like US dollar *leh*. So he said one hundred US dollars to use his ID."

W̶̶̶̶̶̶̶̶̶̶̶̶̶̶̶̶̶̶̶̶̶̶̶̶̶̶̶̶̶̶̶̶̶̶̶̶ Pascual has finis̶̶̶̶̶ he ascends to his room and pulls out his CIA-issued ̶̶̶̶. When he turns it on, he is not surprised to see Balasubramanian's number below a missed call notification. Pascual turns the phone off after noting the lawyer's number and then punches it in to his new phone.

To his surprise the lawyer answers immediately. "You have a new telephone," he says when Pascual identifies himself.

"You sold me on security."

"Very wise. Can you come and see me? I still prefer the face-to-face."

"Sure. Right away?"

"Actually I am in the middle of a rather busy day. Shall we say six o'clock this evening?"

"That would be fine. Is there a new development?"

"I have some information for you. Information that your associates in Langley, Virginia will be very glad to have. I believe it would be advantageous for you to have something to offer them when you approach them on the subject of their refusal to pay you, would it not?"

"It couldn't hurt. What kind of information?"

"Before we get to that, one point if I may. There will be a consideration."

"A consideration?"

"For this very valuable information, yes. You mentioned

money that you are owed, a considerable sum. I thought you might not be reluctant to pass on a very small portion of it to me, in return for this valuable information."

Pascual sags on the edge of the cot. My kind of lawyer, he thinks. "How much did you have in mind?"

"We can discuss that when you arrive. Nothing too shocking, I assure you. But I think you will find the information I have for you to be worth a modest consideration."

"Can I have a teaser? A sniff of the merchandise?"

"Of course. It concerns your friend Mr. Dexter Fang and certain people in his network."

Pascual listens to his heart beating for a few seconds and makes a decision. "Very well. I'll be happy to discuss the matter. I'll see you at six o'clock."

"I look forward to it," says Balasubramanian, and rings off.

■■■■

The heat has begun to ease a little when Pascual steps outside. He remembers evenings like this in Damascus, the city stirring, almost sighing with relief after the intense heat of the day. The heat here is damp and heavy, so different from the scorched Syrian air, but the feeling is the same. With evening comes a rise in spirits, the cheerful prospect of release from toil, of food and drink and ease.

The faces are different here, too, alien but beginning to individualize, to take on character, assert themselves. Again Pascual deploys what tradecraft he has, idling through the mall on New Bridge Road, halting abruptly, reversing direction, noting who comes up the escalator after him. He is reasonably confident nobody has been watching him since he was installed in his bolt hole, but he has learned that confidence can lead a man over a cliff, and he is determined to take care.

He dawdles through Pearl's Hill Park, becoming sure he is clear. Slipping over the back wall of the bungalow garden was the key; since then there has been no point at which the watchers could have picked him up again.

By the time he reaches the entrance to Balasubramanian's building, Pascual is thinking about Dexter Fang's network and the negotiations ahead. In the lobby a uniformed security guard gives him the eye from behind a desk, barely responding to Pascual's nod. The elevator disgorges two Chinese who brush past him without a look, office workers on a beeline to the bar or the teahouse or wherever Chinese workers go at the end of the day. On the third floor the door to Balasubramanian's office is closed; Pascual gives a light tap on the glass with a knuckle before pushing it open, less disheveled this time and hoping to make a better impression on the pretty secretary.

The anteroom is empty, no sign of the secretary, pens lined up neatly on her desk and the chair shoved in, computer screen dark. The door to the inner office stands open. "Mr. Balasubramanian," Pascual calls.

There is no answer. Pascual stands still for a moment, not alarmed, merely waiting. A pleasant smell reaches his nostrils, the aroma of India: turmeric, coriander, ginger, grilled meats. Apparently a hard-working lawyer has treated himself to takeout for dinner at his desk. Pascual hopes there is enough for two.

That would compensate for the absence of the secretary. He advances to the door of the inner office and stops.

The meal lies on the desk in a foam container, chunks of chicken on a pile of rice and vegetables, all bright yellows, reds and greens. Balasubramanian's chair is pivoted away from the door, his head and shoulders visible over the back, and now Pascual is alarmed, because the man has had ample time to swallow, wipe his lips and respond to Pascual's call. And yet the seconds go by, and both Pascual and the man on the chair remain motionless. The lawyer is sitting erect, head up, elbows on the arms of his chair, apparently not in distress but sitting completely still.

Leave now, thinks Pascual. You were never here.

Instead Pascual walks slowly around the desk until he can see Balasubramanian in profile, see the half-closed eyes and the trickle of blood from one corner of his mouth. Those would explain the utter stillness; Pascual cannot understand how the man could be holding his head up until he sees the skewers, long wicked slivers of bamboo that no doubt arrived with the chicken, now re-purposed and driven with force, two into the chest and one straight up through the soft underside of the jaw into the brain, enough of the length remaining beneath to support the head on the incline of the chest.

Pascual remains frozen, heart pounding, for only a few seconds before his brain starts working again. I saw them, he thinks, remembering the two Chinese exiting the elevator, and I have seen them before, two nights ago. I should have recognized them instantly but I am a fool, the classic westerner unable to tell one Chinese from another. The next thing he thinks is that too many people have seen him, starting with the two Chinese, who might at any moment decide that coming back for him would round out a tidy evening's work, and ending with the security guard in the lobby, who will no doubt be able to give the police an accurate description of him.

He briefly considers playing good citizen, making an ally of the guard by descending immediately to report the crime. Briefly, because there would be a lot of explaining, and while Pascual has no institutional loyalty, he can see no advantage to himself in further antagonizing certain people in faraway Virginia by frank explanations that would blow at least a part of the CIA's operations in Singapore sky-high.

Rather the opposite. Pascual finds a stairwell at the end of the hall and makes use of it.

▪▪▪▪

"I got away clean. I think." Pascual is panting slightly, as much from the shock of the past few minutes as from the physical exertion of trudging along Chin Swee Road, traffic roaring past, covering his shouts into the phone. "I went out the back way and there was a path into the park. I'm pretty sure nobody followed me."

"You'll be on the CCTV cameras," says Mr. Tan in his ear.

"Can't be helped. The killers will be, too. Let the police sort everyone out. Look, the point is, the killers must have been monitoring my phone, the old one. That's the only way they could know about the lawyer. And that means they have been watching my movements and listening to my conversations. So they know about Mrs. Eng, they know I'm working with Dexter, they know all about my business here. It's time for me to get the hell out, and you need to warn Dexter, warn Mrs. Eng. I don't think they'll be listening to your phone. I never called you on the compromised one. Call Dexter and have him meet me somewhere again. No, wait. Don't call him. Take him a message, or send someone with a message. Tell him to meet me somewhere. You pick the place, call me back and tell me where and when. And tell him not to bring his phone. That's important, absolutely crucial. Don't bring any phones and make sure he's not followed."

This is met by silence. Just as Pascual is wondering if his phone has dropped the call, Mr. Tan says, "Very well. What will you do in the meantime?"

"I don't know. Walk, I guess."

Mr. Tan is not one to lose his head in a crisis; he could be discussing the menu for dinner. "Let me suggest something better. Find a taxi if you can and have it take you to a hotel in Geylang called the Green Jade. I will call the manager there and instruct him to give you a room. The registration will be in my name, I will pay for the room. I will have Mr. Fang meet you there."

Pascual manages a ragged laugh. "Mr. Tan, I will be eternally in your debt."

"Not at all, Mr. Rose. The Green Jade. In Geylang. Go there now."

# 13

Geylang is a Singapore Pascual has not seen yet: not many high-rises, block after block of nondescript two- and three-story walkups that could be in any city on earth. Cheap hotels, convenience stores, hair salons, Indian, Thai and Chinese restaurants, a dentist, a tattoo parlor, a mosque. The wealthy do not live here, and tourists do not come to the Green Jade Hotel. It stands on a corner, peeling stucco painted a sickly green in keeping with the name, a mere two stories with air conditioners above drip marks at every window and a recessed entrance. Night has fallen and idlers cluster around the entrance, some Chinese and some something else, all men. They fall silent and stare as Pascual makes his way past them, nodding politely. Inside, the desk man is Chinese, and to Pascual's relief he appears to be expecting him. "Mr. Tan sent me. I'm Mr. Rose." The man nods and hands Pascual a key.

Pascual sits on a swaybacked bed in a room lit by ghastly fluorescent light and indifferently cooled by a clattering air conditioner, second-guessing every decision he has made since he was twelve years old. He wants out, he wants to go home, and he wants a home to go home to. Most of all he wants to figure out whom he can trust. Mr. Tan is a probable. Dexter Fang is a maybe; as far as Pascual can see, their interests are aligned, but there is clearly an information gap, and Pascual is not prepared to tolerate it any longer.

One thing Pascual no longer cares much about is a mythical million dollars. You should have listened to Sara, he thinks.

Because Fang is only a maybe, Pascual goes out into the hall and sits on the stairs up to the third floor, around the corner from his room, and listens. Other guests come padding up the stairs and shuffling along the hall; doors open and close. When Pascual hears knocking, he peeks around the corner and sees Fang standing at his door listening, unaccompanied by Chinese hit men or police. Fang turns at the sound of Pascual's approach and scowls at him. "What the hell is going on? Why is a courier knocking on my door at dinnertime with orders from you by way of Mr. Tan?"

Inside the room, door locked, Pascual waves Fang to the single chair and sinks onto the bed. "Do you have your phone with you?"

"No. Just a cheap prepaid phone with a SIM registered to a former employee, now deceased. I keep one or two handy. But I'm not clear on why you think my phone's compromised."

"Because mine was. And if my phone was infected, yours could be, too. Anybody I talked to could be infected. All they need is your number to hit it with a zero-click exploit."

"That seems unlikely to me. I have top-of-the-line encryption on all my phones."

"I was told I had that, too. But my phone was compromised, and it got a man killed."

Fang raises a hand. "All right, stop right there. I'm going to ask you again. What the hell is going on?"

"The lawyer's dead. Somebody killed him, maybe five minutes before I got to his office."

"Good God."

"I think I saw the men who did it, and I think he was killed to stop him from giving me information. He claimed to have something that would interest Langley, and he was going to sell it to me. The only way someone else could have known about that was if they were monitoring his phone. Not mine. When he made his pitch, I was on a different phone I'd just gotten. But how did they know to monitor his? I had no connection with this guy before I called him the other day. They must have seen everywhere I went and heard everyone I talked to on the phone I brought to Singapore with me. How it got compromised, I don't know. But they knew the lawyer was going to talk and they knew where to find him. If you have a better theory about how they knew that, let's hear it."

Fang frowns. "I see no reason to assume it was your connection that led to his being targeted. If he was in the business of selling information, there could be any number of people with an interest in silencing him. I don't even see that it's necessary to assume a hacked phone. Someone talked. What do you know about this fellow? If he was a criminal, peddling information, he was most likely betrayed by some other criminal. The source of the information, for example."

"That's possible, I suppose. But are you willing to bet on it? He offers to sell me the information, and within a few hours he's killed. I would think operational security would require us to assume that was cause and effect."

Fang greets this with a stone face. After a moment he says, "Why didn't they wait for you and kill you, too? If they knew you were coming."

"Maybe just because killing one of us was sufficient. Look, the point is, everything is blown. Everything."

Fang doesn't like it, but his grunt says he will accept it, at least provisionally. "So what do you suggest we do?"

"The first thing we do is ditch every phone anybody used to talk to me since I got here. Everyone I talked to could be compromised. For that matter, it could have gone the other way. My phone could have been compromised via yours."

Fang shakes his head. "No, really. I think that's impossible. Mr. Campbell and his people are very good. We dealt with the Pegasus threat when it was first revealed, and those vulnerabilities have been fixed on all my phones. My people run MVT on our phones regularly. They update the IOC's all the time. And they've developed equivalent tools for the Pegasus variants coming out of China now. So I'm fairly confident I haven't been hacked. But what I can do is have all our phones checked. I'll do that tomorrow."

"Thank you. You'll have to have someone collect my phone from the hideout where Mr. Tan stashed me. You want to know what the information was that this dead lawyer was offering to sell me? He said it concerned 'Dexter Fang and certain people in his network.'"

Fang sits erect on the chair, hands on his thighs, sweating a little in his batik shirt, a sour look on his face, a frog on a lily pad contemplating a snake undulating silently across the pond. "Certain people."

Pascual nods. "I have no idea who he might be referring to. I have no idea about a lot of things in this situation. Like how you got involved with the CIA, to start with. Like who you answer to in that circus. And dammit, I think I deserve some explanations. If I don't get them, I'm out of here. As in, off the reservation, going rogue, in the wind and to hell with the agency and all its designs. Am I making myself clear?"

Fang blinks a few times, then sighs softly. "Very clear. Of course you deserve some explanations. I'm just not sure I'm authorized to give them."

"Who is?"

Fang frowns at the floor for a moment and says, "Give me till tomorrow morning. I'll have some answers for you, I promise."

"I may not have until tomorrow morning. The police could be looking at security camera footage right now and wondering who the hell this is walking into Balasubramanian's building about the time he was killed. Or they're looking at his phone and seeing my number. They could be looking for Pascual Rose as we speak. What are you going to tell them when they come to you asking about me?"

There is nothing inscrutable about Fang's expression; it shows full-blown alarm. After a moment Fang stands with great effort, levering his considerable bulk off the chair, goes to the window, parts the slats of the blind with a finger, looks out for a few seconds and finally turns. "I suppose I will have to tell them you have disappeared and I have no idea where you are. I will have to disavow you."

Pascual is not surprised. "Well, thank you. That's admirably frank. Where does that leave me?"

"What happens if you simply go straight to the airport and fly out tonight? I think the odds are in your favor. We don't know if the body's been found yet, and even if it has, I don't think the Singapore police work fast enough to identify you tonight."

"Who knows if I can get on a flight tonight? Meanwhile, they get a look at the lawyer's phone and see my name, the first thing they look at is who's on standby tonight out at the airport. Look, I could have called the cops myself. I didn't, because for reasons that are not clear to me I'm still invested in this operation you and our so-called mutual friends are running. But if I wind up in a police interrogation room, you better believe I'm going to tell them everything I know."

Fang looks at that for a few seconds and says, "Yes. So obviously the solution is to keep you out of sight, put you on ice for a while."

"That works for me. Where?"

"I think you are probably safe here for the night. I trust Mr. Tan's judgment. Tomorrow I will have transportation for you."

"To where?"

"That remains to be seen. To a place where you'll be beyond the reach of the Singapore police, in any event."

"That would be good," says Pascual.

An electronic chirping startles them both and Fang claws a

cell phone from his shirt pocket. He glances at the screen, jabs, puts it to his ear and answers in Chinese. A brief conversation ensues, and Pascual can tell from the look on Fang's face that it is not good news. Fang goes from annoyed to frozen to alarmed in very short order. He turns away from Pascual and alternately listens and growls into the phone a few times, then finally ends the call and turns back with a troubled look on his face. "That was Archie," he says. "There's a problem."

"What sort of problem?"

"I don't know. He was parked not far away, waiting for me to call. Now he says he had to move. He says if I can make it to the Shell station on Geylang Road, he will pick me up there."

"I hope Archie was using an anonymous phone, too."

"Archie only ever uses anonymous phones." Fang slips his phone back into the pocket. "I think you should come with me."

"Why?"

"Because Archie said it's time to reconsider our position."

"What does that mean?"

Fang heaves a great sigh. "It means he agrees with you that everything is blown."

# 14

Of course, thinks Pascual as he and Fang make their way along a narrow street toward Geylang Road. The hotels should have tipped you off.

Nightfall has brought out an aspect of the neighborhood that Pascual had not expected: along some of the side streets lie rows of houses with brightly lit and garishly decorated entranceways, women in very short skirts and very high heels lounging under the lamps, and on one long block they passed scattered streetwalkers, calling softly to them as they passed. Fang is visibly uncomfortable, and Pascual wonders how long it has been since the man took a simple stroll through the streets of the city where he lives.

"We're to wait in the convenience store," says Fang as they approach the Shell station on brightly lit Geylang Road. "When he is able, he will pull in as if he is buying petrol, and we should be ready to jump in."

Pascual has stopped trying to control events. Everything is blown, people are dying, and the chauffeur appears to be running the show. Deep waters, and Pascual is all too aware of what else may be swimming in them. They wait for the light to change and cross the broad boulevard to the station. Inside the store Fang buys a packet of salted fish skins to justify their presence. They stand looking out through glass and watching the traffic, Fang crunching his way through the packet. He offers some to Pascual, who declines. His stomach has not recovered from the sight of Balasubramanian's aborted last meal.

Fang has finished his snack by the time the Mercedes pulls up at a pump and Archie gets out, looking their way. Fang pushes out into the heat, Pascual following. They pile into the Mercedes, Fang in front, and Archie rams it in gear and pushes back out into traffic. He and Fang go at each other in Chinese for a minute or so while Archie steers swiftly through light traffic back toward the city center, eyes constantly flicking to the mirror. When they fall silent Pascual says, "So what's the story?"

Eyes on the road, Archie says, "I've been spotted."

"How?" says Fang. "Please don't tell me your phone's been compromised."

"No. I think it was good old-fashioned surveillance. We know they've been tailing us off and on. They've probably got us all on video. And I think they made their move tonight because they finally got a good enough take for the facial recognition software. I was parked down at the end of Lorong 14, and they came down the block and tried to box me in. I had to go up over the curb and along the grass strip to get to Guillemard Road. Didn't do the suspension any good. I was lucky to get away."

"And you're sure you shook them?"

"As sure as I can be. I just hit the gas and got into traffic. I knew they wouldn't risk a chase. I did a few circuits through Katong and Marine Parade to make sure I was clear before I called you. But I've definitely been made. It's time to move."

Pascual waits a beat and says, "Made by who?"

Nobody answers. After a moment Fang says, "Mr. Rose would like a fuller account of what's going on than the one he was given."

Archie says, "Mr. Rose, the best thing you could do is have me take you straight to the airport right now and get on the first plane out."

"We've already discussed that and decided against it."

Fang says, "There is a possibility the police are looking for him, or will be soon. He might be arrested at the airport."

"Then the less he knows, the better."

Fang says, "I'll leave information control to you. But I think the only solution is for him to disappear for a while. And the most comfortable way for him to disappear would be to go with you."

Archie works on that. "How soon can we get out?"

"As soon as Singh can have the plane ready. Tomorrow morning, probably. I've got a couple of meetings tomorrow, but I can reschedule."

"You're coming, too?"

"We need a pretext for the flight. I'll take Renata, too. I'm not sure what we're going to need at the other end. She can make herself useful in any number of ways."

Archie concentrates on his driving for a moment and then

says, "All right, the first thing she can do is meet us somewhere to switch cars. The faster I can be rid of this one, the better. Have her meet us in the car park behind Orchard Towers. Say the second level. We'll leave this one on the top level and walk down. She can take us . . . Where? Where can we lie low while you set up the flight? They'll be watching your flat and the bungalow."

"The villa on Sentosa. It's not in my name. Nobody knows about it. Renata will have to go by my office and get the keys." Fang pulls out his phone.

Pascual is grateful for the courtesy they have shown by discussing all this in English, but he feels they are still some way short of full disclosure. "Can I ask where we're going?" he says.

"Probably Indonesia," says Fang over his shoulder, poking at his phone. "Does that work for you?"

■ ■ ■ ■

"How long will we be gone?" says Renata Taggart, turning from the counter with a freshly poured cup of coffee. She has shed office garb and makeup, and in jeans with her hair in a casual ponytail she is merely a nice down-to-earth Eurasian girl of striking natural beauty. Pascual wonders briefly what personal engagements this emergency has torn her away from; surely the fashionable suitor must have some claim on her time. If she is dismayed to be summoned to duty after hours, she is not showing it; she was waiting as ordered in her BMW coupe in a corner slot when Fang, Archie and Pascual peeked out of the stairwell in the parking garage. She drove them skillfully through the center of town and across the bridge to this gleaming new villa, all planes and angles, steel and glass, in a spanking new development on Sentosa Island, a detached fragment of land at the southern tip of Singapore given over to high-end tourism and exclusive residential enclaves. The house is furnished and provided with a few kitchen essentials, and Pascual suspects this is a bolt hole Fang has had in readiness for some time.

"Hard to say," Fang says. He is perched on a stool in the breakfast nook; behind him Archie has been pacing in and out of the room, hands in his pockets and frowning at the floor. "A week at least, I'd say."

"And why is this necessary?" Renata may be a loyal employee, but her challenging look says she is no pushover.

Fang takes a sip of his coffee before answering. "Because we have attracted some unwanted attention here in Singapore. There has been a breach of security."

"Because of my carelessness?"

Fang shakes his head. "No, no, not at all. Your mistake was trivial, and tonight's crisis has nothing to do with you. The problem is that things have more or less blown up in our face tonight. To put it crudely, Mr. Rose is going to need to stay out of sight for a while. And I think the best place to hide him is Indonesia. I have a lot of resources there."

Pascual notes with interest Fang's failure to mention Archie. He says, "And what's the endgame for me? How do I get home?"

Fang blinks at him. "I don't know. I can't say yet."

Pascual shrugs. "Fair enough. All right, how do we get to Indonesia?"

"We will fly, out of Seletar. I've notified my pilot."

"Where's Seletar?"

"That's the smaller airport, up in the northern part of the island. It's mostly for private jets. The privileges of wealth, of course. I keep Mr. Singh and his Gulfstream on retainer."

Archie says, "They'll be watching Seletar. It's the obvious place. They'll be all over it."

"Who will be watching Seletar?" says Renata, her eyes flicking back and forth between Fang and Archie.

"The bad guys," says Archie. He ignores Renata's puzzled look and turns back to Fang. "There's immigration and border control at Seletar. Can we really circumvent that?"

Fang vents an exasperated sigh. "What do you suggest?"

Archie comes to the table and sits. "Mr. Rose and I go by sea."

Fang frowns. "By sea. What, on one of those ferries to Batam? There will be passport control on those, too. And that only gets you as far as Batam. We need to get to Java."

Archie shakes his head. "On the yacht."

Fang gapes at him. "What, my yacht? The *Jade Empress*?"

"Why not? We'll be two playboy pals of yours, maybe with a couple of girls. We can rent a couple of discreet ones, I'm sure. We go out for a little cruise. When the boat comes back, only the girls will get off. Nobody will notice. Pay your crew a little extra, I'm sure they'll be happy to land us on a deserted stretch of coast not too far from a town."

"Archie, Java's five hundred miles from here. That's more than an overnight."

"We don't have to go all the way to Java. They can shoot

across and land us on Batam or Bintan. That's a day trip. There's an airport on Batam, right? You fly there, and we rendezvous at the airport and fly on to Jakarta."

Fang looks incredulous, but he gives it a few seconds. "Landing you without getting caught would be the trick. There's the Indonesian coast guard to watch out for. But then, smugglers go back and forth under the noses of the coast guard all the time. You could rendezvous with a boat offshore and be at the airport in an hour. We can both start in the morning. By the time you're off Batam, I'll have it set up. I have some contacts there. I'll call the yacht and direct the captain to the best landing spot."

"That should work."

"Forget the girls. Any girl you could rent would talk to anyone who would pay. My crew won't talk. You two will have to get to the Republic of Singapore Yacht Club on your own. I would suggest you call for a taxi. Mr. Rose, I'll have somebody retrieve your luggage from your hideout there in Chinatown."

"I didn't bring any leisure wear with me. I'll show up at the dock dressed for a business-class flight. They may not question me, but they'll notice."

Archie says, "We'll get you some clothes first. And a cheap bag. Take what you need from your luggage and leave it here."

Pascual looks at Fang. "Discard or destroy that phone I left under the pillow. It's got to be infected."

"I've already talked to Campbell about the phones. It will be collected and taken to our security people for analysis, along with mine and Renata's. Campbell will set up new, fully encrypted phones not traceable to us, some of these ultra-secure Katim phones, with international SIM cards. He'll have them for us in the morning. I'll call my captain and tell him to be ready to cast off at ten o'clock. Any questions?"

Pascual hardly knows where to start with the questions, but he says nothing. Fang says, "Very well, then. We can probably be in Jakarta by dinnertime tomorrow."

# 15

Pascual has had a troubled relationship with boats. He enjoys a stiff breeze on a broad reach as much as the next man, but boats of various types have also provided him with several near-death experiences, and he tends to regard them with a skeptical eye. To his relief, the boat he is on today has so far shown no signs of broaching, capsizing or sinking outright.

It is a sleek silver motor yacht with a flying bridge, some twenty-five meters long, captained by an Australian named Kourakis. He is stocky and swarthy, with skin like leather and hair like steel wool. Besides Kourakis there is a crewman who appears to be Malay.

"You'll stay out of sight until I say so," says Kourakis. "You get spotted, I'm the one that gets fined or goes to jail."

"You're the boss," says Pascual from the depths of the sofa where he is lounging in canvas deck shoes and chinos purchased this morning at a Chinatown secondhand store. Archie sits on a matching sofa opposite him here in the lower deck salon. Kourakis stands at the foot of the stairs up to the bridge, having just descended, binoculars in hand.

Pascual was prepared for a day on the high seas; in the event it has taken a mere couple of hours to slip out of Singapore through the fleet of anchored ships and a scattering of small offshore islands and cross the Strait. By the time Pascual felt they had finally left Singapore behind, they were within swimming distance of Batam. Currently they are lying to, a mile or so off the northeastern coast of the island, a flat tree-lined stretch with scattered signs of habitation among the palms: houses, docks and some kind of industrial installation.

"I'm taking a hell of a risk," says Kourakis. "I see any sign of Indonesian coast guard, it's off."

"This is why Dexter pays you the big money," says Archie.

Kourakis vents a gruff laugh. "Lot of good it'll do me in an Indonesian jail."

"So if we run into the coast guard, we go downstairs and hide in the bedrooms and you give them the cover story. Would they search the boat?"

"They might if they don't buy the cover story."

"Which is what, again? Remind me."

Kourakis nods toward a coastline just visible on the horizon to the east. "In theory I'm headed for the resort on Bintan over there to pick up friends of Mr. Fang. My port clearance certificate from Singapore doesn't mention any outbound passengers, which is why you had to hide below when we left. When I get back tonight, if anybody asks why I have no passengers I'll just have to hope they buy the story about Mr. Fang's friends not showing up on Bintan."

Archie shrugs. "Sounds airtight."

Kourakis turns back toward Batam, near at hand. "As long as nobody spots you two slipping over the side and heading for shore. God knows who's watching us right now."

Archie says, "Mr. Fang will take care of any problems on the Indonesian side. He has good connections here."

Kourakis is squinting out across the water toward the shore. "Yeah, money works wonders in this part of the world, or so they say. Right. Off you go, then. This looks like your taxi." He hurries up the stairs to the bridge.

A small boat has come around a spit of land and is puttering toward them. No more than four or five meters long, it is covered amidships by a blue canopy and powered by an outboard motor. Pascual makes out one man at the stern and another at the bow. He and Archie drag their luggage out onto the open rear deck. They stand shading their eyes as the boat creeps slowly toward them. Pascual looks up at the bridge to see Kourakis scanning along the coast to the south with the binoculars. Pascual looks and sees nothing but a few small craft like the one approaching them.

When the boat finally arrives, Kourakis yells down to its crew in what Pascual assumes is Indonesian. The man at the stern yells back, and Kourakis motions them around to the stern. He yells down to Pascual. "They're from Fang, all right. At least they say they are."

The two men in the boat are Indonesian, both in shorts and wearing baseball-style caps, the one at the bow shirtless. The helmsman maneuvers the boat skillfully to pull in at the stern, shielded from view on land. Kourakis's crewman catches a line tossed by the man at the bow and holds it while the man at the stern uses the motor to nudge the stern of the boat close to the yacht. There is no rail at the stern of the yacht and it is a simple matter for Archie and Pascual to toss their bags into the boat and then step onto it.

"Thanks for the ride," says Pascual, looking up at Kourakis on the bridge.

"You were never here, mate," says the Australian, shaking his head. "Never saw you two in my life."

The shirtless man waves Pascual and Archie to seats under the canopy, gabbling in Indonesian, as the boat pulls away from the yacht. Pascual is grateful for the shade. The shirtless man goes to sit by his partner in the stern. Archie says, "I wonder how many middlemen were involved in this transaction. I think Dexter's connections are mainly on Java and Borneo."

Pascual is intent on the shoreline ahead, terra incognita and far out of his comfort zone. Palm trees, a scattering of houses, little better than shacks, boats pulled up on shore. The spit of land from behind which the boat appeared is just ahead. The helmsman cuts the motor and the boat slows and begins to drift. The shirtless man ducks under the canopy and walks toward the bow between Pascual and Archie. He wheels and squats and says, "OK, you pay now." He holds out his left hand palm up and slaps it with his right.

Archie and Pascual exchange a look. Archie says, "Already paid."

The shirtless man juts his chin toward Archie. "You pay now. Pay transit."

Archie shakes his head. "Mr. Fang pay."

"No pay. You pay. One thousand dollar. Or you swim."

A stalemate ensues. The boat drifts, Archie and Pascual exchange another look, the man at the stern chuckles softly and murmurs something to his companion. The shirtless man reaches under a thwart and pulls out a machete. He hefts it, grins and says, "You pay now."

Pascual runs through options at lightning speed: jump and swim, throw the bag in his face and start swinging, pay up. Archie sighs. He pulls out his phone and says, "One minute."

The shirtless man jerks the machete back, cocking for a blow, and Pascual grips the handle of his bag. Use it as a shield, he is thinking, knock him over backward and hope Archie can punch his weight. Archie coolly holds up a finger, putting his phone to his ear. The shirtless man snarls in Indonesian. Archie starts speaking Chinese into his phone. Everyone freezes. Archie hands the phone to the shirtless man, who lowers the machete and takes the phone with a deeply suspicious look. "Mr. Fang," says Archie.

The man listens. The look on his face goes from suspicious to surprised to totally blank and winds up at sullen in the space of fifteen or twenty seconds. He tosses the phone back to Archie and growls something to the man at the stern. Then he clambers to the bow of the boat and spits into the sea. The man at the stern restarts the motor and resumes putt-putting toward land.

"Really bad pirates," says Archie. "If they were any good, they'd have just killed us, taken our money and thrown us in the water, and told Dexter we didn't show up."

Pascual's pulse is just beginning to slow. "Thank God for incompetence," he says when he finds his voice.

"Welcome to Indonesia," says Dexter Fang, emerging from the passenger side of a Toyota SUV parked in the shade, a hundred yards or so up a dusty road leading away from the squalid little cove where Pascual and Archie were landed, littered with beached small craft and surrounded by a variety of ramshackle structures, some on stilts in the water. "I'm sorry for the unpleasantness," says Fang. "I'll have a word with my local contact about these ruffians. I take it there was no more trouble after I dropped his name?"

"Not a bit," says Archie. "What's he got on them?"

"He more or less runs the smuggling in this part of the island. They depend on him to buy the stuff they bring across from Singapore and forge the paperwork for the sand they take over there."

"Sand?"

"Singapore imports a lot of sand, for construction. Illegal dredgers get a lot of it from beaches and rivers in Indonesia. The traffic's been outlawed, but that just means more profit opportunities for smugglers. Well, not our problem. The plane's waiting."

The driver of the SUV is tossing Pascual and Archie's bags in the back. Pascual says, "How far is the airport?"

Fang points through the trees. "Less than a mile that way. You could walk there. Hop in."

A short drive takes them up the road and into a town of sorts, an unruly variety of trees shading widely spaced concrete houses with tin roofs, painted pastel colors, some with small neat gardens. Smuggling is not a bad living, at least for some, to judge by the cars parked here and there. They turn onto a highway that runs straight as an arrow away from the sea, and in a few minutes they are negotiating traffic circles and access roads to what looks like a sizable modern airport. "Indonesia's eighteen thousand islands," says Fang. "Without air travel we couldn't have a modern country. Any island of any size has an airport. This one has all the mod cons, including customs and immigration, but fortunately we'll be allowed to drive right up to the jet, so we'll be able to finesse that and get you two aboard." Fang beams one of his high-wattage smiles. "You won't appear on the flight plan, so if we go down, your disappearance will be a mystery forever, but that's the price we pay. We'll just swing by the VIP hall to pick up Renata and we'll be on our way."

Half an hour after Pascual was contemplating jumping into a tropical sea to escape a machete-wielding buccaneer, he is watching Renata Taggart climb into the back of the SUV, looking like a million Singapore dollars in white jeans and a light green jacket. "Hello, gentlemen," she says. "How was your passage?"

Archie and Pascual exchange another look. "Uneventful," says Archie.

"Stimulating," says Pascual. "A nice introduction to local culture."

▪ ▪ ▪ ▪

The Gulfstream is roomy and luxurious, a flying hotel suite. Singh the pilot is dark and glowering, with a military air. Pascual spends the flight with his face pressed to a window. When it is not the sea beneath them, it is a swath of nameless island or perhaps a fringe of Sumatra, and for all Fang's talk of a modern country, there is a lot of trackless unmodernized green below. Pascual tries to ignore a faint but growing sense of dread. He is being drawn farther into an alien space, the mysterious East, spice islands and pirate havens, Joseph Conrad territory, pursued by people who solve problems by ramming a spit into a man's brain. He is beginning to regret his decision not to throw himself at the mercy of the Singapore police, and he has had to admit to himself that one reason he did not was the lingering prospect, however delusional, of a million-dollar payoff.

You have always been a slow learner, Pascual thinks.

The sun goes down in a conflagration, and the jet descends through the abrupt tropical darkness toward an extravagant spread of lights on the horizon. What Pascual knows about Jakarta is that it is sinking, an exploding megalopolis built in a coastal swamp. There is plenty left above the waves, he sees as the jet banks into its approach; a distant cluster of skyscrapers looks solid enough in the midst of a vast spread of lights tracing the haphazard street patterns of explosive urban growth.

On the ground a black Mercedes is waiting for them. They have taxied to a cluster of buildings removed from the main terminal, and the engines have been cut. Fang ends a call on his cell phone and says, "All right. As this flight originated on Batam, we will not have to go through border control procedures here. Renata and I officially entered Indonesia on Batam this morning. You two are still in Singapore, for all anyone knows. My Jakarta chauffeur is waiting and nobody will question or even notice two extra passengers getting off the plane. We've landed at Jakarta's second airport, which is much more convenient to the motorway, and we will avoid some of the notorious Jakarta traffic. Our first stop will be a town east of here called Telukjambe. There is a tolerable restaurant there. After dinner we will proceed. By bedtime we'll be at our destination."

"Which is where?" says Pascual.

Fang smiles. "A place like you've never seen before. The Javanese highlands."

■ ■ ■ ■

Bedtime is fast approaching, Pascual feels, as the long stressful day begins to catch up with him. He drains the last of his very nice single-malt scotch and steps to the edge of the veranda to take in a draft of the cool night breeze coming across the valley, bringing intimations of vast spaces in front of him. The day that started in Singapore is finishing here, in a house on the side of a mountain somewhere between Subang and Lembang, two towns which this morning he didn't know existed, at the end of a long drive in the dark along winding roads through haphazardly lit villages, always climbing. Pascual's expectations have been confounded; his vision of Java was a steaming tropical island with waving palms and shimmering rice paddies, but what he could make out in the dark as they drove reminded him of mountain regions he has seen elsewhere: not very prosperous clusters of habitation crowding the edge of the road, glimpses of forested slopes against the sky, black on slightly less black. The final stretch brought them through a district of discreetly spaced, noticeably more opulent dwellings, to this white stucco villa with a tile roof and an encircling veranda, opening in back onto a large garden sloping away into the dark. Inside are nicely appointed rooms for living, dining and lounging on the ground floor, and enough comfortable bedrooms and fully plumbed bathrooms upstairs to accommodate them all. They were received by a houseboy, a serene elderly man in the black felt cap of a devout Muslim, and his silent wife. Somebody in these hills has money, Pascual can see.

A step sounds behind Pascual and Renata says, "Mr. Fang would like to see you." Pascual follows her into a large room, furnished with thickly cushioned bamboo furniture and decorated with lush plants in brass pots. Fang is planted in an armchair at the end of the room nursing a drink. Archie is at one end of a long sofa; Renata settles onto the other. Pascual drops gratefully into an armchair opposite Fang. "Would you like another drink?" says Fang.

Pascual sets the glass down on a table at his elbow. "No, thank you. This one is going to knock me out in about fifteen minutes. That should be just enough time for you to put me fully in the picture of what you three are up to."

"We three." Fang chuckles. "It's really just me and Archie. And I suppose it's only fair to bring you both into the circle." Fang looks at Archie. "Are we agreed on that point?"

Archie says, "If you are completely sure that everyone in this room can be trusted."

In the slightly chilly silence that follows, Fang appears to give that careful consideration, gently swirling the ice cubes in his glass. Finally he drinks, swallows, levels a look at Archie and says, "I trust Mr. Rose because he came to me when he could have gone to the police. He could have blown us sky high and been on his way home by now, but he did not betray the operation. I trust Renata because she has worked for me for three years and handled the most delicate matters with great skill and discretion. And because her father and mine were friends, and so there are bonds of family. So yes, I think they can both be trusted with full disclosure. In fact, I think we owe it to them to come clean, as the expression goes."

Renata is staring gravely across the room at Fang. "Come clean about what?" she says.

"About the true nature of this enterprise Mr. Rose has come to Singapore to help us with."

Renata's eyes narrow. "You mean that there's something even more disreputable about it than setting up shell companies to funnel laundered money to clients you are reluctant to discuss? I would have thought that was enough risk for a respectable man like you."

Fang concedes with a gesture, looking a little shamefaced.

"I am very grateful for your discretion, Renata. And when I told you that these questionable maneuvers were being done with the best of motives, I was telling the truth. There's just an element I left out. And that element is extremely sensitive. I have been reluctant to tell you, but if you're going to be on the team you need to know what's at stake."

Pascual raises his arm to point at Archie. "It's about him, isn't it? Maybe it's time to tell us who he really is."

Archie does what Pascual least expects: he laughs. He looks a little ridiculous in his black-framed glasses with the mop of hair flopping on his forehead, but he is deadly serious as he says, "Bingo, Mr. Rose. Yes, it's all about me. I am a fugitive, and the people who are after me have a lot of resources and a reputation for being completely ruthless."

"And who are they?"

"I'll give you a hint: They come from a country with a billion and a half people and one political party." Archie turns to Fang and says, "I think probably the cat's at least halfway out of the bag for both Mr. Rose and Renata at this point. You might as well tell them who I am."

Fang draws a deep breath. "Well, how to put this? Archie is the most wanted man in China."

# 17

A few seconds tick off the clock. A look of wonder spreads over Renata's face and she says, "You're Chee Dongfeng."

Archie nods. Abruptly he takes off the glasses with one hand and sweeps the hair out of his eyes with the other. Renata gasps softly. "My God."

"Yes. Archibald Chee to most of the world, as seen in a thousand news photos. Very recognizable." He lets the hair fall back and puts the glasses on. "I can't tell you how much I hate the hair hanging in my eyes, but it does change the look. So you got it, congratulations. Now please keep it under your hat. My life depends on it. You, too, Mr. Rose."

Pascual says, "I have no idea who Archibald Chee is, so I'm not likely to tell anyone. But I know how to keep my mouth shut."

"Good." Archie looks at Renata. "You obviously know who I am. Would you like to tell Mr. Rose?"

Renata composes herself and turns to Pascual. "Mr. Chee is the founder of Yuanzang." When Pascual merely looks blank she adds, "That's one of the top internet search engines in China, the closest rival to Baidu."

"Ah. Forgive me, I don't do much surfing in Chinese."

Fang says, "All you need to know is that even being number two in China means you're a pretty big deal. Our boy Archie here has built Yuanzang into a major internet company, branching out into all kinds of interesting things, much like Google. It has made him a very rich man. A billionaire, in fact."

Archie gives a modest wave of the hand. "Unfortunately it has also made me into a target. You may have heard something about the government's crackdown on the so-called tech tycoons."

Pascual says, "The party decided they had amassed too much wealth and proceeded to cut them down to size. Is that it?"

"More or less. There has been an avalanche of new regulations, sabotaged listings on foreign exchanges, intrusive investigations, crushing fines, arbitrary detentions. Valuations have sunk and people have lost billions. They've been pressured into making confessions of wrongdoing and professions of loyalty. Some of the biggest names and most successful entrepreneurs in China have been . . . what's the expression? Brought to heel."

"And now it's your turn, is it?"

"It was going to be. That's why I chose to disappear."

"Ah. You're one of the disappearing billionaires."

"The most prominent one," says Fang. "There has been speculation about Archie in the media for weeks. It's been assumed that he has been detained by the authorities for the usual treatment, a lecture on the facts of life and some coaching in contrition, along with the extortion. But there are also rumors he's suffering from a fatal illness, or had a nervous breakdown, and he's in a sanatorium somewhere."

Archie says, "Unlike the others, I disappeared preemptively, before I was called on the carpet. I could see what was coming. So I started planning my escape. I paid a lot of money for a genuine passport under the name Zhang Wei, which in China is like John Smith, and flew out of Shanghai three months ago."

Pascual frowns. "And you made it as far as Singapore. Was taking a job as Dexter Fang's chauffeur part of the plan?"

Fang clears his throat and says, "Archie came to me for help. We are actually distantly related. My branch of the family went to Indonesia, his stayed in China. Getting himself out of China was only half the battle. What he needed from me was help in getting his money out. I was happy to help my cousin in his hour of need. But he had to stay out of sight. So I hired him as my chauffeur. I'd just fired one, as it happened. Fortunately Archie is a pretty good driver."

Archie says, "I drove a cab in Los Angeles when I was at USC. I needed the money because unlike a lot of my classmates I didn't have a rich daddy paying for everything. It was pretty good training."

Fang says, "Actually, not having a rich daddy has turned out to be an advantage. Archie doesn't have any close family back in China who can be held as hostages."

Archie puts on a rueful look. "The only woman I ever wanted to marry was a sorority girl from Pomona. And she wouldn't have me."

Fang's belly shakes as he laughs. "Poor Archie. The only hostage they have is his money."

Archie says, "As you can imagine, my finances are quite complex. And the greater part of my assets are still in China and thus extremely vulnerable to confiscation, though I've been quietly moving money out for a couple of years now. In China there is no law but the party, ultimately."

Pascual tries to digest all this. "So you went to the CIA for help."

Fang and Archie trade what strikes Pascual as the look of two men making sure they have their stories straight. "Not exactly," says Archie. "I went to Dexter first. I knew I could trust him, and he has a lot of useful resources. After Dexter and I had come up with the basic idea, just to explore options, I contacted an old friend from college who's done some interesting things in IT. And it turns out he has CIA connections. That's how it happened. I talked to my friend, and the next thing I knew I was in Honolulu, talking to people from Langley. They drew up the whole scheme. They didn't mention anyone like you, but I suppose you were part of what they called 'diversionary tactics.' They were very concerned with security."

"I can imagine. Who's the friend?"

"I can't tell you that." Archie raises his chin a few degrees. "Security, you know."

Pascual looks at Renata, who is observing intently, and then back at Archie. "All right. Why don't you just fly to Honolulu or Los Angeles or Washington, D.C. tomorrow and set up operations there? It sounds like whatever salvage you can do at this point will have to be done remotely anyway, and you'd be safer there, wouldn't you? How long were you planning to masquerade as a chauffeur?"

"Until I saw which way the wind was blowing. I'm not sure where I'd be safe now. The Guoanbu has a long arm."

"The Guoanbu?"

"The Ministry for State Security. They have abduction teams they send out to grab people they want overseas. They kidnapped a friend of mine from a hotel in Hong Kong and took him back to China for trial. And there have been abductions in other countries, as well. I decided that staying out of sight was the best option. But somehow they got onto me in Singapore. They have a big presence there, of course. I think they must have suspected I'd contact Dexter and started watching him. And eventually they spotted me. Probably with surveillance cameras and facial recognition software. I thought I could beat that with the glasses and the hair, but I guess not. I'll have to find a different disguise now."

A gloomy silence follows. "Speaking of security details," says Fang, "my Jakarta man will be bringing a team up here tomorrow. Just three or four men to keep an eye on things without being too obvious. This is not a bad district to hide in. It's a resort area, full of vacation homes for rich people from Jakarta and Bandung, so strangers don't attract that much notice. You should be all right here for the moment. Tomorrow Renata and I will go back to Jakarta and work from my office there, to show whoever might be interested that there's nothing going on but business as usual. Campbell will have a forensic report on those phones by tomorrow, and we'll see where we stand. Obviously at some point Archie has to figure out where he's going to wind up, and Mr. Rose is going to have to find a way to get home and get paid. In the meantime, I don't see any reason why we can't proceed as planned. We have one account up and running, and Archie can start moving money into it, so that you can then move it on to various destinations I've prepared, nicely scrubbed. We can see if the financial plumbing works."

Pascual frowns. "You don't think that will attract attention? Especially if the police are looking for me?"

"As of an hour ago, Singapore news reports on the lawyer's death make no mention of you. If the police are looking for you, they're not broadcasting it. I think we have accomplished more or less what we set out to accomplish. We have established a channel for some of Archie's money to begin flowing from its original hiding place to another, via Pascual Rose's accounts. Meanwhile, we just need to keep Archie off the radar while we explore alternatives. I would think the main thing to worry about would be betraying your location here. Campbell can advise us on security issues."

In the silence that follows, Pascual makes eye contact with the other three in turn and sees the same wary reserve in each of them. "And we can do this all remotely, from here?" he says finally.

Fang smiles. "Technology is a wonderful thing. Ask Archie. He developed a lot of it."

■■■■

"Watch out for snakes. They come out at night."

Pascual turns to see Fang stepping out onto the veranda, glass in hand. Pascual has wandered some ten or twelve steps out onto the grass, listening to elusive snatches of distant music and inhaling the complex, alien smell of tropical highlands. "What kind of snakes?"

"Cobras, pit vipers. Various others."

"Ah." Pascual walks back toward the veranda, watching where he puts his feet. He goes up the steps and says, "Thank you. Perhaps I'll just go to bed after all."

"You'd have to be very unlucky and step on one or something. They're generally shy and try to avoid humans."

In the light from inside Pascual can make out the smile on Fang's face. "I won't push my luck."

"That's wise."

"Can I ask you a question?"

"Of course."

"Are you sure we're safe here?"

"As safe as I can make you. The house belongs to an associate of mine who owes me a favor. If anyone succeeded in following us from the airport, I believe we eluded them by switching vehicles in Telukjambe. The phones Renata and I brought with us were guaranteed clean by Campbell and his technical wizards as of this morning. We are at this point off the radar of anyone who might be interested in my movements. As for the people in my employ, I trust them completely. They are all from families that have served mine for generations. Yes, I believe we are safely hidden here."

"All right, that's reassuring. One more question. Have you had time to think about your network?"

"I beg your pardon?"

"The lawyer who got killed was going to sell me some information about certain people in your network, remember?"

"Ah, yes. Certain people. Well, yes, I've thought about it. I think the most likely thing is that he was referring to Archie."

Pascual nods slowly. "Yes, I suppose so. You would know more than I. I'm still feeling my way in the dark out here." He turns to go inside. "Thanks for the tip about the snakes."

# 18

In the morning what was a vast darkness full of formless threats resolves itself into a range of rolling green hills stretching away under a gray sky, with a scattering of white villas with red tile roofs among clusters of trees. There are palms and ferns, but also to Pascual's surprise some conifers, including three cypresses at the corner of the hedge-enclosed garden of the villa. The morning is cool, and Pascual finds it hard to believe he is standing within a few degrees of the equator. He turns and goes back into the house.

Renata is on the sofa where she sat the previous evening, focused on her phone. From a front room comes Fang's voice, speaking what Pascual assumes is Indonesian, as it is certainly not Chinese. He follows the sound and finds Fang and Archie with three Indonesian men, neatly groomed but casually dressed in jeans and untucked shirts, none very large but all wiry and fit. They could be gymnasts or judo contestants but for the impassive, unimpressed look Pascual has come to associate with the professional hard case.

"Mr. Rose." Fang beckons. "Come and meet the security team. They'll make sure nobody bothers you while you're on vacation here. This is Subroto." Pascual shakes hands with the eldest, maybe in his late thirties, his high cheekboned face starting to show the miles. "And here's Eko." This is the most muscular of the three, with a fierce low-browed look. "And Hasan." The youngest, still a bit baby-faced but not the type of boy you want to pick a fight with, to judge by his sullen expression.

Fang makes a sweeping gesture, the impresario. "All former Kopassus. That's the army's special operations force. They all speak some English," says Fang. "Right, boys?"

In a staccato accent Subroto says, "Call in artillery and call it a day." The other two give it a token laugh.

Archie says, "God, let's hope there won't be any artillery involved." He is lounging in an armchair, hands clasped on his belly, giving the former commandos a skeptical look.

"I don't think there's going to be artillery or anything else alarming," says Fang. "They're just here for insurance. They'll bunk in that back room upstairs, and there'll always be at least two on duty. They've got that fancy SUV out front, and they'll keep an eye on the neighborhood. They'll be in constant communication with each other and with me. As long as you have to lie low up here, they'll make sure you don't have anything to worry about."

"Do they have guns?" says Archie.

There is a moment of awkward silence, and then Subroto lifts his shirttail to reveal the grip of an automatic.

"Great," says Archie, with a nod. "Let's hope you don't have to use it."

"Amen," says Fang. "All right, then. Renata and I are going back to Jakarta this morning. I'll work there for a few days, and this will all look like a routine trip. Meanwhile I'll work some contacts and ask some discreet questions and try to find out if it's safe for Pascual Rose to show his face in Singapore. Archie, you and I will talk, all right?" Archie mutters a few words in Chinese by way of reply. Fang turns to Pascual and says, "By the way. I talked to Campbell just now. His cyber wizards examined all our phones. And guess what? You were right. Your phone was infected with a Pegasus variant out of China. Mine and Renata's were clean."

Pascual contemplates this. "Out of China. Not a surprise, I guess. The question is then, how did it get infected? They had to have my number to deliver the attack, right?"

Fang shrugs. "These things are beyond me. It might be good for you to talk to Campbell at some point. Well. We'll be in touch. For the moment, I think you can relax and enjoy a little leisure."

Pascual is remembering other enforced vacations with time heavy on his hands. He turns to the security detail and says, "Do any of you play chess?"

■■■■

Hasan, it turns out, plays chess quite well, making moves with quick angry swipes after half a minute's thought. They play on a beautiful wooden chess set produced from a cabinet in the back parlor by the houseboy, the pieces figures from Javanese mythology, intricately carved out of two types of wood, light and dark. Time has darkened the lighter wood until white and black pieces are nearly indistinguishable. With that confusion adding to the long-standing weaknesses in his game, Pascual quickly loses twice. He shakes his head, extends his hand to Hasan, and goes in search of Archie.

He finds him in front of the villa talking to Subroto, standing next to the Hyundai SUV that brought the team from Jakarta. Archie greets Pascual with "Want to come for a little tour of the district? The boss here says we'll be OK as long as we don't make a public spectacle of ourselves."

This appeals to Pascual immediately. Subroto summons Eko with a brief phone conversation and gets behind the wheel, Eko taking the shotgun seat. Archie and Pascual get in back. "We're not that far from Bandung, which is a major city," says Archie. "But the town just down the road should have an internet connection, which is all I'm after today."

"There's none at the house?"

"None that's nice and anonymous. And until I'm confident Dexter's connection to this place can't be traced, I'm not going near it. Fortunately the internet's everywhere now, even in Indonesia. Every little town will have an internet café or two."

Pascual is absorbed in the sights for a time, other villas passing by, the valley opening out on their left, the strangely untropical vegetation still suggesting higher latitudes. "Is there a way I could send a message to my wife without giving away our location? I don't have an e-mail account anymore."

"There are anonymous e-mail services. But anything you send could be traced to our location if someone is monitoring her account. Is that likely?"

"I don't think so. In any event it would not be obviously from me. We've worked out a sort of code for messages. I've been more or less off the grid for a couple of years."

"That's damn hard to do these days."

"Tell me about it."

"Who's chasing you?"

Pascual smiles. "Who isn't? I've made a lot of enemies. I seem to have a talent for it."

Archie cocks an eyebrow at him. "Should that make me nervous?"

Pascual looks out the window. "I kept some very bad company for a while in my youth. Then I had a change of heart and sold them all out. I've been trying to atone, or at least not do any further damage, ever since. But half the world considers me an irredeemable thug and the other half a contemptible snitch. Both with some justice."

Archie chuckles softly. "I salute a fellow outlaw."

A long downhill stretch, modest houses crowding the edges of the road, brings them out onto the valley floor. The road levels off and is lined by trees; roadside stands offer fruits, bottled water, sundries. The shacks proliferate and suddenly they are in a town, Subroto piloting the SUV carefully through traffic composed largely of weaving motorbikes.

The main street of the town is crowded with shops, all boasting exuberant signage in a mixture of languages. *BUAH SEGAR, GENNIUS PHONE, MASAKAN PADANG, LOVE CELL.* The internet café is squeezed between an electronics stall and a perfume shop; the café portion consists of a tiny counter behind which a youth dispenses soft drinks. Deafening rap music pounds from a speaker. The youth has enough English to negotiate terms and direct them to one of four laptops on a long table, two of them occupied by youths absorbed in games. Archie brings up an e-mail service and Pascual, after a moment's thought, types in Sara's address, the subject line *Hola* and in Spanish the message *Java even more beautiful than they say*. He signs it *Nono* and shoves the laptop to Chee. "Thanks."

"No problem. Would you mind going for a walk? I need to take care of a little business here. Go be a tourist for half an hour. Or talk to those gorillas."

Pascual opts for the gorillas on security grounds. The SUV is parked on the shoulder across the street, crowding the front of a clothing store and drawing dirty looks from the owner. Subroto is behind the wheel; there is no sign of Eko. Pascual climbs into in the back. "How long will he be there?" says Subroto.

"Half an hour, he said."

The Indonesian grunts softly and resumes watching the street, checking the mirrors frequently. Pascual gropes for a topic of mutual interest. "How long have you worked for Dexter Fang?"

"Four years. Before that, army, twenty years. I went to Australia two times, Hawaii once. Train with the U.S. Marines. Semper Fi." The stern look relaxes and Subroto flashes a grin. "Mr. Fang, he pay better."

"I'm sure. How many security men does he employ?"

The grin goes away. "Enough."

Pascual steers toward less sensitive information and manages to elicit that Subroto and Eko are Javanese, while Hasan hails from some Sumatran backwater. "But we are all Indonesian now. Indonesia has two hundred eighty million people. Biggest Muslim country in the world. The Indonesian army is number fourteen in the world."

Pascual toys briefly with the idea of asking for Subroto's perspective on Indonesian military depredations in East Timor, but rejects it, and shortly he is relieved to see Archie emerging from the café. Eko magically appears out of a crowd as Archie crosses the street, and they both climb in.

"Back to the ranch," says Archie, "unless anybody has any shopping to do."

Subroto shakes his head and noses out into traffic. Archie says, "Your lawyer's murder is all over the news in Singapore. The police are looking at his connections to the vice trade. There's no mention of Chinese agents or of you, but that doesn't mean they're not looking for you."

"Sooner or later I'm going to have to talk to them."

"Probably. In the short run, there are other things to worry about."

"Such as?"

Archie scowls out the window for a few seconds before answering. "You know who owns the house we're staying at?"

"I just heard what Fang said. A friend of his who owes him a favor."

"Yes. A man named Roosevelt Halim, another Indonesian of Chinese origin. He and Dexter go way back. That's why Dexter trusts him."

Pascual reads between the lines. "You don't?"

"When Dexter told me about the house, I knew I had heard the name. I couldn't quite remember in what connection. So I looked him up just now. It turns out that Halim made his first fortune in palm oil, but he has diversified since then. He has invested a great deal of money in tech companies, some of them in China. It was in connection with one of those investments that I'd heard of him. He has a big stake in a company headquartered in Fuzhou that is developing some AI tools with possible military applications. He is reputed to have ties with people high up in the PLA, the army."

"Does Dexter know this?"

"He will as soon as I can talk to him. He will probably scoff and insist there's nothing to it. But the Guoanbu is obviously focusing on Dexter and his network in their attempts to find me, and here's a member of his network who I would have to say is very vulnerable to Chinese pressure. That is not the man I would choose to hide with when running from the Chinese."

Pascual gives it a moment's thought. "The key question would seem to be, does Roosevelt Halim know Dexter is hiding you?"

"He better not. I've been assuming Dexter's keeping his mouth shut about that."

"What did Dexter tell him about this little house party?"

"Dexter says he gave him a story about a retreat with some business associates. But Dexter has plenty of places of his own for that kind of thing. Halim's got to wonder. And if the Chinese have leaned on him a little, told him to report anything unusual . . ." Archie shakes his head.

They are silent for a time as Subroto steers them out of town and back onto the road that leads to the hills. "They do have guns," says Archie, nodding at the two in the front seat. "And they probably know how to use them."

# 19

Pascual awakes in confusion, unsure whether the crash of breaking glass, the urgent stressed voices in an unknown language, and finally the sharp crack of pistol shots are part of a turbulent dream or a reality that is going to make him very unhappy. By the time he hears someone sprinting down the hall outside his bedroom door, the fog has cleared and he is groping for his trousers. Instinct warns against turning on the lamp; a crack of light from the hall shows under the closed door. By the time Pascual has progressed to shirt and shoes somebody is pounding on it and yelling, "Wake up! Fire! We go now!"

Pascual is more inclined to worry about the shooting, if he did not hallucinate it, but now he can smell the smoke. He has the presence of mind to snatch his wallet from the bedside table and stuff it into his waistband. When he tears open his door he can see the smoke, wafting up through flickering light from downstairs. In the dim glow from the single overhead fixture in the hall he can also see Archie stumbling out of his room across the hall, bare-chested, carrying shoes and shirt, wide-eyed without glasses, hair a wild tangle. Steps sound on the stairs and Eko comes charging up, automatic in one hand and phone in the other, shirtless like Archie but shod, though with laces flying loose. He glances up at the hall light and leaps to a switch to douse the light. Now lit only by the flames below, he runs toward them saying, "You come!"

Archie ducks back into his room. On the floor below, someone is panicking; the voice is elderly and wailing. Pascual remembers the houseboy and his wife; are they just going to leave them? Eko has pushed open the door to the darkened bedroom just past Archie's and is beckoning violently. Archie reappears clutching a shoulder bag. Pascual makes a rapid decision: with both fire and gunshots in play, there is nothing in his room worth an instant's delay. Eko drops to hands and knees, motioning for them to do the same. On all fours he crawls into the bedroom, the other two following. Eko crawls to the window, a lighter shade of black in the dark room, and slumps to a sitting position against the wall. He puts the phone to his ear and growls into it. The wailing voice downstairs fades, receding into distance outside the house. Smoke reaches them and Archie coughs; Pascual's eyes sting. Eko barks into the phone and then stuffs it into his waistband. He reaches up to unlatch the casement window and pulls it open. He cautiously raises his head above the sill. Pascual squeezes his eyes shut, tears welling. When he opens them again Eko is slithering out over the windowsill. Pascual expects to see him disappear, but instead he thumps onto something just outside the window and whispers hoarsely back into the room. "You come!"

Archie does not hesitate. He follows Eko out the window

and Pascual realizes that it gives onto the roof over the veranda at the side of the house. As soon as Archie has cleared the sill, Pascual follows, tumbling onto the tiles. Eko is crouching, swiveling this way and that, both hands on the gun. Voices sound faintly not too far away. Eko grabs Archie by the arm and pulls him toward the edge of the roof. "We go down. You follow me." Without further ceremony he slides over the edge, hanging briefly by his free hand before dropping out of sight.

Archie murmurs, "You have got to be kidding me."

Pascual shoves past him and rolls over on his belly, throwing his feet out over the void. The weight of his legs pulls him down; he grabs at the edge of the tiles but quickly loses his grip and drops a meter or so onto the grass, toppling as he lands but managing not to sprain anything. Prone on the grass, he watches as Eko scans a dark and chaotic visual field, gun raised. There is a scraping noise overhead and a strangled oath, and then Archie hits the ground with a tremendous thump, nearly landing on Pascual.

Eko makes a hissing noise, unmistakably a command to be silent. He is facing the back of the house, frozen. From the direction of the garden come soft voices and a rustling of brush. Suddenly three more shots ring out, from the other side of the house, to judge by the sound. They are answered from the back of the garden; the muzzle flashes light the foliage.

Eko is tugging at Pascual's arm, urging him toward the low hedge that separates the villa's grounds from its neighbor. Pascual thrashes through it, trips and sprawls on the grass. Eko and Archie follow; Eko hauls Pascual to his feet and says, "Run!"

They run. There is enough light for Archie and Pascual to follow Eko across the neighboring lawn and into a clump of bushes, where Eko halts, drops to a crouch and pulls them to the ground. "Wait now."

The shooting has stopped. Indistinct noises come from the direction of their villa, people moving furtively through the dark. A wavering orange glow lights the windows. Pascual lies in a thicket, foliage brushing his face, and remembers Fang saying *You would have to be unlucky, step on one or something.*

Fire and guns and now snakes. Pascual suppresses the urge to bolt, panic pushing at his self-control. Two more shots sound near the villa and then a car engine starts. "We go now," says Eko, slapping each of them on the leg as he rises. "Hurry now."

They follow him around the back of another villa and then cut up through a stand of small trees toward where the road must lie, stumbling in the dark. A light goes on in a nearby house. They reach the road as a vehicle comes roaring up it, no lights showing, reflected light from the now considerable conflagration at the villa dancing on its side. The flashlight app on Eko's phone goes on for two or three seconds, long enough for him to signal and then off again as the SUV skids to a halt in front of them. The three of them pile in and Pascual makes out Subroto at the wheel. He has the vehicle moving before the doors are shut, and then he hits the gas hard.

Subroto careens through the dark for another hundred yards, steering by sheer instinct or perhaps echolocation, before he switches on the headlights. They are tearing past darkened houses at the bottom of a hill before Pascual thinks to ask, "Where is Hasan?"

Subroto steers around a curve, tires squealing. "Hasan covering us. We will find him later."

Pascual's nerves are just beginning to recover from the stimulation of the past couple of minutes when a tremendous boom assaults their ears and the hillsides are lit with an eerie glow. Pascual leaps on the seat; Subroto jams on the brakes and slews to a halt diagonally across the road. They gape for a moment and then spill out of the SUV to look at the fireworks display over the crest of the hill behind them, flaming debris floating to earth through the night sky. Archie says, "What the hell happened?"

Subroto laughs. "Gas," he says. "Gas in the kitchen." He motions for them to get back in. "Bad for the owner, good for us."

■ ■ ■ ■

"They breach the door, throw in a Molotov cocktail." Wherever Subroto learned his English, he seems to have acquired the necessary professional vocabulary. "In front, so we must go out the back. And they were waiting in the garden. Hasan, he saw everything. He fire to pin them, while you ran and I went to get the car."

Subroto has pulled off the road in a grove of trees and doused the lights. The route he has followed for the past ten minutes was meandering and random as far as Pascual could tell, taking them past isolated houses and along narrow lanes, though Eko seemed to be navigating with his phone. Pascual can make out nothing in the dark around them; the closest lights are scattered on slopes in the far distance. Eko is now poking at his phone. He puts it to his ear, waits a few seconds and speaks. His tone at first is calm, but it changes fast, and Pascual does not have to speak Indonesian to know that whatever Eko is hearing is bad news. Eko lowers the phone and brings Subroto up to date; he puts the vehicle in gear and pulls back onto the road.

Eko is talking rapidly into the phone again, quietly but urgently, breaking off every few seconds to speak to Subroto, who has switched on the headlights and picked up the pace. They climb a slope, the trees thinning and lighted windows appearing in the distance. Subroto swings left at a T-junction with a larger road and accelerates along a long stone embankment; Pascual is startled to see the glow of the burning house over the crest of a hill not too far ahead. A siren sounds behind them; Subroto glances in the mirror and pulls to the edge of the road. A police car tears past them, lights flashing. Subroto and Eko confer briefly and Subroto puts it in gear.

Pascual orients himself when they reach the traffic circle which lies just up the road from the villa. The lights of the police car have joined others two hundred yards further on; Pascual can see a crowd gathering, lit by the fire. Eko mutters and points to the right; Subroto wrestles the car through a turn and heads downhill on a lane heading away from the villa. Now he goes slowly; they pass three houses and then there is nothing but the land falling away on their left and the flashing of a light beneath a tree at the side of the road. Subroto accelerates briefly and then brakes hard, the headlights washing over Hasan, who is sprawled on the grass, back against the tree, legs splayed, the hand holding the phone dropping to the grass, the other hand pressed to his side, blood seeping between his fingers.

"Now we have a problem." The look Subroto is directing toward the distant hills says bad things are in store for somebody. Eko has walked a few paces away and is smoking a cigarette, scanning what he can see of the landscape from this clearing in a thicket off the road where Subroto has pulled the SUV. On the back seat of the vehicle, Hasan's body sits canted against the window, motionless; he groaned and died as Subroto and Eko struggled to lift him into the vehicle. The eastern sky is just beginning to lighten. On everyone's mind is the possibility that the people who shot Hasan are still in the neighborhood.

Pascual looks at Archie, who has been talking on his phone and is now holding it out to Subroto. "Mr. Fang wants to talk to you." Subroto takes the phone, grunts into it, and moves away, listening. Archie says, "Dexter's freaking out."

"I don't blame him."

"This is a disaster. If the police get involved, Dexter will get dragged in. And then he won't be able to keep me out of it. Once it gets out that I'm on the run, it's all over for me. The state will start grabbing everything it can."

The look on the dying Hasan's face has so far distracted Pascual from any concerns about Archie's money, but he is glad to have something else to think about. "They know you're on the run already, don't they?"

"They do, sure. But it's not public knowledge, not yet. The party always prefers to control the narrative. If they can grab me quietly and take me back, they can stage a trial and make it all look legal. But if word gets out, then they'll go to plan B. They'll just seize all my assets." Archie exhales and looks at Subroto, talking quietly into the phone a few steps away. "I'm betting the abduction team didn't stick around. If we don't, either, maybe Dexter can cook up something the police will buy."

Pascual says, "I think even in Indonesia you probably have to explain a corpse with a gunshot wound to somebody."

"Sure. But in Indonesia, if you're Dexter Fang, the cops are going to accept whatever explanation you give them."

Pascual shakes his head. "Even if they can stitch it up, I'm not sure that would solve your other problem."

"What other problem?"

"Where are you going to be safe? This was supposed to be a secure hideout, remember?"

"I told you. Halim sold me out. Has to be him. Who else knew where we were?"

"So what is Halim going to say when the police come asking why his house got blown up?"

"I imagine he'll back up whatever Dexter comes up with. Even if he did sell us out, he won't want any more trouble. He'll go along with Dexter."

Pascual is pondering that when Subroto comes to hand Archie's phone back to him. "Mr. Fang." Archie takes the phone and switches to Chinese, moving off. Eko tosses away his cigarette butt and wanders over to confer with Subroto. Pascual spots the stump of a tree and goes to sit on it, too depressed even to worry about snakes. He puts his head in his hands and thinks about early mornings in Badalona far away. Archie ends his call and says, "OK. Dexter's got a plan."

▪ ▪ ▪ ▪

"We'll be in Jakarta in two hours," says Archie. "Dexter's got a hiding place for us. This is one only he knows about."

Subroto is pushing the SUV along a nice, flat, tree-shaded road through lightly wooded country, heading north for Subang. He and Eko are not happy, Pascual can see. Whatever Fang's plan is, it involves pretending that Hasan's corpse is not settling into rigor mortis behind the rear seat. The two have been trading muttered observations and sullen looks since getting their orders from Fang and motioning everyone into the vehicle. Hasan's blood has dried on the seat and on Pascual's trousers, and he and the two Indonesians have expended a bottle of drinking water to clean their hands.

Archie is visibly frazzled, but rallying. His speech has become slightly manic. "Dexter says Roosevelt Halim is furious about the attack and wants the full story. Dexter won't even consider the possibility Halim tipped the Chinese. He says Halim doesn't even know I was there. I still think it's possible Halim talked to someone, but I could be wrong. Anyway, Dexter's going to handle him. He's probably going to have to give him a lot of money."

"How's he going to handle the corpse?"

"He'll just have to work it into whatever story he and Halim cook up."

Pascual remembers Hasan playing chess, vital and intense, now just an inconvenient object to be worked into a lie.

Archie has moved on. "I think the solution's going to involve you."

"Me?"

"That's what you're here for, right? The scapegoat? Dexter says Halim will back him up. They're going to blame everything on the Islamists. And you."

"What the hell do I have to do with the Islamists?"

"The idea is, you're here to cut a deal with Halim to build a resort on Bali. Dexter flew you in secretly so as not to tip the competition. But the Islamists suspected you were scheming with Halim to build a casino."

"What?"

"Halim's a Christian, like Dexter. The Islamists have stepped up their attacks on Christians in the past few years. Halim's had a few clashes with the jihadis, on stupid pretexts, like Halim supposedly promoting prostitution because he sponsors the Miss Indonesia beauty pageant. Gambling's illegal in Indonesia, but that wouldn't stop the Islamists from believing Halim is pulling strings to get the law changed and plotting with a foreign financier to build a casino. The story should fly."

"And I'm supposed to back this up? The thing's full of holes.

How are the jihadis supposed to have found out about the meeting?"

"Any number of ways. Somebody on Halim's staff, somebody at the airport. Remember, Dexter sneaked you in. That will have to come out, but don't worry. Dexter's clout will protect you. The point is, it will explain the attack without bringing me into it."

"Terrific. And I get stuck with the consequences."

"At most you'll get a slap on the wrist, maybe get deported."

"Or maybe get decapitated by a bunch of jihadis because I tried to open a casino."

"You'll be out of Indonesia before the jihadis know who you are."

Pascual can do nothing but gape, then shake his head and look away out the window. Archie pats him on the leg. "Think about this. Dexter's going to have to spread some money around to keep this quiet. To Halim, to a few well-placed officials. He won't forget to include you. I'll make sure you get your piece of the payout."

Pascual goes on shaking his head for a while, but the word "payout" settles into a niche in a corner of his mind, along with the image of a quick deportation and return to more familiar precincts, and as the lush green countryside goes by, he feels his resistance to the concept of being bought off beginning to seem quaint.

■ ■ ■ ■

"This is a very serious matter." The officer intoning this, a leather-skinned whippet in the brown uniform of the Indonesian National Police, sits behind a desk in a large, amply air-conditioned office. He has three stars on his shoulder boards and reasonably fluent if heavily accented English, though he has deployed it only intermittently during this interview, which has been mostly conducted in Indonesian. Across from him sit three men: Pascual, Dexter Fang and a third man some years older and a few pounds heavier than Fang, with Chinese features and sparse black hair combed straight back. This is Roosevelt Halim, who has mostly sat silent, registering his extreme dissatisfaction via a high-intensity glower throughout the proceedings.

"We are aware of that," says Fang, who keeps tugging the conversation back to English for Pascual's benefit. "It resulted in the death of one of my employees."

"And the destruction of one of my residences," rumbles Halim. "Outrageous."

The whippet nods. "And this death should have been reported to the nearest district station. Why did your men leave the scene and drive more than one hundred kilometers to Jakarta before reporting the crime?"

Fang spreads his hands. "Because they were fleeing a violent attack. My men are trained to ensure the safety of their charges above all other considerations. They recovered the body of their companion and evacuated Mr. Rose, removing him from danger before coming to report to me. They proceeded as any well-trained bodyguards would have."

"And it does not appear that they committed any offenses, other than failing to report the incident. Unfortunately, they were unable to give any evidence that would identify the attackers."

The officer scowls for a moment and turns to Pascual. "You are aware that you entered Indonesia in violation of the immigration laws?"

Pascual nods and draws breath to repeat his rehearsed excuses for the third or fourth time, but Fang interrupts. "As I said before, the offense was mine. I wished to bring Mr. Rose into the country covertly for reasons of commercial secrecy and purposely subverted immigration procedures at the airport when my private jet landed. I am of course prepared to accept the legal consequences, including paying a fine and . . . any other fees that may be legally required."

The whippet gives Fang the evil eye for a moment and then resumes speaking in Indonesian. Fang replies, Halim joins in; there is a three-way discussion for a couple of minutes while Pascual sits feeling his nerves being worn to the snapping point.

The Indonesians fall silent. The officer picks up Pascual Rose's Maltese passport, fans the pages briefly and shoves it across the desk. He looks at Pascual and says, "You are released on the recognizance of Mr. Fang. You will not be officially deported. But you will leave Indonesia within three days. He will be responsible for your compliance. Is that clear?"

Pascual nods. "Very clear. Thank you."

Halim leans forward. "And what will be done about the destruction of my property?"

"The investigation has already begun. A unit of the Mobile Brigade Corps and a team from the Criminal Detective Unit have been dispatched to the site. These attacks by religious extremists will not be tolerated."

Halim nods, grunting. Fang and Pascual make eye contact briefly, and Pascual sees what real clout means as Fang gives just the barest hint of a smile.

■■■■

"You owe me, Dexter." Roosevelt Halim taps Dexter Fang on the chest with a thick finger. "I loved that house."

They are standing in an internal courtyard of the enormous walled police headquarters complex in Kebayoran Baru, South Jakarta, two black Mercedes limousines waiting. The noonday sun is brutal after the air-conditioned office, and Fang is wiping his brow with a handkerchief. "Send me a bill," he says. He has found the good grace to look, if not ashamed, at least mildly abashed. "I will make it good."

"You'd better. And someday I want the story, too. The real story." Halim turns toward his car, a chauffeur springing into action to open the rear door.

"Come on," says Fang. "Let's go get some lunch. This place gives me the creeps."

"So what are we going to do with you?" says Dexter Fang, looking at Pascual from his corner of the back seat. The limousine is not moving, stalled in the famously constipated Jakarta traffic. Motorcyclists seep through the interstices; Pascual has been observing a man on a pedestrian overpass just ahead who is eating some kind of fruit and spitting the seeds down onto the trapped vehicles below.

"Put me on an airplane," he says. "Tonight."

"With no entry stamp to Indonesia in your passport you will have an interesting conversation at the airport. There are criminal penalties for illegal entry. But they will probably let you leave. You can always try dropping the General's name. But it would be better to let us smuggle you back into Singapore. We can probably fudge that again without too much trouble, and then you are legal again, nobody in Singapore the wiser."

"Legal and available for police interviews. Don't forget the dead lawyer."

"I haven't been able to forget him, because as it happens, the

Singapore police finally contacted me this morning, asking about you. I told them I had not had any contact with you for several days and didn't know where you were. But I'm afraid you are going to have to talk to them."

"Wonderful. What do I tell them?"

"Just tell them the truth. You were sent here to set up shell companies to fund a CIA operation. Tell them everything just as it happened but keep Archie out of it. They will go off eagerly pursuing the CIA aspect, and then it will all be the agency's problem, and that will divert everyone's attention from the real problem, which is to get Archie to safety. I think in fact you were right all along. That's what you were sent here for."

Pascual files this for further consideration. "So it seems."

"I am sending Renata back tomorrow. You could go with her. I'm afraid I will be tied up here for a few days dealing with the fallout from this. There's a funeral to arrange, among other things. Poor Hasan. I'll have to see that his family is taken care of. And mine, for that matter."

"Yours?"

"What's the next logical step for the Chinese? A kidnapping. 'You get your wife back when we get Chee.' I've put on extra security for my house here, an extra car when the wife goes out. I'd love to think my children are safe where they are, but the Chinese really want Archie, and they've got a long reach. I've talked with my boy in Manchester and my daughter in Versoix, told Campbell to call who he needs to call to make sure they're protected, whatever the cost. And then there will be some tricky maneuvering to control the narrative on this thing. It's going to cost me."

The limo is in motion again, slowly and fitfully, and Pascual watches Fang gazing out the window. "Speaking of fallout, have you figured out who betrayed us?"

Fang's face hardens and he turns to Pascual. "It wasn't Roosevelt, if that's what you're thinking. I know that's what Archie believes. But Roosevelt didn't even know he was there. No, sadly, I think the culprit is probably me."

"You?"

"Yes. You see, a couple of years ago I was having some problems with my Jakarta staff using company cars and vans for personal errands and junkets. Moving auntie's furniture, taking off for a weekend in Bali, that kind of thing. So I had a GPS fleet tracking system installed to cover all my Indonesian vehicles. And I'm afraid it is a Chinese system that is notoriously hackable, according to Campbell. His boffins are looking at it now. That is an obvious vulnerability that the Chinese would exploit the instant they suspected I was sheltering Archie. And when they saw that two of my vehicles had paid a visit to an isolated villa in the hills north of Bandung, I'm afraid that was all they needed."

This is plausible enough, and Pascual sees no reason to contest it. He glances at the driver of the limo, who is stifling a yawn as the traffic grinds to a halt again. "Is there a plan for getting Archie to a safe place?"

"There will be soon, but I'm not sure you're on the list of people who need to know."

"Fair enough."

"He's in a safe place, with a new security team. You'll be joining him shortly. But that will be just for tonight. Tomorrow, it's back to Singapore for you. I think your role really is finished at this point. Things have gone to a different level now."

Pascual is surprised by an intense surge of relief. He has heard no mention of a payout from Dexter Fang, and the original million-dollar bait seems to have been pure fiction, but he decides that with a plane ticket home he will consider himself a lucky man. "Well," he says. "It was fun while it lasted."

■■■

Fang's Jakarta headquarters are located on the forty-fifth floor of a skyscraper looming over a complicated freeway interchange in central Jakarta, carefully isolated by nicely landscaped gardens from any threat of interaction with the teeming neighborhoods around it. Pascual stands at a window, bemused to the point of paralysis by the tumult of the past twelve hours and the sight of a metropolitan sprawl of thirty million people stretching to the horizon. A step sounds behind him and Renata Taggart says, "Impressive, isn't it?"

Pascual turns. Renata is in business mode, sleek and splendid in silk, hair corralled behind her head. Pascual is in the only clothes he now possesses, the second-hand trousers and T-shirt he grabbed when Eko pounded on his door. He is shabby, unshaven and possibly malodorous, but he decides not to care. "If you like skyscrapers," he says.

"They like them here," says Renata. "Jakarta claims to have more skyscrapers than any other city in Asia." She stands for a moment looking out at the spectacle, then wrinkles her nose very slightly. "I don't like Jakarta," she says quietly. "Too ostentatious, too anarchic." She turns toward him. "Well, it will be under water in a decade."

"That's harsh."

She grimaces. "I know. Hard on the people who live here. And some of them are lovely, I shouldn't be such a snob. But I'm always happy to get back to Singapore. I understand you're coming with me tomorrow."

"That's the plan."

"And Mr. Fang tells me you need some clothes."

"Just a single change and a toothbrush ought to do it. Most of my things are back at the house on Sentosa. I assume I can recover them there."

"Of course. I've got a young man from the office here who is ready to take you shopping. There's quite a nice mall near here, with a Dior men's store. And then Mr. Fang will have one of his security men take you to the flat where you'll be staying tonight."

"In a company vehicle, by any chance?"

It takes her a second, but she gets it. "No, he's well aware of that issue now. I think they've made arrangements to get you there without being tracked." Renata pauses with lips parted for a moment before saying, "So awful. Just unthinkable. I've never seen Mr. Fang so disturbed."

"Having an employee shot to death will do that."

"Yes. And not knowing how they found the place. That's the frightening thing." Her voice drops in volume. "Mr. Fang actually asked to see my phone this morning. He was apologetic, but he said he had to check my call log, just for the record. Of course there was nothing, but I'm terrified that it was something I did, even though it was one of the new phones Mr. Campbell gave us before we left. I did use the Wi-Fi at the house, but only to look at some news sites. Do you think I could have given away the location somehow?"

Renata looks genuinely dismayed, and it humanizes her; Pascual is pleased to find that his infatuation is wearing off as the knockout gets knocked about a bit. Beneath the deft makeup job he can see the effects of stress. "I couldn't tell you," he says. "But I have never trusted the damn things."

Renata nods once and is in complete command again. "That's very wise, I'm sure. Well, let me take you to Joyo now. He'll make sure you get what you need."

■ ■ ■ ■

"So how much is Dexter going to have to contribute to the policemen's retirement fund to keep you out of jail and me out of the spotlight?" Archie Chee turns from the window, letting the curtain fall back. For a moment Pascual just stares: with his head shaved and without glasses, Archie is a different man. He is wearing cargo shorts and a black T-shirt with the name of a heavy metal band on it. He could be a street vendor or a casual laborer, just about anything but a world-class tycoon. Outside, a motorcycle roars by, briefly drowning out the gabble of voices drifting up from the canal-side marketplace overlooked by this squalid, cramped apartment on the second floor of a narrow three-story walkup, guarded by a man in the street in addition to the one who admitted Pascual and has gone to sit in the kitchen.

Pascual drops onto a chair, letting his plastic Dior bag fall to the unfinished concrete floor. "That part of the discussion was in Indonesian, so I couldn't tell you. But the General didn't seem to have any trouble believing it was an Islamist attack."

"No, that's pretty plausible, unfortunately. They'll round up a few jihadis and rough them up, and things will be tense again for a while."

Pascual has a brief vision of lies propagating outward like ripples on a pond. He says, "I like the new look."

"It was time for a change. Next, a funny hat, let the beard grow, keep the facial recognition software guessing."

"What does Dexter have in mind for you?"

"That's a very good question. What does he have in mind for you?"

"I'm flying back to Singapore with Renata tomorrow."

"Lucky you. Let's hope you make the flight."

"Why shouldn't I?"

"I'm just wondering how secure we are here. Or can be anywhere that Dexter puts us."

Pascual watches him pace back to the window. "You think he's compromised?"

Over his shoulder Archie says, "I think the Guoanbu is probably all over him, yes. You heard his theory about the vehicle tracking software?"

"Yes. It didn't sound impossible."

"No, it didn't. And who knows what else the Guoanbu has up its sleeve? Are Dexter's guys a match for trained Chinese special ops units? They went through all the motions to make sure we weren't followed on the way here, but why here? What's the connection between this place and Dexter, and is it traceable?"

Pascual contemplates this, dejected. "What's the alternative?"

Archie turns to face him. "If I had a good one, would I be wise to tell you? I don't know you, and Dexter doesn't, either. You were supposedly sent to us by the CIA but then they said no, actually, you're just a phony. Why that didn't set off all Dexter's alarms, I'll never know."

Pascual returns Archie's stare. "Because I was the first target, remember? If I was working for the Chinese, why would they have pulled the stunt with the drugs?"

Archie has no answer for that. He stands looking thoughtfully at Pascual until a faint buzzing sounds and he pulls his phone from his shirt pocket. He answers, listens and after a moment takes a step toward Pascual, frowning and offering the phone. "It's Dexter. For you. He seems to think you're in trouble."

"You have been summoned for a return engagement with the police," says Dexter Fang in Pascual's ear.

"That doesn't sound good," says Pascual when he finds his voice.

"It's not. It means you are going to have to give a fuller explanation of your presence in Indonesia. That is going to tax your powers of invention if you want to keep Archie out of it."

"I can invent all kinds of things. But lying to the police is a risky business. Why can't I just tell them the truth? You said it would work in Singapore."

"The reason you were in Singapore had nothing to do with Archie, as far as you knew. The reason you're in Indonesia is all about him. You're going to have to embellish that Bali resort story."

"I see. What the hell happened? I thought you'd bought yourself a general."

"That's an awfully crude way of putting it. What I thought I had bought was the General's agreement not to look too closely at my business affairs, which were supposedly the trigger for this attack. Probably what happened was, somebody did some research on you, either Roosevelt or somebody in Kebayoran Baru. It could have been Roosevelt, because he's not too happy with me right now, understandably. Anyway, your name brings up all kinds of red flags, and now suddenly the financial crimes people want to know the full story."

"Can't our friend with the three stars overrule them?"

"Not if it brings too much political heat. And Roosevelt can bring that if he wants."

"Have Roosevelt make something up. He knows the territory."

"He already told them the proposition was yours and all he had agreed to was to listen to it. And he's made it clear to me he's not going a step further with that story. Now we have to make sure it's convincing. Either that, or you have to disappear."

A few seconds tick away as Pascual listens to street noises. "I'm not sure I heard you correctly."

"I think you did. Listen, there's no time to waste. I have promised to deliver you back at police headquarters tomorrow morning at eight o'clock sharp. That gives you time to make a decision. Either we put our heads together tonight and flesh out this Bali nonsense, or you slip out and lose yourself in the Jakarta streets."

Pascual listens to the boisterous noises coming up from those streets. "That shouldn't be too hard. What happens to you if I don't show up?"

"Nothing. Not my fault that the notorious con man took to

his heels. I show contrition, I promise to exercise better judgment in the future. It's over for me. But if that's what you choose to do, it means you really have to lose yourself. I can't be complicit in hiding you anymore. My position here is too precarious. If you choose to disappear, there's no flight back to Singapore tomorrow, no more safe houses. Our association has to be at an end."

"That's quite a choice."

"You have a few hours to make it. Call me back only if you want to commit to the Bali story. Good luck."

The call ends and Pascual hands the phone back to Archie, who says, "It's gotten more complicated, hasn't it?"

"Just a bit." Pascual explains briefly. "Dexter seemed to suggest I should just disappear."

"Dexter usually has pretty good judgment in these matters."

Pascual exchanges a long, frank look with Archie. "I could probably talk my way out of it without bringing you into it. Probably."

Archie's look goes sour. "Your choice. You're certainly entitled to put your interests before mine."

Pascual looks for a reason to disagree and comes up empty. "So if I choose to disappear, how do I get out of Indonesia and out of this whole mess?"

Archie's eyes narrow and he cants his head slightly to one side. "You could come with me."

"Where are you going?"

"The States, eventually. Short run, wherever the people who are coming to pick me up decide I should go."

"And who are they?"

"People who have my best interests at heart. You want to come along, you have to trust me."

"And why would you take me with you?"

"Because if I'm not sure I can trust you, I'd rather have you where I can keep an eye on you, instead of here scheming with Dexter."

"And when are they coming?"

Archie looks at the watch on his wrist. "Any minute now."

■ ■ ■ ■

From the window they can see a stretch of the narrow canal and the street that runs along it, lush trees shading the vendors' carts, food stalls under awnings, stacks of crates, racks of second-hand clothing, parked scooters and cars draped in tarps squeezed into narrow spaces. The vigorous commerce of the poor generates a tremendous noise: shouts, laughter, the purr of creeping traffic. "In flood season this is all under water," says Archie. "It's a slum, really. Anyone who can afford it moves to higher ground. Not one of Dexter's luxury properties. I don't know what his connection with the place is, but I think it's a matter of time before the Guoanbu people find it. So we're leaving, as soon as I get that call."

Pascual looks over his shoulder toward the kitchen. "Are our bodyguards just going to let us go?"

"I doubt it. We'll have to con them somehow. I don't want them to get in trouble with Dexter, but I don't want Dexter knowing where I'm going, either. It's time to break that link. Now that the Guoanbu knows he's been hiding me, they can pressure him in a million ways, and he'll have to cough me up eventually. So it's best that he doesn't know where I am."

Pascual has been pondering what is best for him. He has no doubt that further engagement with the Indonesian National Police, quite apart from any consequences it may have for Archie Chee, will complicate his life immensely and in unpredictable ways. So do you trust Archie's judgment enough to throw your lot in with him? As Pascual is posing himself this question, Archie's phone buzzes.

Archie answers, listens, says, "OK. We'll be ready. Just before the bridge, next to the stall with a blue awning selling second-hand electronics. Across from the food cart. Look for the guy in the Metallica T-shirt. Give us five minutes." After a pause he says, "Yes, there are two of us. I'll make introductions when you get here." He ends the call and looks at Pascual. "All right." He nods in the direction of the kitchen. "The fellow in there doesn't speak much English. But he's easygoing and anxious to please. In three minutes I'm going to send him across the street for a couple of orders of *pisang goreng*. While he's gone, we'll grab our stuff and go down and stand just inside the street door. If he comes back with the snacks before the van gets here, we'll just have to pretend we came down for fresh air and hope we can jump in the van when it gets there without him and the other guy making too much trouble. But if the van gets here first, he'll never see us leave. We're looking for a green van with *Asiasphere Logistics* on the side."

Pascual knows this is one of those decision points that have a way of ambushing him at intervals in his life, and he is keenly aware he has shown a genius for making the wrong decision. He rapidly decides that, all other considerations aside, he would probably prefer Archie's company to that of a team of Indonesian financial crimes investigators. With a faint but familiar sensation of ignoring his better judgment he says, "Sounds like a plan."

■ ■ ■ ■

"What's *pisang goreng?*" Only now does it occur to Pascual to ask the question, standing inside the security grille that masks the recessed entrance to the building, watching through the bars as across the street their bodyguard chats with his partner, who has wandered over from his station beneath a tree to join the cluster of people around the food cart with *GORENGAN* inscribed on it.

"Fried bananas." Archie is looking to their left down the narrow, teeming street. "Where's that damn van?"

Pascual can smell the bananas now, and they are weakening his resolve. Is he really going to drive off blindly into the unknown, not even getting to taste the *pisang goreng*? He gropes for a reason. You can have the fried bananas, he reminds himself, but the police come along with them.

The woman running the food cart is fishing the golden delicacies out of the fryer with a sieve, the boy beside her shaking out a paper bag. The bodyguard chooses this moment to look over his shoulder. He stiffens when he sees Pascual, looks puzzled, and nudges his partner. "Shit," says Archie.

"Relax," says Pascual. He waves and puts on a cheery smile. He pats his stomach and licks his lips. The bodyguards smile back.

"Here they come," says Archie. He stoops to pick up his bag.

Pascual waits until the guards are distracted by the process of paying for the food before he picks up the plastic shopping bag with his brand-new clothes. Archie steps out into the street and waves. Mistake, thinks Pascual, as this instantly gets the attention of their keepers. It takes them about three seconds to read the situation and start across the street, but by then it is too late, as the green van is pulling up in front of the house, blocking their view. The side door with *Asiasphere Logistics* in big gold letters slides open and a man inside is beckoning. Archie stumbles on the step and falls in headlong, Pascual leaps in after him as the van starts to move again, and then the shouting begins. The door is hauled shut and the van picks up speed. Through the rear window Pascual catches a last sight of their former bodyguards, standing forlornly in the street with two paper bags full of fried bananas.

"How likely are they to come after us?" The accent is American, the man somewhere on the downside of forty but leathery and sharp-edged, with just a fuzz of blond hair on his skull, his blue eyes startling in a sun-darkened face. He is looking over his shoulder from the front passenger seat. The man behind the wheel is Indonesian, as is the man in back with Pascual and Archie. Having swung left to cross a bridge across the canal, the van is making decent speed along the opposite side, heading back in the direction from which it came.

"I'm texting Dexter now to call off the dogs," says Archie, thumbing his phone. "They had a car somewhere nearby, but it will take them some time to get to it, I would guess."

"So no worries," says the Yank. "We've got a pretty good lead, and there's no such thing as a high-speed car chase in Jakarta." He twists a little more to shift his gaze from Archie to Pascual. "So who are you?"

"I'm Archie's valet," says Pascual.

The Yank frowns; Archie laughs. "This is Mr. Rose. He's with the good guys. He's in Indonesia illegally and the police would like to talk to him, which would be inconvenient. If we can get him back to Singapore, that would be good."

The Yank is giving Pascual the eye. "Singapore's not on the flight plan, I'm afraid."

"He's not in a hurry. Are you, Pascual?"

Pascual laughs weakly. "I have a feeling it wouldn't make any difference if I was. What is on the flight plan?'

"Top secret," says Archie. "Even I don't know."

"Do I get to know who I'm traveling with? Or is that a secret, too?"

The Yank says, "I'm Frank, pleased to meet you. This is Gus and that's Amin back there. They actually work for Asiasphere. I work for somebody else."

Pascual gives this a second and says, "Somebody headquartered in Virginia, by any chance?"

"Oh God, no." Frank the Yank scowls. "Private sector. Why, is that who you're with?"

"Not anymore," says Pascual.

Archie's phone is making noise, and he swipes and puts it to his ear. "Dexter. You got my text." He listens for a moment and then, falling back on the seat, launches into a torrent of Chinese. Pascual watches storefronts go by. They are still following the canal; there are fewer trees and bigger buildings. Everyone listens to Archie arguing with Dexter. Finally Archie ends the call and says, "Dexter's not happy, but he'll get over it. All I told him is that I'm with friends and he's off the hook as far as being responsible for me. I told him I'll contact him when I'm sure I'm in a safe place."

Frank twists around to look at him. "You'll be safe where we're going," he says. "You might as well be on the moon."

This does not sound ideal to Pascual. Archie says, "Do me a favor, will you, Frank?" He leans forward, holding out his phone. "Toss that into the canal for me." Frank nods, takes the phone, waits for an opportune moment and flings the phone out the window. "Thanks," says Archie. "I don't want to take any chances. If Dexter's phone is compromised and they get my number, they could track me if they have access to the tower data."

"The Chinese?" says Frank. "I wouldn't bet against it."

Pascual has been assuming that they are headed for an airport, but their route is not taking them toward either of the two Jakarta airports of which he is aware. Instead they have veered away from the canal and plowed slowly through increasingly wider but more congested streets in a southwesterly direction, and now they appear to be negotiating the entrance to a shopping complex at the base of a skyscraper. Gus pulls to the curb at a set of revolving doors. Frank bumps fists with Gus and says over his shoulder, "Out you get. We're here."

Pascual and Archie follow Frank through a vast lobby to a bank of elevators; in less than a minute Pascual's ears are popping as they shoot toward the top floor. Pascual has given up trying to make sense of things.

It is not until they leave the elevator, wait while Frank confers with someone in an office, and finally follow a uniformed guard up a set of stairs and out into bright sunshine on the roof of the building that Pascual suddenly understands.

The helicopter is already visible, half a mile away and closing fast. Pascual's stomach flutters as he watches it come. An executive jet is one thing, but boarding this frail craft will be an act of faith. It is a mere bubble with a rotor and a green tail. Pascual looks at Archie, who gives him a manic grin and says, "This is how you beat the traffic." Pascual notes that Archie has broken into a sweat. The sound of the engine becomes audible above the roar of the vast city.

The noise swells as the chopper slows and hangs motionless for an instant before positioning itself for a landing, the pilot clearly visible now, in sunglasses and headphones, working his stick. He brings the thing down gently on its skids, the rotor wash sending dust flying. Frank slaps Archie on the arm and motions him forward. There are four seats in the craft; Frank ushers Archie and Pascual into the rear two and takes the seat in front by the pilot. There is some shouted conversation between Frank and the pilot, and the chopper lifts off.

Pascual's stomach is just strong enough to be absorbed in the view as they soar out over the megalopolis, but he notes that Archie's eyes are squeezed shut, his fingers clenching and unclenching around the handles of his bag. They fly in a southerly direction, the vast city stretching away into the haze. A couple of minutes into the flight Archie opens his eyes, takes a deep breath, makes eye contact with Pascual and grins. "Wow," he shouts over the engine noise. "Don't look down."

Pascual leans toward him to be heard. "Where are we going?"

"To the moon. You heard the man. We'll know when we get there."

"These are your friends, right? And you don't know where they're taking us?"

Archie laughs. "I sent out a distress call. This is the response. They didn't give me an itinerary."

"Who the hell are they?"

Archie says, "Long story, and I'm not going to lose my voice shouting at you. I'll explain everything when we get there."

After twenty minutes they begin to descend. Ahead an airfield has come into view, densely packed neighborhoods crowding it on every side. There is nothing resembling a terminal in sight, just the long runway and a few hangars. As they approach, Pascual can see small planes and a few helicopters parked. The pilot brings the chopper in smoothly and they descend on a square of tarmac with a large H painted on it.

"All right, boys, let's go," says Frank. "We've got a connection to make."

■■■■

"I was betting on Australia when we took off," says Pascual. "But we're flying east." Far out to the north, Pascual can see the shimmering blue of the Java Sea. Directly beneath is the island itself, checkerboards and parquets in green and brown, tight clusters of red tile roofs, the occasional brown river snaking through. He has had his face pressed to the window since they took off, after a hurried transfer to this sleek twin-engined Cessna jet. Frank has gone to commune with the pilots up in the cockpit, leaving Archie and Pascual to enjoy the comforts of the cabin, plush seats and a fully stocked galley. Archie has provided himself with a beer, but Pascual has opted for sobriety, out of an obscure feeling that his wits will be tested in the next few hours.

"There's nothing east of here except more Indonesia," says Archie. "I think I know where we're going."

Pascual waits, but nothing follows. "Want to share that?"

Archie's brow wrinkles as he appears to ponder the question. "I told you I sent out a distress call. The guy I sent it to has fingers in a lot of pies. One of them is mining. I'd bet we're going to one of his facilities."

"This is the old friend from college?"

"That's right."

"And why would we want to visit one of his mines?"

"To make it hard for the Guoanbu to find us. They'll be tracking any kind of commercial transportation and any places I frequent or have been known to favor. I think the idea is to lay low in the jungle until my pal figures out the best way to get me to a safe haven, along with as much of my property as we can salvage."

"And how long do you anticipate this will take?"

"Don't worry, he can probably arrange transport back to Singapore for you."

"That would be good. I have fond memories of Singapore."

■ ■ ■ ■

By the time the jet begins to descend, a black night has fallen and Pascual can just make out a few sparse clusters of lights on a coastline in the distance ahead. As far as he can tell, they have flown down the entire length of Java and left it behind. They have been over land and water alternately for the last half hour. There is enough of a moon to allow Pascual to make out a jagged skyline of dark peaks above a long stretch of white beach. The lights of a runway stretch away from the beach toward an eerie glow in the hills. The jet banks, lining up for the approach.

"They've got a lot of lights on," says Archie. "Not exactly off the grid, are we?"

Thirty seconds later they are touching down. The airport is even less elaborate than the one they took off from, a single isolated tile-roofed building to one side of the runway next to a small tower. The jet taxis to an apron in front of the building and shuts down. A white four-door pickup is waiting for them. "Almost home, boys," says Frank, waving them out onto the tarmac. Pascual takes in a lungful of the night air, full of mysterious scents: alien vegetation and the nearby sea.

"Where are we?" says Archie, stretching after three hours on the aircraft.

"You're on the beautiful island of Sumbawa. Home to a million and a half Indonesians and one of the largest copper and gold mines in the world. And there's some pretty good surfing, too, if you're into that." Frank greets the Indonesian driver and herds them into the rear seat of the pickup. "Just a short drive and there'll be food and maybe a couple of cold ones."

Pascual is so far out of his comfort zone that even the prospect of cold beer fails to raise his spirits. The pickup goes out a gate and turns right onto a paved road that takes them gently uphill, the headlights showing thick brush on either side. They go for less than a mile, top a rise, and there are bright lights ahead. A sign says *Selamat Datang Welcome – Townsite* beneath the name and logo of a multinational mining company that even Pascual has heard of. "Your friend owns this?" he murmurs, leaning toward Archie.

"Enough of it to give him the clout to get us here."

The truck pulls up at a security booth; there is a brief conversation and the barrier arm rises. They roll past a parking lot full of buses and then a small complex of office buildings, and two hundred yards further on they are suddenly in what appears to be a suburban town, lamplit streets lined with houses, a mini market, flowering trees, tennis courts. They pull up at a building with a roofed veranda and multiple doors, like a small motel. Frank pushes his door open. "Here you go, fellas. The guesthouse. Let's get you checked in and see what we can do about supper and those beers."

The sun has just cleared the steep green peaks to the east, and the morning is still cool, birds with absurdly bright plumage skirmishing in the trees overlooking the veranda. "I think we have landed on our feet," says Archie, settling onto his chair with his second cup of coffee. "This beats that slum back in Jakarta, doesn't it?"

Freshly scrubbed, clad in yesterday's purchases, Pascual is refreshed after a night's sleep but still dazed. Twenty-four hours ago he was fleeing gunshots in the Java highlands. "I had visions of a hut on stilts, a hundred miles upstream from civilization, headhunting tribesmen leering at us in the firelight. Instead we're in Pleasantville, USA."

They have been given neighboring rooms with a view of what to Pascual looks like a village green, quiet residential streets stretching away beyond it. Children are playing on the other side of the green; a gardener is trimming a grass border with clippers.

Archie sips coffee and says, "It's good to have friends in high places."

"Are we comped for the rooms, or are we going to get a bill?"

Archie laughs. "If we get a bill I'll pay it, don't worry. Maybe we can get someone to take us up to the mine today. It's supposed to be pretty impressive."

"All of this is here because of the mine?"

"That's what pays for everything. The company spent two billion dollars on all this. There was no infrastructure, so they built it. Roads, electricity, water. Sumbawa was one of the poorest islands in Indonesia and now it has the highest per capita income in the country. It triggered the development of the whole west end of the island. Rapacious capitalism at work."

Pascual has no objection in principle to capitalism, or to multinational corporations as long as they behave themselves, but he mistrusts enthusiasm. "What does it do to the environment?"

"I don't know." Archie gestures vaguely toward the interior of the island. "Ask all the people who got jobs if they care."

"You sound like a company shill."

"I'm a realist, that's what I am. I saw what rapacious capitalism did to China. And you know what? Mostly I approved."

I would too, thinks Pascual, if it made me a billionaire. "So what's the plan now? You mentioned transport to Singapore."

"There will be at least one jet going out today. We should check in with Dexter before we put you on a plane. But I'm not sure of the best way to do that. The Guoanbu has probably stepped up their surveillance on Dexter, and I don't know how good Campbell's people are. We can discuss all this with the big man when he gets here."

Pascual gives him a look. "Who's the big man?"

Archie laughs softly. "I'm not supposed to say. He's flying in today. He'll probably want to talk to you." Archie drains his coffee cup and stands. "I think you'll be interested to meet him. He's a rapacious capitalist. Of the best sort."

▪▪▪▪

Pascual stands with his feet in the Indian Ocean, hands in his pockets and the wind in his face. A few hundred yards out, the breakers come rolling in past a precipitous green-swathed headland rising out of the sea; far away on the horizon white clouds mass. Beyond that is Australia, Pascual estimates, or possibly Antarctica.

It is a long way from Badalona. Pascual turns to contemplate what foreign capital has made of this sheltered bay less than a mile downhill from the mining company townsite. Somebody has built a resort here, bungalows grouped around a main building with tables under an arcade, a garden with flowerbeds and palms, the whole surrounded by a concrete wall to keep out wild animals and impecunious locals. A couple of those locals have built a shack on the beach to sell drinks to surfers and sunbathers. They are staring forlornly at their cell phones, no customers in sight.

Heaven is where you are, thinks Pascual. This morning the formula fails to satisfy. You are stranded in paradise, Pascual thinks, and paradise holds nothing for you. Your presence here is pointless, your existence useless.

After you get back to Singapore, if you get back, then what? Pascual sees that he has been deceiving himself. His life in

Badalona is as unsustainable as this little holiday on Sumbawa. Any life at all with his wife and son may be unsustainable because there is no greater danger to them than his presence.

And that is your penance, Pascual thinks, for a life misspent. He ambles over to the shack, running an eye over the wares. A youth sprawled on a plastic chair puts his phone away and stands, beaming at Pascual. "Hello, mister!"

Pascual is about to open his mouth when he remembers that he has no money. He slaps his trouser pockets. "I'm sorry. I forgot my wallet."

The youth shrugs. "You pay me next time. What you want?"

Pascual guiltily accepts a small carton of apple juice. "I owe you."

"Where you from?"

An excellent question, thinks Pascual, applying himself to opening the carton. I am Lester Gray, an American spy. I am Pascual Rose, a Dubai-based con man with a Maltese passport. I am Pascual March, a failed husband and father of mixed ancestry. The boy is waiting for his answer. "I'm a vagabond," Pascual says. "I don't have a home."

The boy gives him a quizzical look, then scowls. "Everybody have a home."

"Everybody but me." Pascual smiles at the boy and wanders back toward the water's edge, sinking into black depression.

A distant whine sounds, out over the ocean. Pascual sees a black speck grow larger until it is a jet lining up for the approach to the airstrip. He watches it come, improbable and inexorable, hoping that whoever is on it will have something to say about his fate, in one way or another.

■ ■ ■ ■

"Mr. Rose here was sent by the agency to help get my money out. The Guoanbu spotted him and tried to put him out of action. He's been on the run with me ever since." Archie presents Pascual to the man at the end of the table with a raised hand.

"Pleased to meet you." The man at the end of the table nods at Pascual. His voice is a deep rumble. He is tall and dark but not handsome, with a long seamed face, piercing black eyes and a mustache that was in style when he was a young man, three or possibly four decades ago. He sports a green polo shirt and a massive Rolex on his wrist. A silver USB flash drive and a cell phone lie on the table in front of him.

"Likewise." Pascual squirms on his chair. He would have appreciated a chance to clean up a little, but when he arrived back at the townsite gate after an uphill trudge from the beach, sweat soaking his new shirt and sand irritating the skin between his toes, he found Frank waiting for him with a company car and orders to deliver him to this air-conditioned conference room in the main office building of the complex. "I'm afraid you have the advantage of me. Archie here wouldn't tell me your name."

"Well, I'm impressed with his discretion." The man shoots Archie an amused look and turns back to Pascual. "But if you can't figure out who I am at this point, there's no hope for you. I'm Noah Colchester."

"The name rings a bell," says Pascual. "I couldn't say exactly in what connection, except that you are extremely wealthy and somehow controversial."

Colchester smiles, creases shifting in his face. "That's nice and vague. Let's keep it that way for the moment. As for you, actually I'm fully informed. Archie should have consulted me before inviting you to the picnic, but we'll let that pass. I got a full report on you on the way here."

"That's interesting. What did it say?"

"It said you had done exactly what you were hired to do and should not be trusted with any role beyond that. It described you as, and I quote, 'a useful idiot.'"

The air conditioner hums, Archie and Colchester stare. Pascual blinks a few times. "Well. My usefulness is for others to judge, but I'd say the idiot part is pretty well established. Was any mention made of paying me?"

"It was, in fact. But before that happens, we need to decide what to do with you."

"I'm all ears."

"The Singapore police want to talk to you. You appear to be the prime suspect in a murder there. Did you do it?"

Pascual stares. "Why would I kill a lawyer in Singapore?"

"You tell me. How did you get mixed up in it?"

"I walked in about a minute after he was killed. I think I saw the killers on their way out. The lawyer was about to tell me something he thought the CIA would be interested in, about somebody in Dexter Fang's network. For all I know, he was talking about you."

Colchester acknowledges the jab with a brief smile. "I'm not in Dexter's network. But Archie is. Maybe that's who he was talking about."

"Well, that would raise interesting questions about how he knew about Archie, wouldn't it?"

"It would. I think the agency's well aware of the issue."

"Well, that's reassuring. Anyway, Dexter says I should talk to them and tell them the truth, leaving Archie out of it. That won't be hard, since I didn't know Archie existed when I took the job."

Colchester nods. "That's what the people who gave me the report suggested. They stressed that your fee is dependent on just that—keeping Archie completely out of it."

Pascual runs through a few responses and settles for, "Well, I'm glad the fee's still in play. I started to wonder when they told the lawyer I was a con man and not to be trusted."

"I can't speak to that. What I was told was that you were sent to Singapore to test the waters, you did that, and now you need to give the Singapore police a story that accounts for your presence but doesn't involve Archie. I think if you can do that everybody will be happy."

"Happy might be stretching it, in my case. I'll settle for not in jail and on my way home."

"All right. So let's run over what you're going to tell them."

Before Pascual can organize his thoughts sufficiently to begin, there is a faint chirping noise and Colchester holds up a hand. "Excuse me a moment." He picks up the cell phone, taps and puts it to his ear. "Yes?" He listens for perhaps ten seconds, says, "Yes, he's here with me," and after another few seconds says, "All right, I'll tell him." He ends the call, turns to Archie and says, "That was the agency guy in Singapore. Fang called him from Jakarta. He wants to talk to you, and he's quote-unquote 'shitting his pants.' He says it's an emergency."

Archie stares. "What kind of emergency?"

"Don't ask me. Here, use my phone." He hands it to Archie, who taps out a number and puts the phone to his ear. After a few seconds he begins speaking Chinese. He listens, responds, listens some more, and Pascual again recognizes the frozen look of a man getting bad news. He and Colchester exchange a look, Colchester glowering down the table as if any misfortune is Pascual's fault. The conversation goes on for another minute before Archie ends the call and sets the phone gently down on the table. He looks at Pascual and says, "The Guoanbu."

"What about them?"

Archie's mouth hangs open for a moment. "They got Renata."

# 25

Colchester says, "Who the hell is Renata?"

Pascual says, "What do you mean, they got her?"

Archie says nothing for a moment, looking stunned. "She was supposed to fly back to Singapore today. Dexter got a call from Singh, the pilot, saying she hadn't showed up and she wasn't answering her phone. Dexter finally got a call from her. She was pretty calm, but he could tell she was stressed. She said her car was hijacked. She was staying in one of Dexter's properties in Jakarta. Broad daylight. They stuffed the chauffeur in the trunk and put Renata in the back of a van. She told Dexter they were about to put her on an airplane."

Pascual says, "That's not good."

"No, it's not. Then she handed the phone to somebody else. Somebody speaking Mandarin. He gave Dexter the terms. Me for Renata."

That hangs in the air while Archie and Pascual stare at each other.

Colchester tries again. "Who is this Renata?"

Archie flaps a hand, distracted. "Dexter's . . . assistant, chief of staff, whatever he calls her. His right-hand woman. She runs things for him."

"Is she Chinese?"

"No. Singaporean, Eurasian."

Colchester looks skeptical. "I'm surprised they would kidnap a non-Chinese national outside of China. They love to grab western execs as hostages in business disputes, but that's always people who are unlucky enough to be in China."

"I think that's where that plane was headed. Dexter said they told him there was a legal case pending against her in China. Which Dexter says is ridiculous."

"That won't matter. They're good at pulling legal trouble out of a hat." Colchester scowls, drumming fingers on the table. "You for her. Would he go for that? Is she that important to him? You're family, right?"

"Yeah. But she's business."

"She can't be irreplaceable."

"You haven't met her. Dexter says she knows everything, the public stuff and the not-so-public stuff. That makes her the ideal pressure point."

Colchester leans back on his chair, and after a moment the creases shift again in a nasty smile. "Sounds like they've got him by the balls."

"That's more or less how Dexter put it."

"Will he give you up?"

Archie looks shocked. "I don't think so. I think he'll start doing damage control on whatever they squeeze out of Renata.

But it'll hurt him."

"Well, into each life a little rain must fall. Tell Dexter he's going to have to write off Renata."

Archie rouses himself. "That's kind of cold, isn't it? Dexter's really gone out on a limb to help me."

"And it's much appreciated, I'm sure."

Archie's voice rises. "Look, let's think about this. You've got the CIA behind you, right? They must be able to do something."

Colchester inclines his head with a look of deep skepticism. "Why would they do anything?"

"He cooperated with them. They can't just leave him hanging."

Colchester is starting to look faintly exasperated. "What do you suggest they do?"

"Work out a deal or something. There's got to be a way to get Renata back without me having to go back. Give them this." Archie points at the flash drive lying on the table.

Colchester shakes his head. "They'll send you back first. Anyway, the Chinese will know we could just copy the data. Why would they go for that deal?"

Archie's eyes widen and Pascual can see him starting to realize the dimensions of his problem. "There's got to be something they can do."

Colchester sighs. "I'll tell you what needs to get done right now, Archie. We have to get Mr. Rose here back to Singapore with an airtight story, and we have to get you and your data to the U. S. of A. Those things have to get done pronto."

Archie turns a pleading look on Pascual, who has nothing to

give him. Archie's expression firms. "Let me talk to Dexter." He picks up Colchester's phone and jabs at it, puts it to his ear and in a moment starts speaking again, in Chinese. There is a short conversation, and Archie takes the phone from his ear and looks at Colchester. "Dexter says he can be here in four hours."

"Bad idea," says Colchester. "There's no way the Chinese aren't tracking his plane. Any fool can do that online. He'll bring the Guoanbu with him."

Archie relays this into the phone with a look of alarm. He listens and then looks at Colchester again. "Dexter says he's not an idiot. He'll turn off the transponder. He says don't do anything until he gets here."

▪ ▪ ▪ ▪

Pascual sits watching Archie pace, hands in his pockets, up and down the path in the garden behind the guest house. The sun is in the west, sinking toward the horizon beyond which lies Java. Pascual toys idly with one of the chess pieces that distracted him and Archie for a couple of hours until Archie swept them off the board in disgust and strode out into the garden.

Pascual has heard no further talk of flights to Singapore and is wondering if he has simply been lost in the shuffle. Archie comes up the steps onto the veranda and drops onto a chair. Pascual waits a few seconds and says, "Tell me something."

Archie turns his head slowly. "What?"

"What do you have that the CIA wants?"

Archie's face goes blank. "Why would you think I have anything they want?"

"They're an intelligence agency, not a human rights NGO. If they want to get you to a safe place, I'm guessing you have something they want, maybe on that flash drive."

Archie gives off a little puff of laughter. "You're a smart guy, Mr. Rose."

"Don't tell me if you'd have to kill me afterwards."

"I suppose it's not really a secret. Anyone who takes a close look at my holdings will figure it out before too long. There is some intellectual property involved."

"If it's not really a secret, why is the Guoanbu so anxious to stop you?"

"Oh, the nature of the IP isn't a secret. But the actual content is. That's what's on the flash drive. But they'd want to stop me even without that. They want me on trial for financial misconduct in Beijing instead of giving talks in Berkeley or D.C. about how bad the regime in China is."

Pascual ponders, his gaze going away across the green. "Why do you need to deliver the flash drive? Can't you just send the content electronically?"

Archie frowns at him for a moment, and in his face Pascual can see the tussle between the need for security and the urge to hold forth. "Number one, there's a whole lot of content. Number two, if you try to send it, then it's out there where the hackers live. And I don't want to make it even more vulnerable than it already is. Basically I'm maintaining an air gap. The hackers can't get to it as long as it's in my pocket and not connected to anything."

Pascual waits for more but sees that the need for security has give him. Archie's expression firms. "Let me talk to Dexter." He picks up Colchester's phone and jabs at it, puts it to his ear and in a moment starts speaking again, in Chinese. There is a short conversation, and Archie takes the phone from his ear and looks at Colchester. "Dexter says he can be here in four hours."

"Bad idea," says Colchester. "There's no way the Chinese aren't tracking his plane. Any fool can do that online. He'll bring the Guoanbu with him."

Archie relays this into the phone with a look of alarm. He listens and then looks at Colchester again. "Dexter says he's not an idiot. He'll turn off the transponder. He says don't do anything until he gets here."

■ ■ ■ ■

Pascual sits watching Archie pace, hands in his pockets, up and down the path in the garden behind the guest house. The sun is in the west, sinking toward the horizon beyond which lies Java. Pascual toys idly with one of the chess pieces that distracted him and Archie for a couple of hours until Archie swept them off the board in disgust and strode out into the garden.

Pascual has heard no further talk of flights to Singapore and is wondering if he has simply been lost in the shuffle. Archie comes up the steps onto the veranda and drops onto a chair. Pascual waits a few seconds and says, "Tell me something."

Archie turns his head slowly. "What?"

"What do you have that the CIA wants?"

Archie's face goes blank. "Why would you think I have anything they want?"

"They're an intelligence agency, not a human rights NGO. If they want to get you to a safe place, I'm guessing you have something they want, maybe on that flash drive."

Archie gives off a little puff of laughter. "You're a smart guy, Mr. Rose."

"Don't tell me if you'd have to kill me afterwards."

"I suppose it's not really a secret. Anyone who takes a close look at my holdings will figure it out before too long. There is some intellectual property involved."

"If it's not really a secret, why is the Guoanbu so anxious to stop you?"

"Oh, the nature of the IP isn't a secret. But the actual content is. That's what's on the flash drive. But they'd want to stop me even without that. They want me on trial for financial misconduct in Beijing instead of giving talks in Berkeley or D.C. about how bad the regime in China is."

Pascual ponders, his gaze going away across the green. "Why do you need to deliver the flash drive? Can't you just send the content electronically?"

Archie frowns at him for a moment, and in his face Pascual can see the tussle between the need for security and the urge to hold forth. "Number one, there's a whole lot of content. Number two, if you try to send it, then it's out there where the hackers live. And I don't want to make it even more vulnerable than it already is. Basically I'm maintaining an air gap. The hackers can't get to it as long as it's in my pocket and not connected to anything."

Pascual waits for more but sees that the need for security has reasserted itself. "Well, you've delivered it now. Which means, I assume, that the CIA is going to have it before too long."

"No doubt. But the Guoanbu will still want me in Beijing. And if they get me, and they find out I passed what's on the flash drive to the CIA, that's it for me. I'll get a bullet in the back of the neck."

That kills the conversation and they sit in silence for a time. They become aware of the sound simultaneously and their heads turn to the west. Archie steps off the veranda for a clearer view and shades his eyes with his hand. Pascual follows, and he spots the jet first, far out over the ocean, steadying for the approach. "Dexter's here," says Archie.

••••

"What the hell are we going to do?" Dexter Fang has aged ten years in a day. He sags on a chair across from Archie at the conference table, his eyes going from Archie to Noah Colchester and back. His considerable belly heaves beneath his shirt with each breath.

Colchester is leaning back on his chair, legs crossed. "If it was up to me, I'd be in the air right now, with Archie on board. As for you, you're going to have to make a decision about damage control. Do some triage."

"I can't give up Archie. That's not happening."

"You're right about that. I won't let it. You're going to have to let this woman do her worst. How bad can she hurt you?"

Dexter sighs, seeming to deflate on the chair. "Pretty bad. Renata knows where all the bodies are buried. That's a figure of speech, of course."

Colchester nods. "Sure. How many bodies are there?"

"Well, quite a few, depending on how we define a body. The man I talked to said there were two ways that Renata could be freed. Number one, they will exchange her for Archie. Number two, Renata can leave any time she pleases, as long as she gives satisfactory answers to a list of questions they have."

"Like what?"

"He wasn't too specific, but I know what they want. Crucial business information. All the stuff I try to conceal from competitors. And, uh, I'd have to add, regulators, tax men, that sort of person. The tax stuff, the Seychelles companies and the Liechtenstein trusts. And the payoffs in Jakarta, the palms I have to grease and the retirements I'm funding. They'll be very specific. They'll want code names, account numbers, passwords, the works. And she's in a position to give them, or at least tell them where to find them."

Colchester grimaces. "That was indiscreet. Never give an employee that much power."

"Thanks for the advice," says Dexter, coolly. "Anyway, they'll verify everything before they let her go. And then the Chinese will basically own me."

Colchester's eyes narrow and a wicked smile shifts the creases. "That might not be entirely a bad thing. If the agency had a guy like you, a major financial player in a crucial part of the world, that the Chinese *thought* they owned, that could have some real possibilities."

Dexter looks blank until he realizes what Colchester is suggesting, and then his expression firms. "Forget it. I'm not going to be a double agent for the CIA and the Guoanbu. That's not happening, either."

For an instant Colchester looks as if he wants to argue the point, but it passes. "Well, OK. You've shot down Plan A and Plan B, then what's Plan C?"

Dexter looks at Archie, who gapes back at him. Colchester sits watching both of them. Pascual sits perfectly still, hoping he has been forgotten. Dexter looks at Pascual and says, "Mr. Rose. What would you recommend?"

Before Pascual can answer, Colchester is pointing a long index finger down the table at him. "Hang on a second. What is this man doing here?"

Pascual gives him a blank look and says, "I'm just waiting to hear about my ride to Singapore."

"You're not going to Singapore until we're sure you've got your story straight. And we've got another crisis to deal with right now. So be patient."

"Why shouldn't he be here?" says Dexter.

"Because the agency says he's served his purpose. As of now he's deadweight."

Archie says, "He was almost dead, period, along with me the other night. And he took all the risks in Singapore. He's been with us the whole way, and he's pulled his weight."

Dexter says, "I want to hear his answer to my question."

Colchester's eyebrows rise and he raises his hands in surrender. "Suit yourself. OK, Mr. Rose, what do you recommend?"

Pascual has nothing at all to recommend, and the last thing

in the world he wants is to take any more risks and pull any more weight. But Dexter and Archie have given him their confidence, and Renata is in distress somewhere. And he is starting to have his fill of Noah Colchester. He says, "I think the logic is fairly simple. If you don't want to give up Archie, and you don't want Renata to talk to the Chinese, you're going to have to get Renata back."

"How do we do that?" says Dexter.

"I have no idea." This is met with silence. When Pascual realizes they expect more from him, he says, "Where is this swap supposed to take place, if you go for it?"

"We didn't get that far."

Colchester says, "Could she be talking now? Maybe it's all over, already."

Pascual says, "I'd guess the Chinese are counting on Dexter throwing Archie to the wolves. Renata's their backup plan. They'll keep her on ice till they see what's happening. Can we communicate with her? What are the arrangements?"

Dexter sighs again. "Here's what I was told. When we have made a decision, we are to contact them at a number I was given. From the prefix I think it's a landline in China. We will be given instructions then."

"I see." Pascual stares out the window. The sun has set and the steep hills are black against an indigo sky. Forget it, he thinks. Not your fight. He says, "So you can't really plan anything yet. But you can look at the logic, and like I said, that's simple. You either have to get Renata back without giving up Archie, or get Archie back after they've given up Renata. Which do you think would be easier?"

"Once they have Archie, we'll never get him back."

"So how do you get Renata back? You can always try sending your ex-commando guys in to rescue her, I suppose. Are you willing to risk that? You've already seen what happens when the shooting starts."

Dexter's face goes hard. "My hope would be to avoid a fight by deploying overwhelming force, as in getting some help from the security forces."

Archie says, "But we'd have to know where Renata is. And if she's in China, it's all over."

Pascual nods. "So the other way to do it would be to threaten the Chinese with something they really want to avoid. Archie, does the Guoanbu know you're intending to hand over the contents of that flash drive?"

Archie says, "I know they're worried about it. That's one reason they're anxious to stop me."

"So what if somebody like me, for example, showed up and made them an offer they couldn't refuse? I've got the drive, having stolen it from you while you were on the run, and if they don't release Renata to me, I will go and sell it to the Americans. That would be entirely in character for me."

Pascual waits to see which of the three men will stop staring dumbly at him and speak first. As it happens, it is Colchester, who says, "Not a fucking chance. That drive's not going anywhere. And you're not getting anywhere near this."

Pascual turns an unperturbed look on him. "Can I ask you a question?"

"What?"

"Are you an officer of the Central Intelligence Agency?"

Colchester juts his long jaw at Pascual. "Of course not. What's your point?"

"I'm just wondering who put you in charge of this operation."

Colchester's eyes widen and for an instant Pascual thinks the man is about to come down the table after him. "I'm in charge here because Archie contacted me for help. I consulted Langley and was delegated to come out and see what was going on. The agency will be fully informed and any necessary decisions will be made in Langley. And just for the record, on these premises I'm the boss because I own the place, and you're not only a useful idiot who has outlived his usefulness, you're an uninvited guest. So mind your manners."

"I wasn't aware I'd been discourteous. I was asked a question, and I was trying to come up with an answer. But if nobody wants to hear it, I'll be happy to shut up."

Archie says, "Take it easy, Noah." He turns to Pascual. "Go on."

Pascual ignores Colchester's glare and proceeds. "First of all, what's the status of the data on that flash drive? Is it something you could retrieve by sitting down at any computer with an internet connection?"

"Not anymore. They got to my security people. My access has been terminated. I can't log on to the server anymore."

"So if you lose that flash drive, you're no longer a threat to hand over the data. But anyone who has the drive is."

"That's right."

"Provided, of course, he convinces the Chinese that the data has not been copied."

Colchester picks up the flash drive and closes his fist around it. He says, "The data on this drive will be copied before anybody pries it out of my grasp. I can assure you of that."

Pascual shrugs. "OK, be my guest. Just for God's sake don't let word get out that you've done it. If I approach the Chinese with a deal, they've got to believe taking possession of the drive will be the end of it."

Dexter says, "You'll have to prove to them that you really have the data. They won't let Renata go until they've checked out what's on the drive."

"It will take some careful setup. Probably involving an intermediary trusted by both sides. Maybe your friend Halim? I'll insist on Renata being released to him, and then I'll let the Chinese look at the drive. If they authenticate it, they give the word for Renata to be released. If they don't, they take her back."

Dexter blinks, Archie frowns. Colchester vents a sigh of exasperation. Archie says, "There's a better way. You could run the data through a hash generator. That would spit out a thirty-two-character identifier for each file that's unique to the specific file that gets hashed. There are any number of hashing algorithms. You can use them to verify the integrity of a downloaded file. If one bit of the file has flipped due to a transmission error, the hash will be different. You could easily generate the necessary hashes and SMS them to the Chinese. Then they could be certain that the files are genuine."

Pascual says, "I'd need your help with that. But it sounds like it could work."

Dexter says, "But wait a minute. You'll never be able to prove the data hasn't been copied. Why would the Guoanbu go for that deal?"

"If they're really worried about the data getting out, it would be risky to call my bluff. I could just walk away and go sell it to the Americans."

There is a brief silence and Archie says, "They'll just kill you."

Pascual waves that away with a gesture that is much more casual than he feels. "They'll have to locate me first. And I will tell them that if anything happens to me, the person holding the drive has instructions to deliver it to the American embassy in Singapore."

"And who is that person? You don't want to have the thing on you if you talk to the Guoanbu face to face."

"I would hope to be able to conduct the whole thing remotely. By telephone and video conference if necessary. I'd use a cut-out to deliver the device."

Colchester says, "They'll laugh all this out of the room. They'll know it's a scam. To start with, why would you give a damn about Renata?"

"Because her rich boyfriend in Singapore is distraught and paying me a ton of money to get her back. That would also be in character for me. I saw a chance to cash in and contacted him."

Pascual is getting tired of being stared at, but it gives him leisure to consider what he has just proposed and wonder what on earth possessed him. "You have a very twisted mind," says Colchester. He turns to Fang. "I'm telling you, Dexter, with the Guoanbu as your silent partner, you'd be positioned to be the most influential double agent in history. Look at it as an opportunity."

Dexter just stares at him, and as the blood drains slowly from his face, Pascual can see him contemplating the end of his existence as an autonomous agent. "An opportunity," Dexter says, quietly.

"Now wait a minute," says Archie, startling them all by slamming a hand down on the table. "Dexter, this is your family's future you're talking about." He turns to Pascual. "How would you approach the Chinese? What's your story?"

Imbecile, thinks Pascual. Why couldn't you keep your mouth shut? He gazes into a corner of the ceiling for a moment, organizing his thoughts, and says, "Up to the point where you contacted Mr. Colchester here, I'd tell it pretty much the way it went. We were still in Jakarta when Renata was snatched, and Dexter brought us in on the crisis management. Being the scoundrel I am, I saw an opportunity to cash in, exploiting the confidence he has so unwisely granted me. I obtained the contact number from Dexter, surreptitiously, of course. I swiped the flash drive out of your bag when you were asleep, or in the shower. I was then flown back to Singapore, having outlived my usefulness. Since I wasn't sure the Chinese would pay, I contacted Renata's fiancé there, having made his acquaintance, again through Dexter's unsuspecting generosity. I asked him how much it was worth to him if I could spring Renata. Being the devoted lover he is, he came up with a big number. Then I contacted the Chinese."

A dead silence reigns for at least ten seconds. Pascual is about to push away from the table and make a nonchalant exit when Colchester says, "There's not a chance in hell Langley will go for anything like that. You're just angling for a score, for real. You'll sell Archie out for a payday from the Guoanbu."

Pascual gives him an incredulous look. "If you're worried about that, all you have to do is fly Archie out of here tonight. I'd have to know where he is to sell him out."

Colchester reaches for his phone. "Well, that settles it. Archie, go pack your bags. I'll tell my guys to be ready for takeoff in half an hour."

Archie raises a hand. "Chill, Noah. I'm not going to throw Dexter to the wolves. And there's still a few billion dollars in China I think I can salvage. I think we at least have to talk about all this with Langley."

Colchester scowls at him for a few seconds and then turns his glare on Pascual. "It's time for you to go take a walk," he says. "The grownups and I have things to discuss."

When Archie and Dexter come up onto the veranda they find Pascual sitting with a tall cool drink at his elbow, listening to the whispering of the tropical night. It is in fact the third tall cool drink Pascual has had. He is pleasantly drunk and hoping to pass out into a dreamless sleep before too long. He says, "Want a screwdriver? The houseboy can fetch you one, for a small consideration. I don't know where he gets them, but they work."

Archie solemnly shakes his head. Behind him, Dexter looks as if he is sleepwalking. He acknowledges Pascual with the barest of nods and shambles off down the veranda toward his room. Archie watches him for a moment and turns back to Pascual. "Noah says Langley will rule on all this by tomorrow. He says he will strongly recommend taking no action to rescue Renata."

Pascual shrugs. "No surprise there. What happens to me?"

"You will fly out tomorrow with Dexter to Jakarta, and then on to Singapore. Noah will brief you on what story to give the police."

"What about you?"

Archie smiles a grim little smile. "I am being rescued. I will fly with Noah back to San Francisco, via Guam and Honolulu. With the flash drive."

Pascual watches the smile fade. "Congratulations, you made it."

"Yes. It remains to be seen how much of my fortune I'll be able to salvage, but at least I should be able to make it to a safe haven. Leaving Dexter . . . what's the expression? Up shit creek without a paddle."

Pascual studies Archie's face in the dim lamplight. He sees a man genuinely dismayed by the consequences of his actions. "Tell Dexter not to go for the double agent thing. Tell him to start putting his affairs in order and get ready to live in mere comfort instead of obscene luxury. He'll be happier."

"No, he won't. I think he'd still like to rescue Renata. But if that's not possible, he'll be the most enthusiastic double agent the CIA ever had. He'd rather be blackmailed by the Guoanbu than be poor."

Pascual frowns. "So tell me, now that I've met the guy. How is it that your pal Noah has such tight connections with the CIA?"

Archie pulls over a chair and sits. "He was an early mover and shaker in Silicon Valley. Among other things, he developed a platform for data analysis that uses AI to integrate and analyze huge masses of data and detect unusual patterns. Very useful for the military and police to spot terrorists, money launderers and so forth. The CIA loves it, and loves Noah. He works pretty closely with them. Especially on China stuff. Noah has a bit of a thing about the Chinese. I kid him about it. He thinks China is the archenemy. And as much as I hate to say it, at least under the regime we have now, I think he's right."

"I see. And what's on that flash drive?"

Archie sends a quiet little laugh out into the night. "You are just determined to breach security, aren't you?"

"I'm just curious. You said it wasn't really a secret."

"I did, didn't I? All right, you know what quantum computing is?"

"I've read a little about it. I can't say I really understand it, especially after three screwdrivers."

"The screwdrivers may actually help. It's weird stuff. To tell you the truth, I don't really understand it either, but here's all you need to know. It's going to blow the cryptography that keeps digital communication secure right out of the water, maybe in just a few years. Once they get the engineering problems solved, and they're not that far away, the public-key cryptography that most current IT uses will be obsolete. That system relies on very complex factoring problems that a classical computer would take millions of years to solve. But quantum computers are orders of magnitude faster than classical computers. A quantum computer will be able to crack those problems in a few minutes. Nothing will be secure."

"Terrific. What do we do, go back to invisible ink and the signet ring in the melted wax?"

"What we do is develop post-quantum cryptography. That means cryptographic algorithms that can't be solved even by a quantum computer. The research division of one of my companies has been working on this for several years. And just recently they came up with one based on multivariate polynomials that has been proved to be secure."

"Wow. Congratulations."

"Don't congratulate me. It's a major crisis for me."

"Why?"

"Because it instantly implicates me in national security. It means an end to my autonomy and my integrity. I'm not just a businessman anymore, free to pursue my interests. I'm part of the war machine."

Pascual strives to concentrate through a vodka-induced fog. "How so?"

"If China can secure its digital communications but nobody else can, China has a huge advantage in warfare of all types. And look at the guy in charge. He knows China has a narrow window to become top dog before demography starts to work against it. If he gets a huge tactical advantage within that window, it brings war that much closer. As for me, I'd rather everybody was able to secure their digital systems. I like that world a lot better. But that makes me a traitor."

This has a sobering effect almost strong enough to cut through three screwdrivers. Pascual gapes for a moment and says, "Good God. I can see why they're anxious to stop you."

"And not stopping me won't be the end of it. I'll be dodging the Guoanbu for the rest of my life. The party has a long memory. I'll be like Salman Rushdie after the fatwa, always looking over my shoulder."

Archie stares gloomily off into the dark. Pascual says, "So why are you doing it?"

"You mean why am I committing treason? And possibly suicide?"

"If you want to put it that way."

Archie shrugs. "I love China, believe me. But I don't like the party. Never did. I hate it. The Communist Party of China takes credit for all the development China has seen, but that development was made possible only when the party abandoned what they claim is their reason for being—communism. The only part of communism it retained was the police state. So it's the greatest instance of institutionalized hypocrisy in history. I say to hell with it." He stirs on the chair and looks up and down the veranda. "I might go for that drink after all. Who do I talk to?"

▪ ▪ ▪ ▪

A surfer is riding a not particularly big wave making its way listlessly in past the headland. Pascual watches until the wave expires and the surfer hops off into waist-deep water, looking bored. A better spectacle is on offer up the beach to Pascual's right, where a party of Australians, including a couple of young females in remarkably exiguous beachwear, are laughing and drinking on the sand. A car horn sounds behind him.

He turns to see a company car pulling to a stop at the edge of the beach. The doors open and Dexter and Archie get out, the Indonesian driver remaining behind the wheel. Dexter beckons, and Pascual trudges across the sand to join them.

"We're leaving," says Dexter. "Archie brought your things from the room."

Archie holds up the shopping bag Pascual brought from

Jakarta. "I grabbed your clothes and your toothbrush. Did I miss anything?"

Stunned, Pascual says, "What, you mean right now?"

"Singh has the plane ready to go. Make your goodbyes and jump in the car."

On the short uphill run to the airstrip, Pascual looks at Archie and says, "When do you and Colchester head out?"

Staring straight ahead, Archie says, "I'm not going with Noah. I'm coming with you."

Pascual can only gape for a moment. "With his agreement?"

"Without his knowledge. He's expecting me at the office in ten minutes for a video call with Langley."

Pascual blinks stupidly. "OK, you're going to have to bring me up to date."

From the front seat Dexter says, "Archie and I spent the night talking about this. Langley will never go for your scheme to get Renata back. They *want* the Guoanbu to blackmail me. They'll see that as a win, because they assume I will agree to be a double agent. But my first responsibility is to my family and what five or six generations of my ancestors have built up, in Indonesia and elsewhere. So I've got to try to spring Renata. I think your idea is a good one, and we're going to put it into action, just like you laid it out last night."

The blood has drained from Pascual's face and the bottom has fallen out of his stomach. The car is slowing for the airstrip gate already, and these two madmen are making him put his money where his mouth is. Pascual scrambles to order his thoughts. "Why is Archie coming along? He's not involved in the plan. He should go with Colchester. At least he'll be safe then."

Archie says, "Your plan only works if I'm still on the run. If I go with Noah, word will get out fairly quickly, no matter how hard we try to keep it under wraps. And the instant the Chinese hear even a rumor that I've made it to the West, they'll assume I brought the algorithms with me. And then your plan is dead."

"What about the flash drive? We've got to show it for the plan to work."

Archie pats the bag on his lap. "Right here. It's coming with us. Noah cloned it last night, so he's got what he wants. But we'll be able to hash those files in Jakarta to show the Guoanbu we've got the goods."

Pascual takes a deep breath. "I think you should go with Noah. In fact, I don't think we should go through with this scheme of mine. There are all kinds of things that could go wrong."

Dexter says, "It's a risk, yes. But I'm not going to sit still and let the Chinese squeeze Renata dry and destroy my security and independence. Look, if you need an incentive, I can pay you. All right?"

A gate swings open, the car goes up a short drive past the tiny terminal and control tower, and there is the Gulfstream, waiting on the tarmac, Singh standing by the drop-down steps, phone to his ear. Pascual feels his judgment being tugged violently in varying directions by pride, greed and fear in quick succession. "You don't need to pay me," he says. "I'm on board."

"Good man." The car stops, doors open, Dexter and Archie leap out. Pascual follows, slowly, moving in a light-headed daze. Singh puts his phone away and greets Dexter, who turns and waves Pascual and Archie on. "We're ready to go," he says.

Renata will be grateful, Pascual thinks as he mounts the steps, there is that. He sinks into a window seat and looks out at Colchester's jet parked to one side of the apron, being refueled from a tanker truck.

Renata will be grateful, Pascual thinks, until something goes wrong.

## 28

"Now Noah's the one shitting his pants," says Archie, putting his phone away. He chuckles. "He said that for a genius I'm the dumbest son of a bitch he's ever met."

"He's afraid he's going to lose his big catch," says Dexter. "He was looking forward to delivering you, tied up with a ribbon."

"He'll still get to do that," says Archie. "He's just going to have to wait a little bit, that's all."

Pascual envies Archie his confidence. His gaze strays out the window to the distant sea, forty thousand feet down and a dozen miles or so to the north beyond a strip of verdant flatland. He is huddled with Dexter and Archie around a table in the cabin of the jet. They are halfway along the island of Java, a route that feels familiar now, and by lunchtime they will be in Jakarta.

"Now, where were we?" says Dexter, calling Pascual back to order. "When you return to Singapore, the problem will be to get you back into the country without attracting any notice, as in theory you never left. I think it can be done. The authorities at Seletar are quite used to my coming and going, and they never come onto the plane. Normally we just go into the terminal for the formalities and are waved through. The plane gets towed to a hangar, where it is serviced. I thought it might be possible for you simply to stay on the plane and be sneaked off and whisked away from the hangar with the collusion of the people from the maintenance company. Singh says that is probably possible, though he seemed reluctant to risk it. I told him I would assume responsibility if there are any difficulties."

Pascual frowns. "It seems to me that places a great deal of weight on the discretion of the maintenance company."

"Well, there would be a consideration, of course. Singh and I are on good terms with the ground operations people. Singapore officials are quite incorruptible, but I have found that ordinary working people generally have their price."

Pascual briefly marvels at the worldview of a billionaire and says, "They're also generally the ones who go to jail if they get caught breaking the rules. That would make me very careful. I think I agree with Singh that it's a bad risk."

Fang looks annoyed. "Do you have an alternative?"

"I think so." Pascual digs out his wallet, and from behind his Pascual Rose passport he extracts a second one and slides it across the table to Fang. "This is a perfectly legitimate U.S. passport I was issued by the CIA. I flew to Dubai on it."

Fang opens it and peers at it. "Who is Lester Gray?"

"He's the man the CIA wants me to be when I'm at home. That shouldn't set off any alarms with the Singapore authorities. And I've got the health documents in Lester's name as well. We'll just have to explain how I got from Dubai to Indonesia without any record in the passport."

"I doubt very much they'll check. If they see an exit stamp from Jakarta they'll be happy. And on an American passport you won't need a visa for Singapore. It should work." Fang slides the passport back. "Now, I don't know how much support I can give you. I don't think it's safe at this point for me to try to hide you in any of my properties. You will have to strike out on your own. Of course, that will fit with the narrative we want to sell to the Chinese."

"Yes." Pascual leans back in his seat, remembering desperate days and harebrained schemes from decades ago. I am too old for this, he thinks. He says, "So how does the narrative go? You make the mistake of including me in your discussions after you get the SOS from Renata. I see my chance and make my plans. How do I get the number in China? Doesn't matter. Carelessness on your part, perhaps. You wrote it down and I copied it."

"You'll need the number," says Dexter. "Do you have a phone?"

"No, I'm afraid the one I had got blown up with everything else in your friend's house. I'll get another one in Singapore."

"How are you fixed for money?"

"I've got a few thousand dollars in cash left. That should give me some mobility and buy me a phone or two."

"If you need more money, contact me and I can arrange to have some delivered to you. As long as you don't go too far off the beaten path."

The hollow roar of the aircraft is the only sound, permeating Pascual from head to toe, for a long minute as three men contemplate the brink of the precipice they have resolved to leap off. "Sounds like a plan," says Archie.

■■■■

On the ground in Jakarta there is an air of crisis. Dexter has been on and off the phone for the last hour of the flight, giving instructions in Indonesian. He disembarks in the normal way on the tarmac and is whisked away in a black SUV, a second vehicle carrying at least two armed men following it. Archie and Pascual remain on the plane until it is moved inside a hangar, where another SUV is waiting. They transfer to it, shielded from public view. A half hour later they are reunited with Dexter in a third-floor conference room in a massive steel and glass building in a sprawling business park less than a mile from the airport. Lunch is waiting for them, laid out on the table. "Paranoid, maybe," says Dexter at the head of the table. "But after what happened to Renata, I'm assuming that anything or any place associated with me could be under observation. Mr. Rose, you will be going back to the airport directly after lunch. Singh says he'll be ready to go in an hour. You should be in Singapore by mid-afternoon."

Archie says, "I'll need a laptop and a few minutes to generate those identifiers for a couple of sample files."

Dexter says, "I can get you access to a computer just across the hall."

"OK." Archie turns to Pascual. "Then you'll take the flash drive. Once you have a new phone, contact me and I'll text you the hashes."

Pascual swallows a mouthful of *nasi goreng*. "I'll need your number. How am I supposed to have gotten access to the files, to hash them? Isn't the drive encrypted?"

Archie frowns. "Good point. How about this? I generated

the hashes to give somebody in the States a teaser. I was careless enough to mention this to you and even worse, I left the file open when I came in for lunch. You had already grabbed the flash drive, you'd gotten a duplicate drive to switch for it, and you saw your chance to download the hashes while I was eating. It doesn't say much for my security consciousness, but the Chinese won't look at the story too closely. They'll be too freaked out when they see the hashes to worry about anything but keeping the lid on."

Pascual nods. "They'll almost certainly ask me if I know where you're hiding. Obviously I can't know that, or I'd simply sell them the location. But it would add authenticity for me to give away the places I've seen. The room by the canal, for example. So be aware."

There is an uncomfortable silence. "You have experience betraying people," says Dexter.

"It's what I do best. How do I communicate with you?"

"I'll give you a number for a secure phone not traceable to me."

Archie says, "How is it going to work? How are you going to make the switch?"

"That will depend on circumstances. We have no idea where Renata is. If they've taken her to China, things will be complicated."

Archie says, "I'd expect them to go where they have assets. I know they've got some big operations around the islands. They could stash her in one of their installations."

Everyone contemplates that for a few seconds. Archie says,

"You'll have to be very careful. I wouldn't trust the Guoanbu to play it straight."

Dexter says, "For God's sake don't do anything to put Renata in danger."

Pascual sets down his fork and looks Dexter in the eye. "I will do my utmost not to put Renata in any more danger than she's in. But you have to understand, if the Chinese start trying to complicate things with further terms and conditions, or if they start questioning the setup, it's off. That will be my call and mine alone. If I decide to bail, it's over."

There is a brief silence. Archie says, "Well, then I guess you'll just have to convince them you have the goods, but no scruples to go with them. Your reputation should help."

The thought depresses Pascual. "Yes. I'm just the man we want. A scoundrel."

# 29

Return journeys always seem to take less time than the voyage out, Pascual thinks, watching the islands pass below him. Far ahead he can make out the smear on the horizon that must be Singapore. He has dozed for much of the flight, sprawled on the couch that occupies one side of the cabin, and now suddenly the curtain is about to go up on the play.

On the approach the smear resolves into a Singapore of tiny cars crawling past towering high-rises, vast and opulent and, after Indonesia, feeling like home. Not for the first time in his life Pascual is astonished at what he has gotten himself into. In the private jet terminal at Seletar, his heart skips a beat or two as a gimlet-eyed functionary from the Immigration and Checkpoints Authority scans Lester Gray's passport electronically and then compares his face with the photo and leafs idly through it before handing it back to him. A quick rummage through his Dior bag is enough for him to clear customs, and he follows Singh to a waiting car.

The driver of the car is Chinese, evidently accustomed to

# The Archipelago Game

chauffeuring Singh, who greets him with a nod and turns to Pascual. "Where shall I have Toby drop you?"

"Somewhere I can change U.S. dollars to Singapore," Pascual says.

Toby nods, expressionless. On the long drive into the heart of the city Singh says little, absorbed in his phone. Pascual runs through what passes for his plan. Can he chance a hotel room, or will that instantly alert the police? Will Mr. Tan help him again? Or will that alert the Guoanbu? All his contacts in Singapore lead back to Dexter Fang, and that connection is demonstrably insecure. Improvisation will be needed.

They turn up Serangoon Road, a thoroughfare lined with jewelers, pawn shops, South Asian restaurants. Toby drops Singh at a high-rise two blocks down a side street and then maneuvers around a couple of corners and pulls up in front of a shop with a large sign proclaiming MONEY CENTER. Over his shoulder he says, "You change dollars here, good rate."

In ten minutes Pascual has five hundred Singapore dollars and change to play with and is back in Serangoon Road asking the way to the nearest taxi stand. This proves to be in Race Course Road, a short hike away. In half an hour he is paying off the taxi in New Bridge Road, hoping he can remember the way to the widow Eng's house. In another fifteen minutes he is tapping at her back door in the alley.

This is a risk, as anyone monitoring his old compromised phone would have noted him sheltering here, but Pascual thinks it unlikely that anyone would maintain surveillance on the place. The widow is evidently astonished to see him, but beckons him inside. Pascual mimics using a phone and repeats Kenny's name. Mrs. Eng produces her phone and speaks into it, then beams at Pascual and says, "He come, he come now."

Pascual thanks her and gives her fifty dollars, which astonishes her further. She brings him into the kitchen and proceeds to feed him, which he does not resist. When Kenny slips in from the alley, Pascual is halfway through a bowl of steaming fish soup. "Hey, what up?" says Kenny, sliding onto a stool opposite Pascual.

Pascual wipes his mouth and says, "I need another phone. In fact I need two phones. Also not traceable to me. I've got plenty of money. Can you do that?"

Kenny gives a slow shake of the head. "Can, boss. But not so easy second time, *lah*. My friend already asking why you don't want the phone can be trace back to you. He say he taking a lot of risk. So if I ask him again to use his ID, he sure will want more money. Okay or not, boss?"

Cost of doing business, Pascual thinks. He inventories his shrinking stock of CIA-issued hundred-dollar bills and tries to calculate how much he can budget for this. "I have a little over four hundred Singapore dollars. I could give you maybe another five hundred U.S. if necessary. But see if you can bargain with your friend a little. My pockets aren't that deep."

Kenny considers this with all the gravity of a Wall Street tycoon juggling billions in his head. Finally he says, "OK boss, I try. You give me cash first and I come back one hour later."

■■■■

"Boss, this time my friend say he want four hundred U.S. dollar. Now he say each line under his name is two hundred. Then you also want two phones, right? Phone still same price like last time, fifty dollars each, Singapore dollar. This is the change, you want?" Kenny holds out a sheaf of bills. Somewhat to Pascual's surprise and much to his relief, the errand has taken well under an hour.

"Keep the Benjamin," says Pascual. "I'll need those Singapore dollars. Don't leave until I'm sure I've got both phones working."

That is accomplished in short order and Kenny vanishes back into *ah beng* byways. Selecting one of his new phones at random, Pascual texts Archie: *In S'pore, sling me some hash.* In under a minute he receives a text containing a 32-character sequence of letters and numbers along with Archie's note *This should convince them you've got the goods.*

Pascual ponders. Events are predictable only a step or two ahead. At some point he is going to need his cutout, but to arrange it in advance would be to create a vulnerability. Best to make the initial contact with the Guoanbu and see what happens.

He thanks the widow Eng and takes his leave. His heart rate has accelerated. He wanders, a little desperately, knowing he is stalling, looking for a spot sheltered enough from the ambient urban roar to hold a discreet phone conversation. He settles for a bench in a tiny street-corner park, shaded by palms. He takes out the second phone. This time the memorized number he punches in is the Chinese landline. He plugs his free ear with a finger and waits.

The phone rings three times at the other end and then a voice answers in Chinese. Pascual says, "I need someone who speaks English."

He is answered by a burst of Chinese. Articulating carefully,

Pascual says, "Chee Dongfeng. Archibald Chee." He waits, hoping those are the magic words. There is some more Chinese, then silence. Pascual waits. After a minute a Chinese-accented voice in his ear says, "Who are you?"

"My name is Pascual Rose. I have something you want. I took it from Chee Dongfeng."

Silence, then "Who gave you this telephone number?"

"Mr. Dexter Fang was careless with it."

A shorter silence. "Where are you?"

"I am in Southeast Asia."

A long five seconds goes by. "And where is Chee Dongfeng?"

"I don't know. I left him in Jakarta earlier today. But he won't be there now."

"What is this thing you have?"

"I have a flash drive which I stole from Chee Dongfeng. It contains important data that he was planning to give to the Americans."

"What data?"

"I can show it to you. I will text you a hash that you can decode to see a sample. I will do that as soon as we hang up."

The silence goes on for a while this time, and just as Pascual begins to think it is time to end the call before somebody gets a fix on his location, the voice says, "OK, you send." The call ends.

Pascual takes out the phone he used to text Archie and brings up Archie's text. Nervous, his hands unsteady, he painstakingly copies the hash, character by character, into a text addressed to the Chinese number on the second phone. He checks the long sequence of characters twice, hits *Send* and waits. In about a minute the phone buzzes and he answers. "Yes."

"I call you in one hour," says the Chinese voice.

■ ■ ■ ■

A comfortable din of laughter and clinking glassware shelters Pascual on his perch at the end of the bar. Wandering again, he chanced, to his astonishment, on this Catalan-themed tapas bar in the heart of Tanjong Pagar. He takes a sip of *cava* and thinks about the choreography. Once he and the Guoanbu agree on an intermediary, the next step will be to make expectations clear. Pascual is acutely aware that he is trying to blackmail people who are capable of driving a bamboo skewer into a man's brain.

The buzzing of a phone startles him. It takes him a moment to realize that it is the one in his pocket, not the one lying on the bar, that is making the noise. He fumbles it out and answers. "Yes?"

In his ear Archie says, "Did you talk to the Chinese?"

"Yes. I sent them the hash. I'm waiting for them to get back to me."

"Forget it. Forget about your plan. Cancel everything and bail out."

"What? Why?"

"Noah just sabotaged the whole thing by making the algorithms public. He's not saying where he got them, but the Chinese will know. And your plan's dead."

# 30

"Noah knew that would stop us in our tracks. Once the Guoanbu knows the algorithms are out, we've got no leverage. He called me to tell me he'd done it."

Pascual watches his fellow drinkers joke, brag and flirt, all blissfully unaware that fates are being decided as they play. "He did this because he wants Renata to pressure Dexter? He really wants the double agent thing?"

Archie says, "More likely he just didn't want me to risk any exposure to the Guoanbu. He wants me to come running for cover and let him take credit for delivering me. It's a big coup for him. Understandable, I guess."

"So go. It should be over for you. You'll be safe in San Francisco. There's no reason for you to delay that any longer."

"Except that they still have Renata. And you know now they're really going to lean on her."

"But the instant you show up in front of the cameras, they'll know they've lost. They'll have no reason to hold Renata anymore."

"You don't know how they think. They've already made clear to Dexter that if I show up in front of the cameras, they'll bring him down. They'll double down on Renata. They'll use everything she can give them. He might be able to buy his way out of trouble in Indonesia, but not in Singapore. He'll be dealing with political scandals, regulatory troubles and maybe even criminal charges for the rest of his life, or else he'll have to dance to the Guoanbu's music."

Pascual considers this and finds he can summon only limited sympathy for Dexter Fang. "So what are you thinking? What do you do now?"

"We've got a Plan B. We're going to scam them."

"Did I hear you right? You're going to scam the Chinese Ministry of State Security?"

"You got it. We're going to spring Renata."

"How the hell are you going to do that?"

"I'm not going to discuss it over the phone. Anyway, it doesn't involve you, unless you want it to. You can bail at this point. Go and talk to the police, clear up this business with the lawyer, go home."

Pascual massages his aching temple. "That might be easier said than done. If I go talk to the police, will Dexter back up my story?"

"I'm sure he will. I can't vouch for the CIA, though. Noah is not your friend, I have to say. He thinks you're just a hustler, and he told me he's going to make sure you never see a dime from the agency."

Pascual is not astonished to hear this. "Good thing I have a return ticket to Dubai. It looks like that's all I'm going to get out of this whole thing."

There is a brief silence. "Stay with us," says Archie. "I'll pay you."

"What?"

"We can use you. We'll need somebody we trust to work this scheme on the Guoanbu. I'll pay you a million dollars to help us."

Pascual's first impulse is to laugh. He takes the phone away from his ear and looks at it, puts it back and says, "A million dollars?"

"One million. For real. I want you on board. You have skills we need, and you have nerve."

"Archie, my nerve is close to being shot."

"A million bucks ought to restore your nerve a little. Look, Dexter and I are flying back to Singapore tomorrow. Don't do anything till you talk with us. Just stay out of sight tonight and we'll talk in the morning. OK?"

Don't fall for this again, thinks Pascual. Go find the nearest police station and throw yourself on the mercy of the nanny state. He opens his mouth to decline Archie's offer and is surprised to hear himself say, "All right. Call me in the morning."

■ ■ ■ ■

Pascual pays for his drink and goes out into a steamy Singapore evening. Get off the street, he thinks. He needs another bolt hole, one he has not used before. A couple of streets over he finds a tiny two-star hotel in a row of shophouses. A sign offers *$25/2 hours, $10 extension (1 hour)*. Whatever the hourly rate may be intended to facilitate, to Pascual it appeals as a way to get off the street fast. There is only the question of whether hotelkeepers in Singapore have his name on a Call Police Instantly list. Pascual decides that given Singapore's reputation for efficiency in all matters, the risk is too great. He walks on past, but the sight has reminded him of another district where short-term hotel rooms may be had, possibly with less regulation. Again he inquires after the nearest taxi stand and finds it in Neil Road, with a taxi waiting. He tells the driver to take him to Geylang.

The drive proves to be relatively short, the driver giving him the eye in the mirror the whole way. Pascual waits for the pitch, is the gentleman looking for a good time, but it never comes. As he pays off the driver at a corner just off Geylang Road, Pascual notes his look of distaste and decides that the man's interest is moral rather than commercial. Pascual thanks him and gets out, avoiding eye contact.

It suddenly occurs to Pascual that an hour has nearly passed, and that the Guoanbu phone may ring at any moment. Now it is nothing but a liability, and his first move is to turn it off and slip it discreetly into a trash bin as he heads away from the bright lights down a side street.

He wanders a little, orienting himself. He remembers that there were streets with brightly lit brothels and others, darker, where the streetwalkers lurked. It takes him a little time and a couple of turns to find one of those.

In all his misspent life with all its disreputable conduct, Pascual has never paid a prostitute for her services. Now that he wishes to, he finds he cannot bring himself to approach one. He makes his way down a featureless block where several women stand at wide intervals, hip-cocked in their short skirts, perched on impossibly high heels, murmuring quietly as he passes, beckoning with raised chins, deploying professional smiles. All of them are Asian, but not all Chinese; this is where poor Cambodian or Indonesian girls come to seek their hard-won fortunes. Pascual decides he does not have the heart for this. He will go out the other end of the block and come up with a better plan.

It is the youngest and prettiest and saddest, the last one on the block, who finally snares him. She could be anything, Thai or Filipina or Timorese; all Pascual knows is that wherever she was born, she should be there now, doing her math homework or flirting with the boy next door, instead of out here in miniskirt and face paint, earning money for some stone-faced Chinese pimp. He heaves to and says, "Hello, sweetheart."

"Hello, mister. You want to come with me?" Close up, Pascual can see the hardness, the sadness vanishing instantly, replaced by the practiced seductive look.

"I would like that a lot," says Pascual. "Where shall we go?"

"Come with me, please." She is all business, setting a fast pace as she leads him around the corner to a six-story building set back from the road beyond a small forecourt, with the name of the hotel in bronze letters on its façade. The hotel looks entirely legitimate, with the usual certification stickers on the glass door, and Pascual wonders if he has misjudged the possibilities. Inside, there is a lobby with a man behind a counter, and Pascual recognizes the stone-faced pimp. The girl walks up to the desk, holding out her hand as the desk man gives Pascual the once-over. He slides a key across the counter; the girl snaps it up.

"Just a moment," says Pascual. He steps to the counter, pulling out his wallet.

"One hundred Singapore dollar," says the man.

"I would like to discuss the terms," says Pascual.

"One hundred dollar for room. She tell you price. Hand job, blow job, anything you want. You want condom, I sell you. You pay her after."

Pascual extracts one of his dwindling supply of hundred-dollar bills and slides it across the counter, keeping two fingers on it. "I will pay her, certainly. And I will pay a hundred Singapore dollars for the room. But I will also pay you one hundred American dollars if I can stay in the room when we're finished. I want to stay until tomorrow, no registration, no passport, no name. Understand?"

A long unblinking staring match with the stone face ensues. At length the man says, "Two hundred."

Pascual knows he has little leverage. There is a limit to how many flophouses he is willing to walk out of to strengthen his bargaining position. "Agreed, two hundred. But the room is mine until tomorrow morning. Nobody bothers me, nobody knows I'm there. Right?"

A nod is all Pascual gets. "Two hundred. One hundred Singapore dollar for room."

Pascual shells out the cash. The Chinese grunts once and sweeps it out of sight. The girl, who has watched all this without expression, leads Pascual to the elevator.

On the ride up Pascual waits for a cue as to proper etiquette, but the girl simply stares at the floor indicator, looking bored.

On the fourth floor she unlocks a door halfway down a short hallway, and Pascual follows her into a sparsely furnished room smelling of mold, closing the door behind him. The girl marches to the bed, turns and sits. "What you like me to do for you?" she says, with the cadence of a memorized line.

Pascual comes a few paces farther into the room. He has been clutching his ridiculous shopping bag the whole time; now he lets it drop to the floor. "I'm not going to have sex with you," he says.

This alarms her. Pascual watches her stiffen, her eyes going wide, and he quickly adds. "If I have sex with you, how much do I pay you?"

Wary, she says, "One hundred dollar. Singapore."

Pascual produces it and hands it over. "There. We had sex." He fishes out another Benjamin and offers it. "This is for you. Your boss doesn't have to know about it."

The look of alarm slowly fades, and she takes the bill and makes it disappear. "Why you don't want to have sex?" Her voice is flat, toneless.

Pascual sits beside her on the bed. He sighs and then a little breathless laugh escapes him. "Who says I don't?" He puts an arm around her shoulders and pulls her to him briefly. "But not tonight. Go home. Wherever home is, go back." He releases her and she stands.

If Pascual expects gratitude, he is not going to get it. The girl stands facing him for an instant, frowning faintly. She says, "I think you are a crazy man." Then she wheels and marches out of the room, pulling the door to with a bang.

No doubt, thinks Pascual, standing at the window pulling the curtain aside with a finger, looking down into the street, sinking into black depression. A crazy man, as if that excused anything.

# 31

When Pascual awakes, a feeble gray light is showing around the edges of the curtain. He has spent a restless night tossing on sheets of dubious cleanliness, and he is stiff and groggy. He lies for a moment retrieving the events of the past twenty-four hours, and as the fog clears, the anxiety mounts. He considers his remaining phone for a moment and decides to leave it off until he has something to report.

The room is dreary and squalid, but he has no place else to go. He lies for a time with his eyes shut, listening to the slamming of distant doors and the rushing of water in pipes. When he realizes he is not going to go back to sleep, he rises with an effort. The bathroom attached to his room has mold between the tiles and pubic hair in the shower drain. Pascual takes a fast shower and puts on his unwashed clothes. He is suddenly desperate to be out of this sump of misery. Three sharp raps sound on the door of the room.

Pascual freezes. The knock is repeated, followed by a hushed, rapid stream of unintelligible words in a female voice. Pascual rouses himself, strides to the door and opens it to reveal an Asian woman in a housecoat, middle-aged and plump, tension in her face. "You come," she says in a stage whisper. "You come with me, come now." Her hand flaps in a beckoning motion.

Stupidly, Pascual says, "Why?"

"Two men. Look for you. You come now, fast."

Pascual dashes back into the room long enough to grab his bag and his shoes and then rushes out into the hall. He follows the woman away from the elevators toward a door at the end of the hall. Beyond it is a stairwell; the woman descends, Pascual close behind her. At the bottom she opens a door slowly and peeks out, then motions to Pascual. Faintly, Pascual can hear angry voices beyond a closed door. They cross a hall and go into a darkened room with a desk in the corner. The woman beckons him to the desk and turns a computer monitor toward him. The monitor shows a security camera view of the front desk, seen from overhead.

Two men stand at the counter, talking with the man who took Pascual's money last night. Pascual leans closer to the screen and goes cold. Given a chance even Pascual can learn, and he is instantly sure he last saw these two pushing out of an elevator on the night Basil Balasubramanian was killed. Pascual straightens up and exhales.

"You know?" whispers the woman.

"I know."

"He send them to wrong room. Now they angry."

That was a well-spent two hundred dollars, Pascual thinks. "Thank you."

She tugs at his sleeve. "You come."

A door at the back of the room gives onto a cluttered storeroom; at the back of that is a door opening onto a small walled yard. While Pascual hurriedly puts on his shoes, the woman trots across the yard, opens a gate and sticks her head out to look up and down. She beckons to Pascual and points to the left. "You go that way. Geylang Road."

■ ■ ■ ■

Pascual's atheism has never prevented him from appreciating the benefits offered by religious affiliation; in Damascus the relative cool and quiet of the city's mosques were his refuge from the tumult of the streets and the soulless nihilism of the political creed he had embraced.

Nearly forty years later, he is glad for the superficial familiarity with Islamic practices he gained there, as it has allowed him to get off the street and join the sparse crowd convened for dawn prayer here in this mosque on Geylang Road. This is a different flavor of Islam, Malay rather than Arab, most of the men wearing the black velvet cap that was ubiquitous in Indonesia, but the ritual is much the same. The suspicion in the looks he drew on entering was dispelled when he duly removed his shoes, depositing them along with his bag on the shelves provided, then ritually washed hands and feet as prescribed before taking his place in a rank of worshippers and participating in the prayers, slyly watching his neighbors out of the corner of his eye for cues.

After the prayers he lingers, returning nods and smiles and answering a few courteous questions, finally settling in a corner of the empty prayer hall, cross-legged on the floor, the picture of a man meditating on spiritual matters. A few kindred spirits sit alone or in small groups, conversing quietly. Pascual feels a slight pang of conscience as he shamelessly exploits the brotherhood of all Muslims to stay out of sight and plan how he is going to stay alive.

First he has to interpret what has happened this morning. Presumably the spyware was implanted on his phone in the wake of the first call he made; he has no idea how long the process takes, but the phone was turned on for more than an hour. He delayed fatally in turning it off; when he failed to answer their return call they would have identified the corner where he ditched the phone without difficulty. Before the night was out they would have been looking at the limited number of hotels in the vicinity.

Pascual thinks it unlikely that they were there simply to eliminate him. They would have wanted to know why he failed to respond. But once they had extracted an answer, they would have had no use for him. Pascual is briefly light-headed, thinking of the narrow escape he has had.

He could happily shelter here in the corner of the mosque for hours, but hunger and other considerations will not allow it. He manages to stand, knees cracking and back complaining, and makes for the exit. He pauses in the entryway just inside the street door to turn on his remaining phone. He can hear traffic outside, another Singapore morning heating up.

A missed call notice, a voice mail and a text message from Archie are waiting for him on the phone. The text message says *Call me*. Pascual punches the Call icon and Archie answers. "Good morning. Everything OK at your end?"

"The Chinese hacked my other phone in the blink of an eye last night and almost got me this morning. Other than that, everything's OK."

"Shit. Where are you?"

"In a mosque. Trying to decide what to do next. It might be time for me to bail."

"Don't do that. Dexter's got a place lined up to hide us, you and me. You need to get in touch with the fellow at the house there, what's his name, Mr. Tan. He knows the place. We'll meet you there."

"I don't know if that's a good idea. I think it's possible his phone's being monitored. I think all of Dexter's people could be compromised."

"Dexter's using a cutout. We're to communicate with Tan via a neighbor who will walk the message over to Tan. I can give you the number."

Pascual contemplates the prospect of more running, more hiding, more stress. He contemplates the prospect of a long frank discussion with the Singapore police and, optimistically, a long flight back to Dubai with just possibly enough cash to fly on to Spain. He contemplates the prospect of returning to Badalona and Sara's forgiving embrace, empty-handed. He contemplates the recurring, bewitching prospect of one million dollars. You are a fool, he thinks. "Give me the number," he says.

■ ■ ■ ■

"This is the last one left," says Mr. Tan, steering the Toyota down a narrow graveled lane crowded on either side by palm fronds and other exotic greenery. "The last Singapore *kampong*. All the others have been leveled and replaced by skyscrapers."

The metro ride from Geylang to the Buangkok station somewhere in the northeast part of the island, followed by the hike to the rendezvous with Mr. Tan, have left Pascual in a mild daze. "What's a *kampong*?"

"That's the Malay word for village." The lane winds and houses appear among the trees, bungalows with corrugated metal roofs, tucked behind neat picket fences or makeshift plywood ones, potted plants on terraces, laundry hung out to dry, children's toys and bicycles lying in the dirt. To Pascual it looks much like the villages he passed through on Java. Only the glimpses of nearby high-rises seen through gaps in the trees betray its location. "How did this one escape?"

"A stubborn owner who won't sell. Fifty years ago most of the island was like this. Then the government decided we should all live in modern flats with running water. The *kampongs* disappeared one after another in the seventies and eighties. All except for this one." He pulls over at a gate in a wooden slat fence in front of a house with a cinderblock foundation and a rusted iron roof. Chickens scratch at the dirt in a fenced enclosure at the side of the house. Mr. Tan turns to Pascual and smiles. "A long time ago I was in love with a girl who lived here."

He gets out and Pascual follows. A man has come out of the house, a Chinese of about Tan's age, tall and thin, leather-faced and stooped. He and Tan shake hands, a certain amount of banter passes back and forth in Chinese, and Tan beckons to Pascual. "This is Rodney. He will take care of you."

Rodney's hand is callused and his grip firm. "Welcome. You speak Chinese?"

"Sorry, no."

"OK, you try to understand my English, OK?" Rodney cackles.

Inside, the place is crammed with battered furniture, worn rugs, tattered wall hangings, a mirror, a fan, a television set on an ornate sideboard. "This one, your room," says Rodney, pointing through a door into a bedroom with a single bed, an ancient wardrobe and a plastic tub on a stool. "Toilet at back." He points. "You want hot water to shower, you tell me, OK?"

To Pascual it looks better than the Ritz. "Thank you. Maybe later. For now I think I would like to rest."

"Sleep if you want. You hungry, you tell me." He waves Pascual in and leaves him.

Pascual's phone buzzes. The number showing is Archie's. "What's up?" says Pascual.

"We're about to take off. We'll be in Singapore in two hours. Did you get in touch with Tan?"

"I did. I'm here, at the hideout. Very comfortable, off the beaten path."

"Cool. We're on our way. Council of war when we get there."

"Of course it's a gamble. I'm aware of that. My whole life is a roll of the dice these days."

Archie has begun to look a little alarming, wide-eyed and intense, unshaven, the fuzz on his skull just beginning to grow out. He sits across the table from Pascual, noodles drooping from the chopsticks in his hand. Dexter has finished eating and is staring moodily out a window into the deepening twilight. Clattering noises come from the kitchen where Rodney is cleaning up.

"I admire your courage," says Pascual, winding noodles around the tines of the fork Rodney kindly provided him with. "And believe me, I appreciate the position Dexter's in. I'm just wondering how realistic the prospects are."

Dexter stirs on his chair. "I have tried to talk Archie out of this. My first consideration is Renata's safety. I would not put her in danger for anything in the world. But I don't want to put Archie in danger, either, and I certainly don't want to deliver him to the Guoanbu."

"My plan shifts the risk from Renata to me," says Archie. "It will certainly get them to turn her loose, and that takes care of the threat of using her to blackmail you. Then the only problem is keeping them from flying me back to China. And that's a practical problem you should be able to solve."

Dexter looks pained. "If everything goes well."

Pascual looks from one to the other. "What's the plan, exactly?"

Archie answers. "Dexter tells the Guoanbu he's willing to give me up. We arrange a swap, me for Renata. If the swap takes place anywhere in Indonesia, Dexter should be able to prevent them from flying me out. He's got his own security people, he's got clout with the security forces. All he has to do is call in some favors and they'll never be able to get me out of Indonesia. They'll have to release me."

Pascual holds Archie's gaze for a moment. "I'm going to tell you what you told me. They'll kill you."

Archie shakes his head. "Not right away. Not on Indonesian soil. They won't want a diplomatic incident, and they'll want to haul me back for a show trial. If they can't smuggle me out, they'll let me go."

"I'm not sure how you can be so confident of that. A couple of days ago we decided that it would be impossible to get you back if they ever got their hands on you. What changed?"

"Noah messed everything up. He didn't leave us any choice. But Dexter's clout shifts the odds in our favor."

To Pascual, Dexter looks a lot less sure of his powers than Archie does. Pascual says, "How do you know they haven't taken Renata to China?"

Dexter says, "I called them this morning. I told them I'd consider giving up Archie and asked how it would work. They said we'd have to bring Archie to them. They're holding Renata at an installation they have on Sulawesi."

"Sulawesi. Where's that?"

"That's the first big island east of Borneo. You may know it by the name Celebes. They have a big complex there, mines and some smelters. With its own airstrip. But I'm pretty sure I can get it shut down."

"Pretty sure."

"I'm sure."

Pascual shoves his plate away. "So why on earth would you need me?"

Archie says, "People like Dexter don't get their hands dirty. He'd just have his people bundle me into the back of a car and pack me off to Sulawesi. And he'd delegate someone to handle the mechanics of the swap. Someone like you. He'd pay you to be the Judas. And with your reputation, that would be believable, just like with your plan."

Pascual raises a hand. "Except that I've already gone off on my own, with this scheme with the flash drive. They'll wonder how I got reconciled with Dexter so fast."

"Simple. Dexter and I never realized you'd stolen the flash drive. That plan was dead when the data was released, and we never knew it even existed. We brought you in on our scheme, not knowing you'd tried to sell us out."

Pascual sits looking forlornly at the tabletop. He has run out of arguments. Now he only has to make a decision. Through his fatigue and anxiety Pascual is able to discern the degree to which he is now being driven solely by mercenary considerations.

So, he thinks, in the end you are just like anybody else. He looks at Dexter. "So how exactly are you going to stop the Chinese from flying Archie out of the country?"

Dexter draws a deep breath. "I've got some assets on Sulawesi."

"He owns a couple of politicians," says Archie past a mouthful of noodles.

"I don't own them," says Dexter, irked. "I offer them a certain amount of support at election time. That gets me a hearing."

"Like I said, he owns them."

"One of them is the head of the regency in which the Chinese complex is located. I think if he can be persuaded, he would have the power to close the airfield, for example. And to dispatch police to search vehicles and premises."

Pascual says, "I see. Make the swap and then depend on the government to get Archie back."

"Not entirely. I will have my own people on the ground. I think we should be able to prevail in any contest of strength with whatever assets the Guoanbu may deploy."

"Like we prevailed up there in the highlands?"

"With no loss of life. With no shooting, if we plan it right and deploy sufficient force."

Pascual does not like the sound of any of this, but he knows a runaway train when he sees one. He says, "When do we leave?"

"Tomorrow," says Dexter. "Singh is earning his pay this month."

"Are Archie and I going by boat again?"

"I don't think it's necessary. The last time, we were concerned about surveillance at Seletar. Now we don't care if they see us leaving Singapore. They know where we're going. And they won't try anything at Seletar. An operation in Singapore would be a lot riskier than one on their turf in Sulawesi. I think we can all just get on the plane tomorrow, me, Lester Gray and Zhang Wei."

Dexter waits for comments but none come. Archie finishes his meal and shoves the plate away. "It'll work," he says. "The Guoanbu's used to winning by intimidation. They won't be expecting us to put up a fight."

Pascual says nothing, remembering blown operations, lost fights and diverse fiascos he has known. One million dollars, he thinks. He must make sure to discuss arrangements for payment with Archie before the balloon goes up. Sara will be able to use a little of it to cover the funeral costs, presuming a body is ever found.

■ ■ ■ ■

The flight is about twice as long as the one to Jakarta, long enough that Pascual starts wondering about the range of a Gulfstream. Before they reach Sulawesi there is a considerable stretch of sea to fly over, and then a great deal of Borneo. Pascual has read about the despoilment of the island's resources, and as they fly inland he can see brown scars in the green carpet, but there appear to be plenty of trees left; after a while there is nothing but rugged unbroken jungle beneath them, as far as the eye can see. Pascual tires of looking at it. He is already tired of being on this plane; the novelty of executive jet travel has long since worn off.

"Let's hope we don't have to ditch down there, eh?" says Dexter, settling into the seat next to Pascual, drink in hand. "If the crocodiles don't get you you'll wind up married to an orangutan."

Pascual gives the joke the feeble smile it deserves. "I'm a little more concerned with the humans. What's going to happen when we land?"

Dexter becomes serious. "First we're going to have to meet with my . . . contact. We'll be landing at a little regional airport in a place called Morowali, about a hundred kilometers north of the Chinese complex, which is on the coast. First we'll have to go a short way north to a place called Kolonodale, where the fellow lives. I've arranged transport. Subroto and Eko will meet us there. They were keen to be a part of this. We'll stay there for a night or two while we plan. When we're ready we'll contact the Chinese. All you'll have to do is follow instructions, theirs and the local man's, which I will transmit to you. You will actually execute the exchange, and when you have Renata you will take her back to Kolonodale, where you'll be protected, until we manage to get Archie back, at which point we'll fly out of the same airport."

Dexter makes it sound like a staff workshop at one of his companies. Pascual recognizes a man well insulated from the dirt-under-the-fingernails end of his business. "I will need a thorough briefing. I'll need an interpreter, too, unless everyone speaks English as well as you do."

"We'll make sure you have what you need."

"Your two guys, Eko and Subroto. Are they hoping to shoot someone?"

"They're hoping to do what's necessary to complete the job. I don't think they're trigger-happy, if that's what you're suggesting. They're ex-military, well trained."

"They also just lost a friend to the Chinese. I'd make sure they know the idea is to avoid shooting. What are the Chinese likely to bring to the party? What kind of a security presence do they have at this complex?"

"That I hope to find out from my local contacts. It's a big industrial park, a joint venture between a Chinese company and an Indonesian one. It's a huge complex, around 2,000 hectares. There are a number of different plants there, mainly smelting and processing nickel. There's housing for workers and even a luxury hotel on an island just offshore, though it appears to be open only to company personnel, VIPs and so forth. I would bet that's where they're keeping Renata. There are a lot of Chinese workers, so I imagine there will be Chinese security as well. They've got a private airstrip, and that's probably how they brought Renata in and how they're hoping to get Archie out. They've also got their own port. Priority number one is to get the airstrip and the port shut down as soon as the swap takes place. That's where the local authorities come in."

"They won't need approval from Jakarta?"

Dexter smiles. "Jakarta's a long way away and regional politicians have their own little armies. I'm hoping it all happens too fast for Jakarta to even notice."

Dexter stares into his glass for a moment and then drains it. Pascual has been laying off the sauce on general principles, but he is starting to want a drink badly.

# 33

Pascual has seen enough of Indonesia at this point that he no longer fears a great Conradian darkness, but as the Gulfstream comes in low off the sea over a patchwork of paddies and a muddy trickle of river, mountains in the distance ahead, he finds nothing cheering in the prospect. He has been ruthlessly disciplining his emotions throughout the flight and has decided that once he has secured Renata's release he will be under no further obligation. Whatever complications may accompany the task of freeing Archie from the clutches of a ruthless totalitarian state will be no concern of his. He admires Archie's courage if not his judgment, but if he can get clear of the mess with Renata unharmed, he will have won.

The airport consists of a single runway, a small, white-columned terminal and a couple of outbuildings. Upon landing, Dexter, Pascual and Archie wait on the plane while Singh descends to the tarmac to deal with the paperwork, conferring with an official who comes ambling out of one of the outbuildings. When the official has made himself scarce again, a black

SUV rolls onto the apron. Dexter, Pascual and Archie deplane and climb into the SUV to see Subroto behind the wheel and Eko riding shotgun.

A half-hour drive takes them into the hills and then down again toward the sea. They roll into a town nestled on the shore of what looks like a mountain lake, steel blue and ringed by steep green-clad slopes. When Pascual sees a freighter moored to a jetty, he realizes it must be a deep coastal inlet, the exit to the sea hidden by jutting promontories to the north. Subroto pilots the SUV through the town and up into hillside precincts where the houses are larger and farther from their neighbors. He pulls through a gate and onto the forecourt of an elegant two-story house, white stucco with a blue tile roof, shaded by palms.

"This is where the local big man lives," says Dexter. "I now need to engage in some slightly disreputable diplomacy, very discreetly. You will go with Subroto and Eko. When I've made arrangements here and talked with the Chinese again, we'll meet to finalize our plans. It might be tonight, it might be tomorrow."

"Make it tonight," says Archie. "My stomach can't take much more of this."

■ ■ ■ ■

"How's your stomach?" says Pascual, coming out onto the second-floor gallery to find Archie slumped on a chair, staring into the distance. The hotel where they are parked with Subroto and Eko is slightly primitive but nicely situated in the upper reaches of the town, with a magnificent view of the bay and the mountains beyond. A breeze in their faces alleviates the afternoon heat.

"My stomach has finally realized it's no use complaining,"

says Archie. "It says as long as I don't try to put anything in it, it will stop bothering me."

Pascual pulls a chair next to Archie's. "I don't envy you."

Archie shrugs. "I've been lucky in life. Things have worked out for me pretty well. It's about time I had some adversity to face. Probably just karma."

Pascual lets a minute go by, watching boats crawl across the opaline surface of the bay. "I still think you could have gone with Colchester, and nobody would have said you were wrong. I think most people would have, in your place. I think most of the world would vote for you to cut and run."

"I know. I'm an idiot, right? But I owe Dexter. He risked a lot to help me, and he stands to lose a lot."

"I told you what I think. I think Dexter would survive. I think he would come out of it just fine."

"Maybe. But it would hurt him, and it would hurt the family. And hey, we're forgetting Renata. Even if they're not actively mistreating her, the process of forcing her to betray the man who made her career can't be too pleasant."

Pascual is silent, thinking of other female hostages he has known and how they were treated. "There is that. So what do you think your prospects are?"

"I think they're good. What else am I going to think? I think once I'm in Chinese hands, they're going to find it hard to get me out of the country. The question is how they respond to that. But Dexter has a couple of aces up his sleeve, too."

"And what happens when he slips them into the deck?"

Archie smiles. "Then I think we might have some fireworks.

In honor of our foreign visitors. The Chinese love fireworks."

"I don't know if I'd be rooting for that. You'll probably be right in the middle of it."

"Well, we'll see." Archie stands with a grunt of effort and stretches. "All I know is, when I stopped by Subroto and Eko's room a while ago, they were pretty busy."

"Doing what?"

"Cleaning their guns. They had the parts all laid out on the bed."

"Good God," says Pascual, his heart sinking.

Archie grins. "I was glad to see it. I like to see workmen taking good care of their tools."

■ ■ ■ ■

"So there it is," says Dexter. "The Guoanbu is ready to make the exchange at any time. We only have to call to set things in motion."

Dexter has convened this meeting in a corner of the hotel garden, where he, Archie and Pascual and the two gunmen have pulled plastic chairs into a circle beneath an ill-tended tangle of flowering bushes. Twilight is advancing as the sun has dipped behind the mountains. Below them the bay has taken on a deep and shimmering ultramarine hue. "Where do they want to do it?" says Archie.

"At the main gate of the complex. The usual type of control point, a guardhouse, a barrier, a few security people. The idea is, we bring Archie, they bring Renata on their side. They send one person to verify Archie's identity, we send one to verify Renata's. That will be you, Mr. Rose. When the emissaries are satisfied, they return to their respective sides, and at a signal from a security official Renata and Archie change places. Archie will supposedly be under duress, of course. I will have two of my men escort him to the gate and hand him over, perhaps with his hands bound for verisimilitude. Renata will get into the vehicle that brought Archie and be driven away with you, Mr. Rose. Archie will then be in the custody of the Chinese, and the fun will start."

Pascual looks at Archie, who is leaning back on his chair staring into the darkening eastern sky, wearing a faint frown. He turns to Dexter. "How in God's name are you going to get him back?"

"Well, we're going to have help. I've been assured that the Morowali district police will cooperate. The most likely thing is that the Chinese will try to take Archie directly to the airfield and fly him out immediately. The airfield is about three kilometers northwest of the main complex. A pretext will be found, probably involving terrorism, for the police to shut it down. The seaport will also be closed. There is a limited number of road exits to the compound. They will be monitored, particularly the one leading to the airport."

Pascual gapes. "You said this complex covers two thousand hectares."

"More or less."

"That's a huge area. If there was only one exit to monitor, they could still hide him in there indefinitely. You can't keep the ports closed for very long, and sooner or later they'll find a way to get him out of there."

Looking a little discomfited, Dexter says, "That's why we

have to move fast. We'll have men inside the complex. We don't intend to let the Guoanbu get very far once they've got Archie in the car."

"You're going to do what, hijack the car?"

"We'll take control of the vehicle Archie is in, yes."

"Without getting anybody shot."

"That's the plan, yes. We'll confront them with overwhelming force. Remember that I am employing military-trained professionals. I'm sure they will do a competent job."

Pascual thinks briefly about the array of skills that competence in military affairs comprises and what proportion of them involve shooting people. "OK, so you'll have Archie in your custody again, and you'll be somewhere inside a two-thousand-hectare industrial installation, surrounded by Chinese security guards. What happens then?"

Silence reigns. "Tell him about the helicopter," says Archie.

Dexter clears his throat. "There is a helicopter landing pad two hundred meters inside the main gate. We have arranged for a helicopter to land there to evacuate Archie and my men within five minutes of the exchange."

To Pascual this sounds like delirium. He says, "Sounds like the timing will be tricky."

"We will be in close communication with the pilot. The helicopter will be positioned nearby, ready to land at the complex at very short notice. You and Renata will depart without delay. You will be driven directly to the airport here. That should take less than an hour. Archie should be here before you. He will find a private jet waiting for him to take him on the first leg of his journey to the US. When you and Renata arrive, we three will fly out immediately and return to Singapore."

The light is going fast and the evening breeze is picking up, rustling the flowers above their heads. Pascual keeps his face carefully blank as he scans four faces waiting for him to say something, remembering his resolution to wash his hands of everything once he has Renata clear of the mess. He feels he must raise a final point. He turns to Archie and says, "Why won't they just kill you at the first sign of trouble?"

Archie shakes his head. "They want a big public trial in China. They'll make an example of me before they put a bullet in the back of my head. These guys we'll be dealing with are expected to bring me back alive."

"I hope they're good at what they do."

"We all do," says Dexter. "Now. The Chinese suggested we do this at dawn tomorrow. I don't like that idea because they could stack the deck any way they want under cover of darkness. I'm going to suggest high noon. That's in the middle of the day shift, so there will be some coming and going but not too much. That will also give us the morning shift change to get our people into position. At shift change you have thousands of workers, all dressed identically in white uniforms and yellow hard hats, walking from the parking areas where they leave their motorcycles in through the gates. Subroto and Eko here will be among them."

The two professionals do not show any reaction, and Dexter goes on. "They will be in position near the main gate shortly before the time agreed on for the exchange. We will be in constant communication with them. Mr. Rose, you will be picked up here an hour before the exchange. I'll notify you by phone."

"All right." Pascual is seeing a Dexter Fang he has not seen before, authoritative and decisive in crisis mode. For a moment he thinks the thing might possibly fly; after all, this man has built and administered a financial empire that stretches across Southeast Asia. He knows how to pull the strings of influence and has no doubt engineered other intrigues, coups and machinations.

Pascual finds this is not quite enough to inspire confidence.

Dexter exhales heavily. "All right, then. I'm going to call the Chinese now. All of this is provisional, subject to their agreement, of course. I suggest you all take this opportunity to get some food, get some rest."

For a moment nobody moves, and then Archie says, "I am a bit hungry, now that you mention it."

# 34

"The hard hats and work suits were easy, but Dexter wasn't able to get them IDs at short notice. They'll have to hide somewhere or keep moving to avoid security. Of course, that gives them an opportunity to scout things out."

Archie is staring out the windshield of the SUV as it pushes slowly through an endless stream of identical figures in yellow helmets and white jackets and trousers, some trudging along the side of the road, others weaving through traffic on motor scooters. Ahead rises a nightmarish tangle of columns and girders, gigantic elevated conveyors crisscrossing over the road. "My God," says Archie. "There are thousands of them. You could slip a whole army in there with this crowd."

Pascual says nothing. He and Archie have been driven along the entire seaward perimeter of the complex, one of Dexter's stone-faced toughs at the wheel and another in the passenger seat, and the scale of the place has struck him dumb. Chinese capital has spread an industrial leviathan over a rugged corner of a tropical island, leveling hills, slicing through ridges, laying down mile-long ranks of immense metal hangars, fencing off mountains of red earth in vast yards, pushing long jetties out into the sea. "Where's the gate?" Pascual says finally.

Archie points. "Just up this road here and around the bend. There shouldn't be much traffic once shift change is over. Anyway, I think the Guoanbu probably has enough clout here that they can stop traffic, clear the road. There shouldn't be too much trouble handing me over."

"No witnesses," Pascual says, unable to resist a growing sense of dread.

"I hope not," says Archie. "If things go my way, the fewer people that can say what happened, the better. And if I lose, witnesses won't help."

▪▪▪▪

High noon. Pascual never saw the movie, but he is aware that the hour signifies crisis. His watch says there are twenty minutes yet to go, but the proceedings have begun. The stone-faced tough, who Pascual has learned is named Harto, grunts once and takes his cell phone from his ear and stows it. He turns to Archie and says, "We go now. Hands, please."

They are on a patch of gravel behind a concrete garage, the most solid building in the thin crust of ramshackle shops and houses lining the coast road a mile or so north of the complex. At their backs is the sea, freighters riding offshore. Archie holds out his hands and Harto produces a pair of plastic cuffs and slips them onto his wrists. "Not too tight," Archie says. "I'm not going to fight you." He tests the give in the cuffs, straining the plastic. The other tough, still nameless, is motioning Pascual toward the SUV. He climbs into the back, followed by Archie. The two toughs climb in front and doors slam.

On the short drive back toward the complex, Archie watches the tin-roofed shacks go by and Pascual watches Archie. He says, "If things go according to plan, we won't see each other after the exchange."

Archie turns to look at him. "No, I guess we won't." He smiles and extends his bound hands toward Pascual. "Thanks for everything."

Pascual clasps both hands. "Don't thank me till you're sure I did you a favor."

"I'm sure. You could have bailed and you didn't. Listen, I had a talk with Dexter last night. If anything happens to me, he'll make sure you get your money. We've got your wife's coordinates."

"Thanks." Pascual writhes a little, thinking how it was only the money that kept him from bailing. He thinks the chances are good that he is sending Archie off to a gruesome fate, and he is going to profit from it. He says, "I appreciate that. We'll talk when you get to the States."

"You got it." Archie releases his hands and falls silent.

At three minutes to noon Harto steers the SUV up the branch road that leads to the main gate of the complex. On the left is an elevated roadway raised on thick columns like an expressway ramp and on the right a sheer rock wall where a ridge has been shaved to accommodate the road. Parked on a concrete apron at the turnoff is a dark blue Toyota pickup with a rack of police lights on top. Harto raises a hand in greeting as they pass it. He takes the SUV around a curve and there is the main gate, an arched metal canopy shading a twenty-yard length of road with a stop sign before it, a security hut to the left. The SUV eases to a halt fifty yards or so shy of the canopy. There is no traffic in sight. Harto turns and says over his shoulder to Pascual, "Now we wait. When Chinese come, you go talk to them."

Pascual nods. He looks at Archie. "Well. Now I get to go play Judas."

Archie manages a grin. "If you're Judas, who does that make me?"

Pascual gets out of the SUV into the intense noonday heat. It is like stepping into an oven. He walks a few paces forward and stops. Under the canopy two men in uniforms stand looking at him. One of them goes to the door of the security hut and leans in for a moment before returning. A third man comes out of the hut, looks at Pascual and goes back in.

Nothing happens for a long minute. In addition to the heat Pascual becomes aware of the immense diffuse roar rising from the vast industrial complex beyond the gate. Just as he is considering trying to move things along by going to talk to the men under the canopy, a car appears beyond it, approaching the gate. A Mercedes sedan, it draws up to the far end of the canopy and stops; one of the uniformed men goes to speak to the driver. A man gets out of the passenger seat and another out of the back. They come forward with the uniformed man and stand under the canopy, looking at Pascual.

Pascual takes his cue and starts walking. He is glad to reach the shade of the canopy. The two men are Chinese, in short-sleeved shirts, nondescript. They could be office personnel rather than agents of a ruthless spy agency. One looks to be in his thirties, the other perhaps in his late fifties. The younger one says, "Mr. Rose?"

"That's me."

"You have Chee Dongfeng with you?"

Pascual nods. "In the car behind me. You have Renata Taggart?"

"In the car. You will go and look, we will go and look."

Pascual raises a finger. "One of you will go and look. And first you will show me you have no weapons." Pascual is thinking that for a million dollars, he is at least going to do a thorough job.

The Chinese appear surprised, but after an exchange of looks and a few quiet words the older one steps forward and raises his arms. Pascual gives him a quick and inexpert pat-down and then steps back, raising his own arms.

The younger man shakes his head, looking amused. He tosses his head in the direction of the Mercedes and says, "You look."

The rear window on the driver's side goes down as Pascual approaches. When he reaches it he bends down to see Renata Taggart in the back seat, hair tied back in a ponytail, eyes wide. "You," she says. "I thought it might be you." She looks tired, strain and the absence of makeup revealing a different woman, still striking but human and vulnerable. "You're giving them Archie?" she says.

"That's the deal," says Pascual. "Dexter wants you back."

"Dexter doesn't want me talking to the Chinese, that's what Dexter wants." The smile is gone.

"I don't blame him. Are you all right?"

"I'm fine. The cage was nicely gilded. Nobody molested me."

Pascual straightens up. "OK, I'll tell them you're the genuine item and then we'll get you out of here."

He walks back under the canopy and nods at the Chinese. "She's the one. You can turn her loose."

The Chinese is looking at him with contempt. "Not yet. You wait here till my man comes back."

Pascual waits, looking at the SUV where Archie is presumably being inspected. After a few seconds the rear door opens and the older Chinese steps out. He comes trudging very slowly back up toward the gate, wiping his brow with a handkerchief. When he reaches the shade of the canopy he says something in Chinese to the younger man, who turns to Pascual and says, "OK. You go back, send Chee. We send the woman."

"Pleasure doing business with you," Pascual says, stepping out into the sunshine. He walks briskly back to the SUV and says to Harto, "She's fine, everything's ready. Time to hand him over."

The two toughs instantly pile out of the vehicle. Pascual stands back and watches as Harto's partner helps Archie out of the back seat. Archie is wearing the look of a condemned man, with a thousand-yard stare. The toughs stand on either side of him, each grasping an arm. As they urge him forward, Archie resists for a moment, looking at Pascual. He says, "You know who that was? That was Li Chung, my partner in the first company I ever started. He taught me everything I know. He was like my father. They let him out of jail to come and identify me."

Pascual can see there is no acting talent involved in this

picture of desolation. "Good luck," he says.

"No sweat. See you in Davos sometime." The bravado fails to match his expression. The toughs lean into their work and Archie lets himself be propelled toward the gate.

Not your problem, Pascual thinks, bitterly, as he watches Archie go. Beyond him Renata is making good time coming toward him, in flat shoes, jeans and a casual striped top, overnight bag in hand and a purse slung over her shoulder. She could be getting off an airline flight, striding toward the taxi rank. As she and Archie pass, she says something to him, very brief, not slowing. Archie replies, twisting to speak to her over his shoulder. She keeps marching, eyes fixed on Pascual now. When she reaches him she says, "They'll kill him."

Pascual nods. "Eventually." He is listening hard for the sound of a helicopter. He and Renata watch as Harto and his partner hand Archie over to the opposition. The driver has emerged from the Mercedes and come forward to take charge of Archie along with the younger Chinese. Archie barely misses a step as he is transferred, and now he is in Chinese hands. Harto and his partner are already coming back toward the SUV. "He should have written off all his money and just run," says Renata.

"Easy for us to say. We've never had a billion dollars to lose."

Beyond the gate, the Mercedes makes a three-point turn and heads for the gate from which it emerged. Above the diffuse ambient roar of the industrial park, the sound of an engine coughing to life is suddenly heard, harsh and loud, from somewhere just out of sight. It sputters, steadies and becomes the whuffing beat of a helicopter engine. Pascual stiffens. The noise is coming from just beyond the high overgrown bank on their left, from inside the complex.

"So," says Renata. "That's how they're getting him to the airfield. I wondered. The helicopter was sitting there on the pad when they brought me up from the hotel. He'll be on a plane in ten minutes and he'll be in China in three hours."

Pascual stands frozen. Of course, he thinks. Why wouldn't they have a helicopter, too? And why would they drive three kilometers to the airfield when they could fly?

Renata is staring at him. "What's the matter?"

Instead of answering, Pascual looks to the sky, because now another sound is claiming his attention. He is hearing helicopters in stereo, as he looks out over the sea and sees a chopper coming in at speed, making straight for them. As it draws near and slows, pulling up and circling, two or three hundred feet up, he recognizes a familiar craft, a bubble with a rotor and a green tail. "There," he says, pointing. "That's the one Archie's supposed to be on."

# 35

Harto and his partner have reached them and Harto is waving them to the SUV, urgently. "We go now." Pascual is staring dumbly at the green helicopter, now hovering above them. Renata is climbing into the SUV, looking back at him. Harto says, "Quick, we go!"

Pascual casts a last glance at the chopper and follows Renata into the vehicle. "What do you mean, the one he should be on?" says Renata as he flops onto the seat.

"It's a rescue attempt. Dexter's got a plan to spring him before the Chinese can get him out of the country."

Renata's appalled look shows Pascual what she thinks of that. Harto puts the SUV in gear and wheels around in a U-turn, tires squealing, to speed back down toward the coast road. Renata says, "They'd better move fast."

"Not our problem," says Pascual. "We're out of it. Whatever happens with Archie, you're going home." Whatever happens to Archie is going to happen in China now, Pascual thinks.

The police vehicle at the turnoff has not moved. Harto is

slowing for the intersection with the coast road when the gunshots sound faintly behind them, a few sharp cracks piercing the ambient rumble. Harto and his partner exchange a sharp look. Harto lets an ore truck and a covey of scooters pass and swings out onto the road. Somewhere behind them there are more shots, and the chuffing of a helicopter engine swells, changes in pitch, and ends in a booming crash. Harto and his partner loose off loud exclamations. "Oh, dear God," says Renata.

Harto steps on the gas. On their right the yards spread out toward the port: mountains of ore, scattered buildings, distant cranes. A phone warbles and Harto's partner pulls it out of a pocket and puts it to his ear. He listens and responds, his voice rising. He relays something to Harto; there is a brief back-and-forth and Harto jams on the brakes, slewing to the side of the road. He leans on the horn, sending scooters into the weeds as he pulls a reckless U-turn to head back toward the branch road.

"Where are you going?" Pascual shouts.

"Subroto need help. We go back."

This is disaster, and Pascual is not going to stand for it. "No. You take us to the airport. That's your only job. Subroto can take care of himself."

Harto is picking up speed fast. "He need help, we help."

Pascual sees that nothing he says is going to make a difference. He says to Renata, "I'm sorry. Blame Dexter."

Renata says nothing, only puts a hand out to steady herself as Harto takes a curve. When they reach the turnoff, the police car is just starting to crawl up toward the gate. Harto tears past it. At the gate a guard comes running out of the security hut and holds up a hand, then jumps out of the way. Harto speeds through the canopied stretch, brakes hard just inside the entrance to the complex and then cranks the wheel to turn up a short stretch of road running up a slight incline.

The disaster comes into view as they speed toward it: a large helicopter, light blue, sits canted over, the blades of the rotor twisted and broken, the body of the chopper partially resting on top of the Mercedes into which Archie disappeared only a few minutes ago. The front part of the car is crushed under its weight. Two bodies lie on the tarmac, a few feet from the wreck. At the edge of the pad a man in a pilot's uniform is bending over Archie's former partner, who is sitting on the tarmac with his hands to his head. Harto jams on the brakes and they skid to a halt.

Subroto appears from behind the pileup, brandishing a wicked-looking machine pistol with a stubby barrel and a long magazine, one-handed. He has shed the yellow helmet and jacket but still wears the white uniform trousers of a plant worker. He is pulling Archie by the arm. Archie looks dazed, bleeding from a gash on his head. His hands are still bound by the plastic cuffs. He staggers as Subroto hauls him toward the SUV.

Pascual has identified the bodies: one is the younger Chinese, the other is Eko. Another submachine gun lies near Eko's hand, and the fallen Chinese is still clutching an automatic pistol. Subroto tears open the door of the SUV and shoves Archie inside. As Pascual pulls him in, Archie murmurs something in Chinese and then, as Subroto and Harto's partner dash to retrieve Eko's body, manages to say, "What a fucking mess." Harto's partner jumps into the front seat, carrying Eko's weapon. Subroto dumps Eko's body into the rear compartment of the SUV and piles in after it. Harto rams the SUV into gear. He wrestles it around in a tight turn to head back down the access road, but stops immediately. Coming up the road toward them at speed is another black Mercedes.

Harto and Subroto confer, Subroto just behind Pascual yelling past his ear. Harto listens to a stream of orders, nods and puts the vehicle in park. The Mercedes pulls onto the pad and stops. Doors open and three men get out. To Pascual they look Chinese; they are in civilian clothes but look fit and imposing. Behind him he hears the rear door of the SUV open. The Chinese advance toward the wreck, taking in the scene. Harto murmurs something to his partner on the front seat. The lead Chinese stops in his tracks and pulls an automatic out of his waistband, his head snapping toward the SUV.

From the rear of the SUV comes a burst of automatic fire from Subroto's machine pistol, pocking the Chinese man's shirt and knocking him backwards. In an instant Harto's partner has thrust Eko's weapon out the window and opened fire on the closer of the other two Chinese. The third makes a dash for the cover of the Mercedes, but Subroto cuts him down and he stumbles, smacks into the front of the Mercedes and goes down hard on the tarmac. Renata suppresses a cry and Pascual swears loudly in his native Catalan.

Subroto yells at Harto and leaps into the back of the SUV. Harto has it rolling before Subroto can pull the rear door shut. He makes for the access road but once again jams on the brakes.

Down at the entrance to the complex they can see the police pickup that was stationed at the turnoff belatedly entering the fray, lights flashing. Harto looks over his shoulder at Subroto and there is another consultation in rapid, high-pitched Indonesian. Harto reverses, spins the wheel and heads for the opposite side of the pad, where an exit ramp shoots off toward the port.

As Harto careens down the ramp, the land falling away on either side, Pascual recognizes it as the elevated roadway they passed under on the coast highway below. Now he can see that it passes over a broad swath of the industrial park and a narrow stretch of water to sweep down on a small island lying just offshore, a steep wooded hump rising out of the bay. Behind Pascual, Subroto is shouting into a cell phone.

Pascual throws a look out the back. As far as he can tell, nobody is following them. The ramp descends in a long graceful curve, providing a view of the immense jumble of installations spreading out on either side and the green hump of the island looming ahead. "Where the hell is he going?" cries Renata. "There's nothing there but the hotel. He's taking me back where I was, the bloody fool."

Pascual surveys the scene below him, a chaotic tangle of roads, ore conveyors, yards, sheds, jetties. "This has got to connect with the highway, right?"

"No. There's no other way off the island. He'll be trapped." She leans forward. "Hey! Driver! It's a cul-de-sac. You're driving into a trap."

Harto ignores her. The ramp makes landfall and merges with a road that appears to follow the shoreline of the island. Harto brakes just enough to avoid a rollover as he swerves onto it. Over his shoulder he shouts, "Helicopter. We meet him here."

"Oh, God, no." Renata falls back on the seat.

"Where the hell is it going to land?" Pascual says to nobody in particular.

"On top of the hotel," says Renata, putting her hands to her face. "There's a landing pad."

Pascual immediately wonders how they are all going to fit in the chopper; he remembers feeling squeezed with four aboard when it plucked him from the rooftop in Jakarta. They are already halfway around the tiny island, a steep tree-clad slope rising on their left and the bay on their right, a village spreading along the far shore. They shoot past a cluster of sheds with a jetty sticking out into the bay, careen around a tight curve, and there a few hundred yards ahead is the hotel, a completely improbable sight after the industrial sprawl they have just crossed.

It is four stories of curving white terraces, a graceful arc open to the sea with the jungle-covered hill at its back. The road snakes up to a canopied entrance. "Oh, God, no," says Renata. "I just left this fucking place."

Harto brakes and they squeal to a halt in front of the entrance. Harto and his partner leap out of the vehicle. Subroto tumbles out of the back, phone to his ear, still shouting into it. Pascual and Renata get out. Renata is fuming, eyes blazing. "Are you out of your mind?" she screams at Harto. "All you had to do was keep driving!"

Pascual is looking skyward. He became aware of the sound of the helicopter the instant he stepped out of the SUV, but he does not spot it until it comes over the crest of the hill behind the hotel, heading seaward as if shot out of a cannon. It passes above them without the slightest deviation or reduction in speed and disappears beyond the hotel. The sound quickly fades. Subroto has stopped shouting but is obviously seething with anger. A bellhop has come out of the hotel and is staring at them. Subroto growls something to Harto and then looks at Pascual. "The pilot say he can't land. He is very scared. He saw us shooting, saw the crash. He say no way José and he go back to the ship. So now we are fucked."

Pascual stares at him for a moment and then does the only thing he can do: he laughs. "Wonderful."

Subroto's look hardens and he says, "Not fucked, not yet. Get in." He waves them back to the SUV. "Quick. Before the police come."

"Where are we going?" says Renata, standing her ground.

Subroto says, "We go back. Nobody can stop us. We have guns."

Calmly, Renata says, "You're a madman. First of all, stop panicking."

"Not panicking." Subroto shoots an arm out in the direction of the mainland. "You didn't see the police? We kill those Chinese."

Renata levels an icy stare at him. "The police will be up there gawping at that disaster for at least another fifteen minutes before anyone comes after us. We've got time to come up with something that actually makes sense. First of all, why doesn't somebody cut these stupid cuffs off Archie's wrists and take care of that cut?"

"Thank you," says Archie, blood oozing down the side of his face and onto his shirt. Harto comes up with a knife and deftly slices through the plastic. Archie massages his wrists as Harto's partner splashes water from a plastic bottle onto a kerchief and starts dabbing at the wound.

Renata says, "The police and the dead Chinese are your problem. All we care about is getting out of this place. We have only one chance to get off this island without another stupid massacre, and that's to go back there and take a boat." She points back the way they came. Pascual remembers passing a jetty; was there a boat?

Subroto and the other two Indonesians just stare at her. Renata turns to Pascual and Archie and says, "The Chinese let me take walks twice a day, under guard. Yesterday I walked down there and talked to the man in charge of the dock. It's there in case some fat cat arrives by yacht, but it doesn't get much use. So mostly it's just the people from the village over there who use it, hotel employees who live there and fishermen who supply the restaurant. If there's no boat there right now, he can call for one. If we move fast, we might get across to the village before this place is crawling with police."

Nobody says anything for a few seconds. More people have come out of the hotel to gape. Archie says, "Sounds like a plan." He is pressing the kerchief to his head, most of the blood wiped from his face. "Let's get the hell out of here." He makes for the SUV, tottering a little. Pascual follows and helps him onto the seat.

Behind him Renata says to Harto, "Well, what are you waiting for?" Harto snarls something in Indonesian and he and his colleagues jump for the doors. In ten seconds the SUV is wheeling around in a tight turn and heading back toward the jetty, leaving a small squad of hotel employees open-mouthed.

Harto and Subroto hold another discussion as they cover the short distance to the jetty. Subroto says to Renata, "We go back. You want to take a boat, have fun. I think you are out of your mind."

"Very possibly," says Renata. "But we'll see which one of us lives out the day."

## 36

"Dexter's going crazy," says Archie, taking the phone from his ear. "Subroto called him to report."

Renata says, "You mean those idiots are still at large?"

"Dexter says Subroto found a bridge off the island to the industrial port. They ditched the SUV somewhere and walked out. Dexter says the Morowali police and the national police both are looking for them. The word is, it was a terrorist attack at the helicopter pad."

Pascual has been staring out across the bay at the island and the giant cranes in the port beyond it. He turns to Archie and says, "We're going to have to move soon. We're already the talk of the neighborhood. How long will it take the police to figure out we're here?"

His vantage point is the village across the bay from the island, a cluster of houses, sheds and workshops cheek by jowl along the shore, most with boats moored behind them, the narrow alleys leading to the coast road lined with parked scooters, plastic jerricans, washing hung out to dry. There is a strong smell of fish. The man who brought Pascual, Archie and Renata across in an open boat with an outboard motor has invited them into his home, where they have been received with great solicitude. An English-speaking youth has been summoned to interpret, Archie's wound has been bandaged and they have been offered food, drink and transportation to the nearest hospital. They have declined with thanks and Pascual has spun a tale of an accident, the road off the island blocked due to the helicopter crash and friends on the way to retrieve them. Pascual is fairly certain that nobody believes them. They have removed to a patch of concrete under a plastic awning behind the house and their host, his wife, the youth and a half dozen small children are squeezed together in the doorway, staring solemnly at them. "Ask Dexter if he can send someone for us," says Pascual. "Preferably unarmed."

Archie starts to shake his head and winces. "Dexter says all his guys are on the run at this point, and his pet politician is making it clear he can't expect any more help. The guy's getting pressure from Jakarta to cooperate with the Chinese, and the Chinese are threatening dire consequences if the terrorists are not apprehended within twenty-four hours. I am assumed to be one of the terrorists, of course. So the Morowali police are now the enemy, instead of being on our side. They're setting up checkpoints all around the complex and along the coast road. Dexter says we're on our own. If we can make it to the Morowali airport he can probably fly us out, but he can't even guarantee that."

A moody silence ensues. Pascual says, "So what the hell happened to that helicopter?"

Archie grimaces. "What happened was, they almost got

away with me. The plan was, Subroto and Eko were supposed to hijack the car as soon as it was back inside the complex and run it up to the helicopter pad. And our helicopter was supposed to land and fly us out."

"Where the hell did it come from?"

"From a marine research ship about ten miles offshore. Noah controls the foundation that owns it."

"Ah. Your pal Noah planned all this, did he?"

"Of course we brought him in on it. He's the one with the resources. They had the operation coordinated through a satellite link to Subroto's cell phone. But our helicopter had no place to land with the other one sitting there. And there was no sign of Subroto and Eko. I thought I was screwed for sure. They got me into the helicopter, and then Subroto and Eko came out of nowhere just as it was lifting off and shot out the windshield. I don't think they actually hit the pilot, but he lost control, and the damn thing came down on top of the car. Then it gets a little confusing, because I took a whack on the head when we crashed. There was some more shooting, and then the next thing I knew, Subroto was hauling me out. I think that's when you got there."

Pascual and Renata make eye contact, and he can read what she thinks of the fiasco. She has managed to retain her luggage through all of this, and she looks like a woman who will be writing a blistering letter of complaint to the organizer of this disastrous tour. She says, "Excellent. Maybe your friend can summon a submarine to take us off tonight."

Archie says, "Noah is not answering his phone," and leaves it at that. He looks like a man who is suffering from a severe headache.

Pascual turns to the doorway of the house and addresses the youth, who has been watching, and no doubt listening, impassively. "Who owns that boat with the blue cabin over there?"

■ ■ ■ ■

"Five hundred," says the wizened man in the baseball cap with the MGM Grand logo on it, helpfully holding up five fingers. "Five hundred dollar." The wizened man has been introduced as Dwi. He and the English-speaking youth are perched side by side in the classic Asian squat on a wooden dock behind a tin-roofed cinderblock shed, one of the more substantial buildings in the village. Pascual and his companions are seated on plastic crates hauled out for the purpose.

The youth adds helpfully, "To take you to all the way to Bahusuai. It's more than one hundred kilometers, very far."

"I'm aware," says Pascual. "And that will get us close to the airport?"

The youth nods. "From Bahusuai, it's only a short way. You can take a taxi."

"A hundred kilometers in that boat?" Renata looks skeptical.

The boat in question is moored to the dock. The boat is about ten meters long, with a slightly upcurved prow and a small square superstructure near the bow, painted blue. Posts at the stern support a wooden roof that extends back from the cabin, shading the length of the boat. The deck is strewn with coils of rope and crumpled nets, and the cabin could use a coat of paint. "Is it seaworthy?" says Pascual.

The youth does not bother to relay this to Dwi. Coolly, he says, "Good enough for him. He is a fisherman. Sometimes he is away for two or three days, on the sea. You will arrive to Bahusuai with no problem."

Pascual is beginning to reassess the youth with his accented but smooth English. "If we leave this afternoon, when will we get to Bahusuai?"

The youth passes this on to Dwi, who addresses Pascual at length, with great earnestness. The youth waits for him to finish and says, "He said that you can leave in one hour. After twelve hours you will be in Bahusuai. He said that if you want to go by car, you can arrive there before, maybe. But there are many police on the road today. If you want to go by boat, this is the only boat. He will take you for five hundred dollars."

Pascual holds a silent and very frank conversation by eye contact with Dwi, who he sees is perfectly aware of why Pascual and his party might wish to avoid talking to the police today, and decides that five hundred dollars is probably a very good price.

Pascual runs an eye over the boat again and says, "Excuse me for asking, but why isn't he out fishing now?"

"Fishing is very bad now." The youth points across the bay. "You see that? You know what they do there? They process ore from the nickel mines. Very large mines, which destroy the forest and the farms. And then the factories put poisons in the river which go into the sea and destroy the fish. The mines and factories make everybody rich. Except the farmers and the fishermen. Now the fishermen have to go very far to find fish. And if they don't catch much fish, no money for diesel. So he can't go out until he borrows more money."

Pascual admires the succinct analysis. "Well. Five hundred

dollars should buy enough diesel to keep him at sea for a while." He looks at Archie, haggard and desperate, and Renata, tense but perfectly composed, and says, "I've got the money. I think we should do it."

Archie says, "Let's go."

Renata shrugs. "Why not? What's the alternative?"

The youth says, "You must go soon. We already have lied to the police once. I think they will come back."

Pascual tries in vain to read the expression on the youth's face. "Why did you lie for us?"

"Because you needed help."

The answer appears to be completely guileless, and Pascual nods in acknowledgment. "Well. Thank you." He stands and pulls his wallet out from under his shirttail.

The youth rises from his squat. "And because the police don't need any help," he says, with the faintest of smiles.

■ ■ ■ ■

"I forgot," says Archie. "I get seasick." He closes his eyes and curls into a fetal position on the deck, his head pillowed on a folded tarpaulin.

Pascual has his own discomfort to deal with, not as bad evidently as Archie's, but enough to spoil his enjoyment of a spectacular sunset behind the mountains of central Sulawesi a few miles to port. The smooth, quick run from Singapore to Batam a few days ago had no effect on him, but he is not looking forward to ten more hours of this plodding pitch and roll. The waters of the bay were smooth as Dwi piloted the craft away from the dock, his passengers huddled in the tiny cabin to avoid observation, but as he steered out through the freighters at anchor offshore, a swell began to assert itself.

Dwi has brought along one crewman, a surly-looking pug who has spent the whole voyage in the cabin, peering out occasionally at the passengers with a suspicious look. The passengers have been provisioned with bottles of juice and fish cakes wrapped in newsprint, but nobody appears to be hungry. Pascual and Renata are sitting on the deck with their backs to the starboard bulwark, watching the distant mountains rise and fall. As the sun has sunk, the brisk wind has begun to hint that with nightfall the tropical air might be less benign. "I'm sorry," says Pascual. "I should have put my foot down. The plan was to drive straight to the airport."

Renata shrugs. "Not your fault. And I can't really blame Mr. Fang, I suppose. His plan seems to have worked."

"We're not there yet," growls Archie from the deck.

# 37

"The hotel was actually quite comfortable," says Renata. "Very posh, lots of smiling staff. Built for visiting Chinese nobs, I suppose. But there was nobody there but me. We had it all to ourselves, me and my guards. They kept their distance and I watched a lot of television and took walks and stared out to sea. The worst thing was the boredom."

Pascual can sympathize. The charm of this evening cruise wore off hours ago. His stomach has settled, and the night air is still tolerably warm despite an occasional drift of spray. But the deck and bulwark have grown hard against his tender flesh, and beyond the reach of the boat's weak running lights lies only a massive heaving blackness of sea and sky, alien and impenetrable. Faint scattered lights are visible at intervals along the distant shore, rising and falling with the monotonous thrum of the diesel. Archie has shifted a couple of times but still lies prone. His feeble groans have finally stopped. The single crewman has emerged from the cabin and found a nest of his own to sleep in near the stern and is snoring gently.

Pascual savors the warmth of Renata's shoulder and hip against his. They have subsided into a casual intimacy that involves only fatigue and a need for contact in the dark. Pascual remembers the juvenile *coup de foudre* she triggered in him only a few days ago and wants to laugh. "How do you think they found you in Jakarta?"

Renata is silent for a while and then says, "Who knows? I think they must have simply followed me from Mr. Fang's office. Either that or they got to someone in his organization. He has lots of employees, not all of them well paid, especially in Indonesia, which makes him very vulnerable. I think the Chinese are good at finding weak spots."

"Yes. And as long as you're intimately involved in his business and he has enemies, you're a vulnerability. Take it from me. I'm an expert in this field. I can't live openly with my wife and son anymore. My enemies know who and where my wife and son are, so we've had to create the impression that I have disappeared. It doesn't make for a lot of relaxed family evenings."

"I'm sorry."

"It's a penance for my sins. If you're lucky, Fang won't make any more enemies, and you and your fiancé will be able to have a carefree night on the town whenever you want." Pascual waits a beat and says, "I imagine he'll be worried about you."

"More likely just angry. He'll wonder why I'm not returning his calls. To tell you the truth, we grant each other a good deal of space. And by the way, there's no formal engagement. That's wishful thinking on the part of a couple of mothers and some gossip columnists."

Pascual wants to laugh again as he thrills faintly to the thought of a still-single Renata. "You are lucky to have your personal life discussed only in the gossip columns. Mine is discussed in intelligence reports and conclaves of blackmailers."

■■■■

"I think we are arriving."

Pascual comes fully awake as Renata's words penetrate his shaky consciousness. He has been flailing through vivid and unpleasant dreams. He raises himself to a sitting position, grimacing. Renata is sitting up straight, chin raised, staring toward lights on a shore that is considerably closer than the last time Pascual looked and stretching away at a different angle as the boat swings in toward it. The single crewman has roused himself and is padding forward toward the cabin, scratching under his shirt. The darkness has lessened, and Pascual twists to see the eastern horizon starting to lighten behind them.

A ragged voice says, "Where are we?" Archie rolls over and pulls himself upright. He looks as if he has been flattened by a truck.

"We are approaching shore," says Renata.

Pascual watches the cluster of lights drift as the bow of the boat comes around. He can make out a line of white foam on a beach, a jumble of dark houses, a few lights on high poles, a break in the shore that might be the mouth of a river.

"God," says Archie, tottering as he makes it to his knees. "What a night." He makes his way aft, carefully, picking his way from handhold to handhold, past furled nets and coiled ropes. At the stern he halts and leans out over the water, supporting himself with a hand on a post.

"Be careful," says Pascual, alarmed.

Archie is still for a moment and then pulls himself back inboard, turns and lowers himself to the deck, sitting with his back to the stern. "Can't do it," he says. "Not enough in the belly."

"Take it easy," says Pascual. "We'll be on land soon."

"Thank God. I want to be buried in good solid earth." Archie closes his eyes and lets his head loll back against the bulwark.

The crewman has gone into the cabin and shut the door behind him. The shore is dead ahead now, and the tempo of the engine has slowed. Renata says, "While you were asleep."

Pascual turns to her. In the twilight her eyes are wide. "What?"

"Maybe I'm paranoid, but I'm starting to trust my paranoia. While you were asleep, the captain was talking in there in the cabin. I could hear him."

"So?"

"The other fellow was asleep out here with us. Who was the captain talking to?"

Nobody says anything for a while. "There's a radio," says Pascual. "I noticed it when we were in there with him."

"Who was he talking to on the radio?"

"I don't know. Somebody here who can sell him some diesel fuel? His wife, telling her when he'll be home?"

"Somebody who is willing to pay him for delivering us?"

The silence goes on for a while as the boat plows slowly toward what is taking shape as a sizable village at the mouth of a river, palm trees towering above a scattering of houses. The crewman comes out of the cabin and goes forward, stepping up onto the decked bow of the boat. Pascual stands, makes sure of his balance and walks toward the bow along the starboard side. He halts at the cabin and listens, looking ahead as they near the entrance to the river. He hears nothing from inside the cabin. The crewman looks over his shoulder at him, incurious.

Pascual walks back to where Renata is sitting. She says, "He knows the police are looking for us. He made five hundred dollars off you to bring us up here. How much more can he make by handing us over?"

Pascual looks to the stern and sees Archie sitting motionless, watching them. Pascual says, "Too bad none of us has a phone. We could have contacted Dexter. He could have sent somebody to meet us, or warn us if somebody else was waiting."

Renata's face is close to his in the gloom and they share an intimate look. "No use crying," she says. "What do we do?"

Pascual leans on the bulwark, peering landward, Renata at his shoulder. He says, "You and I go ashore. Archie hides on board until we're sure it's clear."

"And if it's not?"

Pascual runs through scenarios and fails to find a good one. "If it's not, we're trapped, aren't we? Unless we can make it back on board and outbid the opposition, pay our captain to take us farther up the coast."

"That sounds very optimistic to me."

"It does to me, too. Let's see what Archie thinks."

Pascual turns toward the stern and freezes. Where Archie was sitting there is now only a vacant space. Pascual blinks, scans, straining to see in the dark. In the jumble of indistinct shapes at the stern of the boat he finds nothing that could be Archie.

Renata says, "Dear God."

Pascual swears and lurches to his feet. He staggers to the stern. "Archie!"

There is just enough light to make out the heaving immensity of the waves rolling in from the Banda Sea. Pascual looks for a splash, a disturbance on the surface, the flailing of a swimmer in distress. Even with the lightening horizon it is a supremely difficult visual field to scan. Renata pitches up against the bulwark beside him. "He can't be far."

Pascual wheels and rushes forward, stumbling over obstacles. He tears open the door of the cabin to see Dwi at the helm, hand on the throttle, concentrating on his approach. "You have to stop. There's a man overboard." Dwi turns, startled, and Pascual realizes that the words mean nothing to him. Desperately he mimics, sketching a dive into the water. "Stop!" he cries, hoping the word is universal.

Dwi snarls something in Indonesian. His crewman on the bow is leaning down at the windshield, peering in. Pascual points at the stern. Dwi yells at his crewman, who comes around the side of the cabin and looks aft. Renata is gesturing frantically at the water. The crewman goes to join her, takes one look out over the water and turns to yell at Dwi.

Dwi throttles back and begins to turn to port in a wide arc. Pascual goes to the bulwark and cranes to look out over the black water. "Archie!" The boat comes around with painful slowness until the bow points back out to sea. The crewman has produced a life ring from somewhere and is standing on the bow again, ready to pitch it. Renata and Pascual have each taken a side of the boat and are frantically scanning the dark waters, which are beginning to sparkle as the east goes pink, promising a spectacular tropical sunrise.

Ten minutes later the boat has completed a second slow circuit and is dead in the water, rocking on the waves. Dwi has come out of the cabin and is haranguing Pascual and Renata in a language they don't understand. Pascual waves him away, stunned and aghast, looking into the magnificent dawn over the shimmering, unbroken surface of the sea.

# 38

"Could he swim?" Renata breaks a long silence as the boat drifts gently toward a ramshackle jetty sticking out from shore.

"No idea." Pascual has been directing a ten-thousand-yard stare at the distant mountains, glowing in the dawn. "He would have to be a pretty good swimmer to have a chance. Maybe he wasn't as good as he thought."

Renata sits wide-eyed and desolate, bedraggled and vulnerable. "Or maybe he had just had enough," she says. "He couldn't face any more stress."

Pascual takes a last look out to sea. "Who knows?"

"So it's over. All that, and it's over," Renata says in a wondering tone.

"We still have to get to the airport," says Pascual.

The boat contacts the jetty with a gentle thump. Dwi's crewman hops onto the jetty and secures a line to a post. Renata gathers her bag and purse, looking like the distressed tourist again, hoping there will be a decent hotel in this slum. Pascual helps her over the bulwark onto the jetty. He looks back to see

Dwi glowering at him in the doorway to the cabin. Pascual understands that the man cannot wait to be quit of them; he is relying on the vulnerability of their position to deter them from dragging him into a messy business involving police or coast guard. His crewman is already casting off.

A short ramp leads down from the jetty onto a patch of bare earth stretching north along the shore. Pascual and Renata come to rest dazed and dejected, looking at the back of a line of clapboard constructions lining the road that crosses the river on a bridge. A woman is standing on a porch at the rear of one of the houses, long black hair falling onto her shoulder, frozen with hairbrush in hand, gaping at them. No one else is in sight.

"A taxi," Renata says. "Does it look like we're going to find a taxi here?"

"It's a little early, maybe." Pascual spots a gap between houses and starts marching toward it. "I've got some hundreds left. Somebody will take us to the airport."

"The airport is about five miles from here. We could walk it if we had to."

The path takes them up a shallow slope past a deserted restaurant terrace with a dozen or so tables and onto the shoulder of what is evidently the coastal highway. Opposite them are more houses, most built of the same unpainted wood with corrugated metal roofs, high palms and an eruption of tropical greenery filling the spaces between them. Nothing is moving on the road or among the houses. Pascual looks back at the terrace. "We could go sit down and wait until they open the restaurant. They can call us a taxi and feed us while we wait."

Renata frowns at it. "Who here has enough money to afford a meal in a restaurant?"

Tires sound on gravel as a vehicle pulls out onto the highway from between two houses a short way down the road to their right. Pascual and Renata stand frozen as a dark-colored SUV with police lights on top comes slowly toward them. When it reaches them it stops and the doors on both sides open. Two men in uniform step out. The driver gives Renata a head-to-toe appraisal and then addresses Pascual in English. "Where is Chee Dongfeng?"

▰▰▰▰

"I told the officer who picked us up," says Pascual. "He fell off the boat and drowned. We looked for him for a long time but we never found him."

The man across the table from him is peering at him in fierce concentration, his weak English a handicap in this interrogation. He wears the gray uniform of the Central Sulawesi Regional Police with shoulder boards indicating that he is the chief of this small district police station no more than a mile up the road from where they came ashore, and despite his authoritative manner he is clearly out of his depth. "Drown," he says. "Chee Dongfeng is dead?"

Pascual nods. "I assume so. He fell in the water and we never saw him again."

Renata says, "We are on our way to meet Mr. Dexter Fang. Can you please contact him? I will give you a number."

The chief's eyes narrow even more as he contemplates Renata, and whether it is suspicion or merely lust, Pascual will never know, for abruptly the man rises, says, "You wait," and leaves the room along with the second officer who has been watching from a corner. The door slams behind them.

Pascual and Renata contemplate the walls of the bare room. After a few seconds Renata breaks the silence. "So we were betrayed."

"So it seems." Pascual has no energy for outrage. He has been numbly contemplating his prospects for staying out of jail and getting out of Indonesia. "Our friend Dwi, maybe."

"Who else?"

"Anyone back there in the village who wanted to collect a reward. There were lots of people around, and I don't think it was much of a secret where we were headed. Did you see that car that followed us here? It was waiting near where the police were parked."

"The Mercedes? Yes. I couldn't see who was inside, but I'd bet they were Chinese."

"That's a good guess. And a bad sign."

"I suppose we will have to put our faith in Mr. Fang. We'll see just how much influence he has around here."

"If he ever finds out we've been arrested."

"There's a cheery thought."

The door opens and the chief reappears. He comes to the table and tosses two passports onto it, Pascual's and Renata's. "You come now."

Renata picks up her passport and slides it into her purse. "Where are we going?"

"You go with Chinese men."

Renata and Pascual trade a look. "Bad sign," says Pascual. He turns to the chief. "Do you always do what the Chinese tell you?"

Mistake, thinks Pascual instantly. He steels himself for the blow as the man's expression goes stone cold. Discipline asserts itself after a moment and the man says, "I do what my brigadier tell me."

Renata says, "That's very wise. You have to keep the boss happy, right?"

"Brigadier is the boss."

"Of course. And I'm sure he keeps you very busy. Your job is very hard, isn't it?"

The chief gives her a suspicious look. "Very hard, yes."

"And you're not paid enough, are you?"

In the silence that follows Pascual can hear voices murmuring elsewhere in the station, traffic on the road outside. The chief pulls out a chair and sits. "Why you ask this?"

Renata's face is carefully expressionless. "Because I imagine that police officers don't make very much money. You have a very hard job, and you're not paid enough. Do you have enough money for everything you want? Enough to pay for your children's school? Enough to keep your wife happy? Enough to take a nice vacation? In Bali, maybe even Australia? Can you afford that?"

"Why you ask?"

Renata lowers her voice just a little. "Because if you have a computer with an internet connection here, I can move ten thousand Singapore dollars into your personal bank account within ten minutes. Nobody will know. All you have to do is send the Chinese away and take us to the airport. Tell the Chinese Chee

Dongfeng is dead. Tell them you are holding us for investigation. Tell your brigadier there was a mistake and we are not the people you were looking for. But send the Chinese away and take us to the airport. For ten thousand Singapore dollars."

Pascual watches the man's face, the classic Malay features, high cheekbones and blunt nose, jaw muscles working. He can see the struggle going on behind the glittering black eyes. "Twenty thousand," the man says.

Renata says coolly, "Fifteen."

The chief shoves away from the table and stands. "I hope you like China."

"All right, twenty." Renata smiles. "You drive a hard bargain."

Renata's smile works wonders; she has made a new friend. The chief smiles back and says, "Fifteen for me, five for brigadier."

She nods. "Of course. Where's the computer?"

"I show you." He turns to Pascual and says, "Chinese are not my boss. Brigadier is my boss. Chinese, I say go to hell."

"I am glad we can all agree on that," says Pascual, graciously.

■ ■ ■ ■

"Chinese are not happy. But they go." The chief closes the door of his private office behind him, looking a little the worse for wear. He strides to his desk and plops onto the chair behind it.

Renata is sitting on a chair, filing her nails; Pascual is standing at the window, looking out over the forecourt of the station, where a black Mercedes is pulling out onto the road. He turns and says, "Thank you."

The chief grunts in response and taps at the keyboard of the laptop on his desk. He peers at the screen for a moment, taps some more and sits back with a considerably more contented expression on his face. He looks at Renata and says, "You want to go to airport now."

"If possible, yes."

Pascual says, "Can I ask you one more question?"

The chief shoots him an irritated look. "What question?"

"How did the Chinese know we were coming? How did they know where to wait for us?"

The chief looks blank for a moment and says, "I think somebody tell them. They only say Chee Dongfeng come to Bahusuai with boat. I send two men with them to arrest Chee Dongfeng. They bring only you."

"I see. Thank you."

Pascual and Renata trade a look and Renata sketches a slight shrug. She looks at the chief and says, "We should contact Mr. Fang before we go to the airport. May I use your telephone?"

"Please." The chief points to a console on the desktop. "You have number?"

Renata nods. She stands and goes to the desk as the chief punches buttons and hands the receiver to her. She pauses with the phone to her ear and looks at Pascual. "I'm not looking forward to this conversation."

Pascual can only give her a pained look. Renata punches in a number and waits. She says, "Mr. Fang. It's Renata."

Pascual watches her face and can imagine what she is hearing. There will be an explosion of relief and urgent questions. Renata is nodding, waiting for an opening. "Yes, Mr. Rose is with me. We came up the coast by boat during the night. We are at a police station just a few miles from the airport. I think the police will be able to drop us there." She listens for a moment and says, "Mr. Fang, I'm afraid I have bad news for you."

■ ■ ■ ■

The mood is glum in the back seat of the police SUV as it pulls into the parking lot behind the small terminal at Morowali Airport. Renata peers out the window. "Mr. Fang said Singh should be waiting in a white Renault hatchback parked near the administration building. That must be it over there." She directs the driver toward the outbuilding. "He sent him down from Kolonodale this morning to prepare for the flight. Mr. Fang will be along as soon as he and his politician are finished with a few administrative matters."

Pascual looks at her fine profile and sees no sign of irony. "He must have his hands full. A helicopter crash and multiple deaths in a shootout are hard to cover up."

"They can't cover that up. But they'll probably keep Fang's name out of it with no trouble. The Chinese will be happy to call it a terrorist attack and blame the local ecological zealots or perhaps the Islamists. Look, there's the Renault."

The police driver pulls up next to it and is off again practically before Pascual and Renata have finished getting out. The passenger side door of the Renault opens and Singh steps out, phone in hand. "Ah, here you are," he says. "Mr. Fang is on his way. He should be here within half an hour. We should be able to get everyone on board without attracting any notice. If you'll just wait in the back with your companion, he should be here soon."

"Companion?" Pascual steps to the back door of the Renault and opens it.

"What took you so long?" says Archie in the far corner of the seat, disheveled, dirty and grinning from ear to ear.

"I can swim like a fish," says Archie. "I grew up swimming in the Pearl River. Two hundred yards to shore was nothing."

Archie is in high spirits now that the Gulfstream is in the air, Sulawesi dropping away beneath them. Drink in hand, he is holding court at the head of the table, with Fang, Pascual and Renata in attendance. "We looked for you," says Renata. "We went around in circles. Why didn't we see you?"

"First because I stayed close to the boat, right next to it, until it started to turn. Then I headed for shore as fast as I could. I knew you'd be looking farther out. And even if you looked in the right area, I knew you wouldn't see me. It's hard enough to spot somebody in the water in daylight, and it was still pretty dark. The only thing I was worried about was sharks, and I only had two hundred yards to cover."

Pascual shudders. Sharks and snakes; he has had enough of the tropics. "It would have been nice to let us know what you were planning."

Archie shakes his head. "I had to sell it. I didn't know if you were good enough actors to make it convincing. If somebody was waiting for us, I wanted them to be convinced I was dead."

Renata turns to Fang. "You knew, didn't you? You knew when I telephoned you that Archie was alive. I thought you took the news a little too calmly. I put it down to shock."

Fang nods, looking a little sheepish. "He called me as soon as he got out of the water."

"Well, not quite," says Archie. "I hid in a shed till the sun was up and things were starting to open up. Then I found a fellow who was opening his store by the side of the highway, and he let me use his phone. Dexter told me to get to the airport and rendezvous with Singh. I told him that if anyone asked, I was dead, until further notice."

There is a general silence. Dexter lays a thick arm across Archie's shoulders and gives him an affectionate shake. Renata lets her head loll back, eyes closed. Pascual wants desperately to sleep, but there is much to think about. "So what happens now?" he says.

Dexter says, "At this point, priority number one is to get Archie to safety. If the Chinese think he's dead, so much the better. I am going to be under very close scrutiny for a while. So far I haven't been associated with the . . . attack at the industrial complex, but I will be eventually, because one of my men was killed. I'm going to have to answer some tough questions. Even if I can sell a story to the Indonesians that leaves Archie out of things, the Chinese certainly know I'm involved, and they'll be watching, maybe as soon as we get to Singapore. Archie, I think the safest thing might be to contact Colchester and stash you somewhere in Singapore while he arranges things. Or let the CIA people in Singapore take over."

Archie says, "Start with Noah. The fewer people that know I'm in Singapore the better."

"OK. So we hide you. Maybe with Tan's friend Rodney again, if he's still game. I'll call Tan and see if that's on."

Archie shrugs. "That would work. I'm all out of phones, by the way. But it might be safer to use Rodney's anyway. Hopefully I won't be there too long."

Fang nods. "Yes. Now, we've all got some damage control to do. Renata, I'm sure there are people who will be worried about you. You need to decide what to tell them about why you haven't been in touch the past few days."

She gives him a wry look. "Actually, they're used to me going off the radar for a few days from time to time. You may recall there have been times when you've kept me too busy to eat properly, much less chat with a boyfriend. I'll make some calls tonight."

Fang raises his hands. "Renata, forgive me. I owe you more than I can say."

"Please consider the twenty thousand dollars I had to slip under the table to our police friend a partial recompense."

Fang laughs. "Cheap at the price." He turns to Pascual. "Now. Mr. Rose. I think it may be time at last to think about turning yourself in to the Singapore police."

"Yes," says Pascual. "Though I prefer to think of it as coming forward to help."

"Let's hope the police see things the same way," says Archie.

■ ■ ■ ■

At Seletar the arrival procedures are again nerve-racking, particularly because this time Pascual has no luggage; his Dior bag has presumably been appropriated by a chambermaid in a hotel in Sulawesi by this time. But neither he nor Archie triggers any alarms, and the car is waiting for them, Toby at the wheel. "Mr. Fang has given him instructions," says Singh. "He'll drop you at your destination first, since it's nearby."

Mr. Fang has also presumably notified Rodney, who does not seem surprised to see them when Toby drops them at his gate. "Welcome back," he says. "You still hiding from the bad guys, ah? Or maybe the police?"

"Possibly both," says Archie, and reverts to Chinese. He and Rodney chatter away in the kitchen while Pascual goes and flings himself onto his cot.

When he awakes, the room is dark. Through the window he can see a twilight sky and hear the manic twittering of birds in the trees. He lies under the weight of a deep depression and an elusive feeling that he has neglected pressing matters. He sits up on the cot, rubs his face with his hands, and waits for his mind to clear and his thoughts to coalesce. He stands and goes out into the main room of the house.

"Well, well," says Archie. He and Rodney are seated at the table, going at an array of colorful dishes with chopsticks. "Sleeping beauty awakes."

"Has it been a hundred years?" says Pascual, eyeing the food, suddenly weak with hunger. He consumed a packaged sandwich on the plane but has not had a substantial meal in days. He sinks onto a chair, and Rodney dishes up heaps of vegetables and chunks of chicken. Pascual eats with great concentration while Archie and Rodney talk around mouthfuls of food. When he finishes he waits for a break in the conversation and says, "Rodney, do you have a computer with an internet connection? I'd like to look something up."

■ ■ ■ ■

*Singapore firms linked to 1MDB fund flows. . . . The Monetary Authority of Singapore is investigating several Singapore financial institutions that may have been used as conduits for 1MDB-related funds.* . . . Pascual scrolls, trying to get his head around the massive financial scandal in Malaysia, just next door, that has been in and out of headlines around the world for several years. *Fugitive fund manager believed to be in China.* . . . Pascual brings up a search engine and enters a name. He clicks on half a dozen articles, scanning quickly, returns to the search window, enters another name. He scrolls, scans, closes the browser. He sits with his head in his hands, eyes closed.

He pushes away from the desk and returns to the main room. Archie and Rodney have fallen silent, bent now over an archipelago of white and black stones in a game of go. The fragrance of a gently simmering broth comes from the kitchen. Pascual says, "Rodney, I'm sorry to be such a pest, but I need to make a phone call."

Rodney produces a phone and looks away from the board just long enough to tap in the password and hold it out to Pascual. Pascual takes the phone and punches in the number he memorized for Dexter Fang. He goes back into the bedroom and sits on the cot while it rings at the other end. "Who's this?" says Dexter Fang.

"It's Pascual."

"Everything all right?"

"Fine. I just need to ask you a question."

"Very well, go ahead."

"Who knows we're here, Archie and me? Who knows where we are?"

In the silence Pascual hears the muted murmur of the city all around them and closer at hand the gentle click of a stone being set on the board. "Why?" says Fang.

"Call me paranoid. I'm just trying to anticipate, think about possible threats."

"Ah," says Fang. "Well, let's see. I do, for one. And Renata. Campbell knows as well. I thought it best to fill him in. I think that's all."

"Singh and his driver both know. They dropped us here first."

"Ah. Yes, I see. Well, I'm sure they're both trustworthy. Singh's been with me for years, and that fellow Toby is his regular driver."

"Anyone else?" Pascual waits.

"Well, Mr. Tan, of course."

"Yes." Pascual passes a hand over his face. "Of course. Mr. Tan knows."

# 40

"We're not safe here." Pascual hands Rodney's phone back to him. "I think we should leave."

That breaks Archie's concentration at last. He looks up from the board, and under Pascual's steady gaze his expression goes from irritated to alarmed. "Says who?"

"It's a long story. Basically, I think too many people know we're here, and I think one of them is not to be trusted. I think we should move, and I think we should move fast."

"Which one?" says Archie. "Who's not to be trusted?"

Pascual heaves a sigh of frustration. "All I've got are suspicions based on circumstantial evidence. But you've seen how the Guoanbu has been right on top of us all along. Are you willing to take the chance I'm wrong?"

Archie looks at Rodney and back at Pascual. He blinks a few times. "Give me a clue. What makes you think we're not safe?"

Pascual draws breath to speak, but before he can begin, a dog barks three times, sharply, not too far away. Immediately there is a commotion just outside, a fluttering and squawking of waking chickens. Rodney growls something in Chinese. Archie responds, and he and Rodney stare at one another. The dog resumes barking, further outraging the chickens. Rodney straightens up on his chair, frowning.

Three strong raps on the door startle everyone. Rodney stands. He says, "Probably just my neighbor, *lah*."

In a low urgent voice Pascual says, "Archie. Let's get the hell out of here. Now." Pascual gestures toward the kitchen.

Archie is a fast learner and has had a particularly educational week. He rises, jarring the table and displacing enough stones on the board to ruin the game. Rodney reaches the door and inquires loudly in Chinese. He is answered by an indistinct murmur. As Pascual and Archie reach the kitchen they hear Rodney pulling back the bolt.

They can spare no more attention for the front door, however, because immediately on entering the kitchen they are confronted with the spectacle of a man coming in through the fatally unsecured back door from the garden. Pascual has seen this man before, twice, and his scowling face would be alarming enough even if he were not carrying a bright yellow electroshock weapon in his right hand.

Pascual snags the simmering soup pot off the stove without even breaking stride, and before the Chinese sourpuss can manage to raise the weapon, thumb off the safety and fire two electrified metal darts into Pascual's chest, a tsunami of boiling chicken broth hits him in the face, providing a powerful distraction. Between his scream, the clanging of the pot on the tiles and the shouts from the front of the house, there is a great deal of noise as Pascual and Archie flee out the back door.

Outside there is only the tropical night, relieved just enough by distant lamps that Pascual can make out a fence made of corrugated metal that will need to be hurdled. He manages a clumsy leap that deposits him on the other side more or less headfirst while Archie clears it in true Chinese acrobat fashion and hits the ground running. Now there is only a lot of brush to thrash through, no doubt teeming with snakes, and then suddenly a more substantial barrier in the form of a narrow concrete channel protected by railings which has to be gotten over somehow, and then suddenly Pascual and Archie burst out of the jungle to find themselves on a lamplit bicycle path along a canal, the opposite side lined with multi-story apartment buildings, the sky glowing with urban light pollution and startled joggers and cyclists staring at them.

■ ■ ■ ■

"Please, sir. Could I use your phone? It's an emergency." Archie has stopped panting and looks less alarming than Pascual with his torn trousers and muddied shirt, so he has been delegated to approach the cashier in this gas station minimart across the canal and around a corner from the *kampong*. Pascual hovers near the door, keeping an eye out for marauding Chinese, though he imagines that any sensible kidnap team would call it a night after having one member nicely parboiled. Traffic zooms by on the boulevard outside; Pascual is listening for sirens. He desperately hopes that Rodney has suffered no harm. Pascual has caused enough damage, collateral and otherwise, in his life. Behind him he hears Archie speaking Chinese into a phone. After a moment

Archie comes to his shoulder and says, "I talked to Dexter."

"Dexter. Not the police."

Archie shakes his head. "Not the police. You want to go talk to the police, be my guest. Dexter's sending Campbell to pick us up. I'm going with him. You want me to have this guy call the police?"

Pascual balks, at the brink of saying yes. Eventually he will have to have his reckoning with the law, but perhaps now is not the time, not yet. "No," he says. "I'll come with you and Campbell."

■ ■ ■ ■

Campbell is in mufti this evening, in a casual sport shirt and slacks rather than the severe gray suit he wore at the office, but his demeanor is all business. "What happened?" he snaps as Pascual and Archie pile into his BMW, Archie in front.

"We were betrayed," says Archie. He has gone into manic mode, talking fast, his voice sliding into the upper register. "They almost got us. I mean, we had to actually fight our way out. Check the hospitals for a Chinese guy with a scalded face. They knew exactly where to find us. If it wasn't for Pascual I'd be on my way to China right now. He figured it out."

"Figured what out?" says Campbell, whipping back onto the road.

"Who sold us out. Tell him, Pascual."

Pascual is just now starting to believe he might survive the night. He says, "Where are we going?"

"Paya Lebar Air Base," says Campbell. "Archie's got a plane to catch."

Archie says, "Oh, good. So Noah came through."

Campbell issues a gruff laugh. "He came through all right. Right now every Guoanbu operative in Singapore, with the possible exception of those sitting in hospital emergency departments, is rushing to Seletar to keep an eye out for you. Since he published those computer algorithms, you can bet Colchester's every move has been under scrutiny by the Chinese. And they won't have any trouble tracking the jet he's sending to Seletar, or spotting the local CIA assets casually hanging about the Seletar terminal. Meanwhile, you're going to Paya Lebar to hop on a Royal Australian Air Force Dassault Falcon for a flight to RAAF Base Darwin. I went to your quarters and retrieved your Zhang Wei passport and packed you a suitcase. They're in the boot."

There is a silence while Campbell steers smoothly through light evening traffic. Archie says, "Australia. Never been there."

"You'll like it, mate. At least as a jump-off for points beyond. And we Aussies are happy to have a chance to poke the dragon in the eye. Though I understand the people in Langley are a bit miffed. They weren't happy being just a decoy."

Pascual says, "I hate to be a wet blanket, but who knows about this? Who knows where Archie's going?"

Campbell says, "In Fang's entourage? Just me. And you, now. Fang thinks Archie's going out on Colchester's jet."

The knot in Pascual's stomach eases. "That's all right, then."

"He'll be miffed, too. He wanted to see Archie off."

Pascual watches high-rises fly by in the night where the *kampongs* used to be. "And just out of curiosity, why do you trust me?"

Campbell laughs softly. "I didn't, until just now."

"That's a credit to your good judgment."

"Pascual's all right," says Archie. "He's stuck with me the whole way."

"And that's a reason to question mine," Pascual says, and he is gratified when Archie laughs.

▪ ▪ ▪ ▪

In the event there is only Pascual to see Archie off, handing him over to a mixed crew of military personnel and obvious spooks, some Australian and some Singaporean, who are not going to let him go any farther than this anteroom in a suite of offices in the main building of the air base. Campbell is conferring in a low voice with one of the Australian spooks, and Archie is looking dazed as he contemplates his escape. His wandering gaze settles on Pascual and he says, "I'm not sure I'm ready for this."

"It's high time. You've had too many narrow escapes."

Archie frowns. "I've still got a lot of assets that I want to put beyond the reach of the Chinese Communist Party. Hopefully I can still rescue some using the structures you and Dexter set up. If not, what the hell? It's only money. I've got enough put away that I'll be able to eat pretty well."

"That's the spirit." Pascual remembers Archie saying "I'll pay you a million dollars" and waits for him to raise the topic. But people are beckoning to Archie now, one of the men in uniform is picking up his suitcase, and Campbell is coming toward them. Archie has time only to turn to Pascual and say, "Thanks. You saved my life." He grips Pascual's hand briefly but fiercely, and then he is being spirited away through a door which closes behind him with a final clunk.

Campbell says, "Well, then. That's a good day's work."

Pascual turns to him. "You and I need to talk."

# 41

Pascual stands on his penthouse terrace, bemused by the spectacle before him: rooftops and greenery, the ordered chaos of Singapore stretching away south under a leaden sky to the ship-flecked strait and the very fringe of the vast archipelago beyond. A storm is coming, and soon the view will be obliterated by a pounding tropical rain.

He turns and paces slowly across the terrace to go back inside, pulling the sliding door shut. He goes into his living room and surveys the expertly coordinated suite of furniture, warm wood tones setting off the green of the carpet, carved figures in ivory and teak, abstract prints on the walls. He reaches down to turn on a lamp.

Enjoy it, he thinks. It's all yours, until the clock strikes midnight.

The doorbell rings.

Pascual stands with his hand on the doorknob, rehearsing his lines, reviewing his plan, regretting what there is to regret and steeling himself for what is to come. He pulls open the door to see Renata Taggart smiling at him. "Hello," she says.

She has never looked more spectacular, the hair flowing free, the flawless cinnamon skin and the midnight eyes irresistible, the trim figure draped in a burgundy jacket above sleek white jeans. "Welcome," says Pascual.

"Ooh, I like it," she says, coming into the living room. "Who did your decoration?"

"Don't ask me," says Pascual. "Dexter took care of it. He snapped his fingers and the next day I moved in." He waves her to a sofa. "Champagne?"

"Please. Did Dexter provide that as well?"

"He recommended a caterer," says Pascual, pulling the bottle from the ice bucket on the sideboard. "He could have provided hired help for the evening, too, but I thought it would be nicer to keep things *en famille*. I'll just throw everything in the sink and have someone come in tomorrow to clean up." Pascual eases the cork from the bottle of Krug Grande Cuvée and fills two flutes. He hands one to Renata and sits in an armchair at the end of the sofa. "Cheers."

"Cheers." She drinks. "I'm afraid Dexter's not going to be here. He had some family obligation to attend to. He sends his apologies."

The smile fades from Pascual's lips. "Actually, I knew that. I have to confess that Dexter and I set you up. I wanted us to have a little tête-à-tête this evening."

In the succeeding chill Renata stares at him, looking only slightly alarmed. She will be expecting the clumsy pass, Pascual thinks, the superannuated rake overestimating the appeal of money. She has no doubt fended off dirty old men before. "That wasn't very nice," says Renata.

"No." Pascual sets his champagne flute on the coffee table in front of the sofa. "But then neither was betraying Archie to the Guoanbu."

Her look hardens. In the silence the first drops of rain come tap-tap-tapping on the windows. Renata says, "You are delusional, Mr. Rose."

"I don't think so. That's the only explanation for why they were so close to us all the time."

The stare-down goes on for a few seconds, and then Renata leans forward to set her glass down. She stands with great dignity and says, "I am going to walk out of here now. I will expect an apology if you wish to have any dealings with me again."

Pascual nods. "You have my sincerest apologies. I hate to send a woman with such fine qualities to prison, but I'm afraid the authorities will insist."

Renata is completely still for a moment, and then she sits back down, crosses her legs and folds her hands in her lap. "What is it that you think you know?"

"I know that you have been pressured by the Chinese into spying on Dexter Fang. I think this probably began about the time Chee Dongfeng disappeared and the Guoanbu suspected he might come to his cousin for help. They looked for pressure points on Dexter Fang, and they found you."

The rain is in full spate now, drumming on the windows, and beyond the pool of lamplight enfolding Pascual and Renata, the room is dark. "You can't possibly prove that," she says.

"I don't have to. The circumstantial evidence is strong enough to get the most sluggish law enforcement agency to launch an investigation, and the Internal Security Department here does not have a reputation for sluggishness. I'm sure they won't have any trouble finding proof."

"What circumstantial evidence?"

Pascual takes a deep breath. "Well, let's see. The first thing that caught my attention was that business of the parking garage supposedly calling to get the plate numbers of Dexter's cars. I thought that was a pretty trivial matter to come to the attention of a woman in your exalted position. I thought surely that would be dealt with by somebody a couple of levels down. But what really got my attention was when you told Campbell the call had come in three days before, on Tuesday afternoon. I knew that was wrong because you had spent that whole afternoon with me. We came and looked at this place, as you may recall."

Renata's look is incredulous, then contemptuous. "So I was mistaken about the day."

"Maybe. Your call log would show it, one way or the other. Campbell could have checked that when he verified the number. But you never followed up with him, as he requested, and then we were overtaken by events and were off to Indonesia. So it never got checked. Maybe that's what you were counting on. But you could have just kept your mouth shut and let Campbell go on wondering how they identified Dexter's cars. An experienced liar knows you don't lie unless you really have to. My guess would be that you had to go and ask somebody for the license numbers so you could pass them to the Chinese, and you knew that would be remembered, so you came up with the cover story."

Renata has no response to that. She leans forward to pick up her champagne, takes a sip and says, "I'm starting to be entertained."

"I'm glad. The next thing I noticed was when we were at Halim's house, up in the highlands."

"Good God. You're not going to blame me for that bloodbath, I hope."

"Who else? Halim would hardly expose his own property to armed attack, whatever Archie suspected. No, I'm pretty sure they were tracking your phone."

"Nonsense." The word comes after a very slight hesitation. "We all had new phones, remember? Dexter handed out those hackproof phones Campbell had procured, what did he call them? The Katim phones."

"Yes. The fancy new jet-black Katim phones. And yet when I saw you using your phone at Halim's house that day, just before you and Dexter went back to Jakarta, you were jabbing at what looked like a good old-fashioned silver iPhone. It didn't strike me right away, but the penny dropped later. I don't think you were texting anybody. My guess would be that you were turning on whatever feature allowed the Guoanbu to track us. I think they probably gave you the phone, and I think you probably still had it when we got off that boat on Sulawesi, thinking Archie had drowned. That's why they were there waiting for us. You may still have it, for all I know."

Renata drinks champagne and gives him a long pensive look. Pascual tries to enjoy the view, but by this time he knows too much to be charmed. "Your theory is ridiculous," she says. "Are you suggesting I staged my own kidnapping?"

"What better way to deflect suspicion? Somebody would have to take a long, hard look at you before too long, after what happened up in the highlands. You moved to pre-empt that. What I wondered when I heard their terms was how they were aware of the extent of your knowledge about Dexter's affairs. That was supposedly the key reason they wanted you, because you could bring him down. How did they know you were so important? Who gave a Chinese spy agency that much inside knowledge of the Fang family office? You seemed like the leading candidate to me."

Renata sips champagne. "Why, Mr. Rose? Why on earth would I betray Mr. Fang?"

"Because if you didn't, the Guoanbu would turn over to the Singapore financial authorities evidence of your implication in laundering funds from the 1MDB scandal in Malaysia."

That freezes her for the first time, and for a long moment they simply stare at each other as the rain thrums. Finally Renata sets her glass down on the table again and says, "And how did you unearth that supposedly incriminating nugget, if I may ask?"

"I did what everyone does now. I just started Googling. I started with your fiancé, Mr. Fernandes. I knew he was a lawyer, and Fernandes is a common surname for people from Goa in India. It didn't take me too much time to find a link between him and my dead Indian lawyer, Balasubramanian. They were both members of the Singapore Indian Lawyers' Guild, and you can see them smiling at the camera on the Guild's website. And there it was, a link to you."

"Oh, please. That's all you have?"

"Not quite. Balasubramanian was killed to stop him from divulging information about someone in Dexter's circle. What was the information? I wondered where you worked before Dexter took you on. And there you were, profiled in an article in the *Straits Times* four years ago, as an up-and-coming financial whiz at a hedge fund called Asia Hawk Capital. And bingo, it turns out that the former general partner, a fellow called Emerson Chen, got out of town just ahead of an indictment last year and is believed to be in China. There's no indication that you were implicated, but the article says you were Chen's right-hand woman, quote-unquote. Much like the position you hold with Dexter, probably. I imagine Balasubramanian's information was something he got from a fellow lawyer. Maybe someone at the Indian Lawyers' Guild let slip over one too many drinks one night that Rohan Fernandes's girlfriend had consulted him, worried about her exposure to the scandal. Your fiancé would have steered you to somebody in his network, probably. Two plus two makes four, Renata. They came and made you an offer you couldn't refuse."

"That's a lot of clever guesswork. But it's not even close to proof."

"I'll bet Balasubramanian had proof. They wouldn't have killed him unless he'd gotten something concrete. He was a CIA asset. That means he had to have sources that produced information the agency would value. And one of them probably told him something about the pretty Eurasian woman talking with the known Guoanbu agent in the back room of the restaurant, or on the treadmill at the gym, or wherever. Am I close?"

Renata finally blinks. Her chest rises and falls as she sighs. "Close. Actually it was the masseuse at the spa. Those cozy little massage rooms are quite good for confidential conversations." Her eyes narrow. "So why am I here tonight, Mr. Rose?"

"You're here so we can work out a nice, amicable blackmail arrangement." As Pascual sits watching Renata's expression shade to disgust, he feels the old familiar tide of self-loathing rising inside him. Better a ruthless blackmailer than a dirty old man, he thinks, reaching for his glass.

"What are your terms?" Renata says.

"Simple. I get a cut of everything you and Dexter manage to siphon out of China. Archie owes me that much. In return, nobody from the Internal Security Department or the Monetary Authority of Singapore ever needs to find out how you did your best to help the Guoanbu catch Archie Chee and take him back to China to be killed."

Her chin rises a little. "Why on earth do you need me? You're the beneficial owner of those accounts."

"Not for long. My deal with the CIA has always been that I give them the account numbers and passwords and so forth and then they change all the passwords and do whatever they want to do with the accounts until the next time they need me. I'm supposed to get paid but I usually get stiffed, and I'm tired of it. With your kind assistance, I can set up a discreet foundation, in Liechtenstein or some place like that, to take a little trickle of Archie's money and provide me with a comfortable retirement. And nobody will ever be the wiser." Pascual drains his glass and sets it down.

Renata muses on that for what seems a long time, looking down her nose at Pascual, and then her look softens. She leans forward again to set her glass on the table. She rises, walks to the window at the end of the room, and stands looking out at the rain for a moment, arms folded. She wheels and addresses Pascual. "Let me suggest something a little more congenial," she says.

"Such as?" Pascual stands and goes to join her at the window.

In the dim light Renata's face is close to his. "Why limit yourself to what little we can salvage of Archie's money? Dexter Fang's pockets are so deep he won't miss three fortunes, much less two modest ones. Working together, we could feather two nests instead of one. Neither Dexter nor the CIA would ever have to know."

Pascual wants to believe her, gazing into eyes so dark he cannot tell iris from pupil. "Tell me more."

Renata leans a little closer. "First you're going to have to forget this blackmail nonsense. It really would have to be working together. An adversary relationship is much less stable than one based on trust."

Pascual says, "And what would be the basis of this trust?"

Renata smiles, and as Pascual feels the full force of her best, sultriest, wickedest smile, he can hear the muted screams of his better judgment as it pounds on the door of the little room where he has tried to lock it away. Before he knows what is happening, her mouth is on his and he is locked in an embrace with the object of his lustful dreams, eyes closed and sensations of taste, smell and touch taking over.

She makes it last. When she pulls back at last she contrives to look demure and a little abashed. "There could be other benefits," she says.

Pascual knows exactly what is happening, and he congratulates himself on his wisdom and clarity of vision. Nonetheless he says, "Count me in."

"Very well." Renata puts her hand on his cheek, caresses it, runs her thumb over his lips. Pascual pulls her body tight against his, not entirely sure where this is going or where he wants it to go, but determined to make the most of whatever role she wants him to play. "I haven't seen the bedroom," she says, softly.

"Well. Let me show it to you." This is the last thing Pascual expected to happen tonight, and he is flying blind. Be a sport but keep your head, he thinks, even if you can't keep your pants on. He urges her toward the door to the bedroom.

She resists gently, halting him. "Wait for me there. I am going to powder my nose." She kisses him lightly and pulls away, trailing a hand across his cheek.

Pascual watches her walk toward the guest bathroom just off the entry hall, admiring the female form working under the clothes he is apparently about to see removed, stunned at the turn of events. You are no longer in control, he thinks. Is this a problem?

Pascual goes into the bedroom and sits on the bed, thinking furiously. At least take your shoes off, he thinks, and tears at the laces. More to the point, he wonders if what is about to happen will advance the agenda he had for the evening or fatally undermine it. Fleetingly he thinks of Sara far away, who has a forgiving nature and has tolerated a flexible notion of marriage for many years. You are a scoundrel, he thinks. You fancied yourself a cunning blackmailer and she has made a dirty old man of you.

Pascual hears the turn of a latch, a door swinging open. He freezes with shoe in hand, thinking that did not sound like the door to the bathroom. Steps come slowly over the tiles, and they do not sound like Renata's. All of Pascual's alarm bells go off at once.

You are a fool, he thinks.

Pascual comes out of the bedroom to see Renata heading out the door, slinging her purse over her shoulder, and a Chinese man advancing with steady step and implacable gaze across the carpeted living room. This one he has also seen before, and if his partner is not with him tonight it will be because he is recovering from second-degree burns somewhere. This is the young and fit one, and as if that were not enough he is also the one equipped with an automatic pistol with a six-inch-long suppressor affixed to the barrel.

"Campbell!" Pascual shouts the name at the top of his lungs. "Get in here!" Pascual retreats, in full panic mode. He dashes back through the bedroom into the master bathroom. As he whirls to slam the door behind him he sees the assassin just inside the bedroom, raising the pistol. Pascual ducks to the floor, his weight shoving the door home as a shot comes through it just above his head with a loud thwack and a little shower of debris.

He flips the lever to lock the door and rolls to the side, crouching at the base of the wall and looking for shelter.

Bathtub, thinks Pascual. Will it stop a bullet? The door demonstrably will not. He coils for a spring into the tub. The door handle rattles once and then there is a tremendous metallic clang as the door shivers in its frame.

Not that, thinks Pascual. Shooting out the lock is a cinematic trick that never works. A second impact displaces the latch plate slightly with a splintering of wood, and Pascual revises his judgment. The gunman is going to be inside in under five seconds, and Pascual needs to make a fast decision and the right one.

There is a vanity to the left of the door, a sink and a mirror. Moving silently on stockinged feet, Pascual crosses the bathroom as the door shakes in its frame from the force of a kick, the lock almost giving way, and hops up onto the vanity, crouching pressed against the wall next to the door. When the door bursts open the gunman will look straight ahead at the bathtub first before he sees Pascual out of the corner of his eye, possibly giving Pascual the second he needs to make use of this vase full of dried flowers Dexter's decorator has thoughtfully left on the vanity. The door gives way with a splintering crash.

Pascual starts his swing when he sees the suppressor come through the door, so that when the gunman's face appears it is far too late for any useful reaction. The vase and a couple of facial bones shatter simultaneously. Pascual takes advantage of the man's momentary sensory overload to jump down onto the floor, knock the pistol hand aside and, with brute instinct and strength amplified by adrenaline, jab with the razor edge of the broken vase and cut the man's throat as he totters in the doorway.

■ ■ ■ ■

"Where's Renata?" Pascual sits on the sofa gazing at nothing. The rain has stopped and night has fallen.

Campbell slips his phone into a pocket and says, "Looking for a place to hide, if she has any sense. Were we supposed to stop her? You were screaming for us to come help you."

"What took you so long to get here? He could have killed me."

"We were here in less than thirty seconds. You'd killed him by that time."

"I was lucky."

"Or very good." Campbell frowns down at him. "Don't worry about her. You're going to have your hands full with the police."

A man comes out of the bedroom, where he has been surveying the appalling scene, great dollops of blood staining the walls and the carpet. He is Chinese, younger than Campbell but with the same grim, concentrated look. He says, "The case for self-defense should be clear with all those gunshots. It would be better if there were audible evidence of the gunman's presence, but I didn't hear any."

Pascual says, "You got it all on tape, didn't you?"

Campbell nods. "We don't use tape anymore, but yes, we did. Loud and clear. I must say, you were very convincing. If I hadn't known better, I'd have said you really were intending to blackmail her."

"I was trying to get her to say something explicit. Something you could use."

The Chinese man says, "We got enough. None of this is for use in court. We just needed enough to convince my bosses to start a proper investigation. We'll pick her up and take it from there."

Campbell gives a single slow shake of the head. "I'd say she got rather explicit. I was starting to get embarrassed, to tell you the truth. It would have made for an interesting transcript."

The Chinese says, "Things would have gotten really interesting if we'd had you wired up the way we used to do it. Maybe that was her way of strip-searching you."

Pascual fails to appreciate the humor; he is reeling from extremes of stimulation in the past half hour. He wonders where he is going to sleep tonight when the police are finally done with him. "No doubt that's all it was."

# 43

"No charges will be brought in the killing of the Chinese national Gao Bo, as it was clearly a case of self-defense. There is insufficient evidence to charge anyone in the case of the murder of Basil Balasubramanian, though your account and the footage from the security cameras and certain circumstantial evidence strongly suggest that Gao Bo and his partner Deng Jun Hie, who has fled the country and returned to China, were responsible for that killing. You have apparently violated no laws in Singapore, though your reluctance to come forward in the case of Balasubramanian's death unnecessarily hindered the investigation."

"I was afraid," says Pascual, not untruthfully. His stomach is knotted tight, and consecutive nights of insomnia have left him drained and on edge, the psychic fallout from diverse traumatic episodes beginning to tell on him.

The Deputy Commissioner of Police in charge of the Singapore Police Force CID gives him a long skeptical look across the table. "I shouldn't wonder," he says. "You seem to lead a fairly high-risk lifestyle."

"Not by choice," says Pascual.

The skeptical look goes carefully blank. "In addition there is the question of your apparent use of two different passports to enter Singapore. The system flagged a suspicious resemblance between the photos of Pascual Rose and someone called Lester Gray. There are some security officials who are very interested in talking to you, but there has been . . . intervention on your behalf by a certain foreign agency. In the absence of viable criminal charges against you, the best solution for all concerned would seem to be for you to leave the country as quickly as possible. Your visa expires in sixty-nine days, but I would recommend that you depart as soon as possible. I will give you three days. If you have not left by that time, I will ask the Minister for Home Affairs to initiate deportation procedures."

"That won't be necessary," says the man at Pascual's elbow. He is Chinese, nattily attired in a sleek linen suit, impeccably groomed. "Thank you, Commissioner. I will make sure my client complies with your suggestion." He stands and beckons to Pascual.

In the hall outside, the lawyer hands Pascual off to Campbell. "Get him on an airplane as soon as you can," the lawyer says. Campbell nods and takes Pascual by the arm.

In the BMW, pulling into traffic, Campbell says, "Fang wants to see you."

"Any news of Renata?"

"Forget about her, mate. No future in that relationship."

"Don't I know it. But she laid a kiss on me I'll never forget while she was setting me up to be killed. That gives me a personal interest."

Campbell laughs softly. "Well, you can indulge it by going to visit her at Changi Women's Prison when the trials are all over. She's going to be there for a while."

"How did they catch her?"

Campbell takes his eye off the road long enough to flash him a sharp look. "Nobody caught her. She turned herself in, this morning. Contacted the ISD, the counterintelligence people, and threw herself on their mercy."

"You're kidding."

"No. I think she finally realized what she'd done to herself. I'm sure the Guoanbu would have tried to get her out, if she'd wanted to go spend the rest of her life in China and work for them. But if she turned them down, she immediately became a liability to them, and that's not very healthy. At that point she had no good choices. Helping to set you up was a fatal mistake. She probably panicked, or maybe they just upped the pressure. Up to that point, all she'd committed was a few financial crimes and a little espionage, arguably not even against Singapore. But abetting murder, that's serious. They probably won't be able to convict her of capital murder, but with that and the other charges, I don't think she'll still have her looks when she gets out of prison."

"I am sorry to hear it," Pascual says quietly, and he means it. It seems a harsh fate for a good Anglican girl gone astray. He is sad for a moment, and then he remembers the six-inch suppressor coming through the doorway and is less sad.

In Fang's office the view is unchanged, except for the man who sits in the chair where Pascual first sat three weeks ago.

Pascual has never seen him before but knows who he is before he opens his mouth. "Mr. Rose," the man says. "I see we managed to spring you from the clutches of the Singapore police." He is American, fortyish, sandy-haired, blue-eyed and military in bearing, though dressed in a sober gray suit. "I'm Tom Carlson, pleased to meet you. I assume you were satisfied with the lawyer we provided?"

"He seemed to do all right. You must have a whole roster of them. How often do they get killed?"

Carlson waves a hand, casually. "Balasubramanian was problematic. He had great contacts, but he was also starting to develop a penchant for trying to monetize information. That's what got him killed, and I hope it will serve as an object lesson to any other assets we may develop here. So, are the cops done with you?"

"I've been given three days to get out of the country."

"That's pretty generous. We can have you on the seven-fifteen flight to Dubai tonight. I understand you have the return ticket open."

"I do. What about my money?"

Carlson frowns. "Ah, yes. The money. Well, we have to discuss that."

"There's nothing to discuss. I signed a contract. I'm not sure why they told you to throw me under the bus, but before I came out here I signed a contract. Call Langley if you don't believe me. I did what I was told to do, and you owe me a million dollars. Payable on completion of services, it said."

"Well, now. I can only tell you what I was told by those same people in Langley you want me to consult. You may recall that the contract also included a clause that said something along the lines of, should the contractor fail to preserve operational security, the contract is null and void. And lo and behold, here we are in the middle of a full-blown, worldwide media storm, with wild speculation all around about these grisly killings and the involvement of a shady figure named Pascual Rose, with reputed ties to the CIA. I don't think that quite qualifies as maintaining operational security."

"That's what I'm paid for. The reputed but easily deniable ties. I'm a professional scapegoat."

"We don't owe you a penny." The stare Carlson levels at Pascual is the same one he has seen on the faces of Syrian secret police colonels and organized crime bosses. "We'll get you home, but that's the end of it. And don't even think about talking to the media. There are too many ways we can make your life miserable."

Pascual finds he is not surprised. He nods once or twice and turns to Dexter Fang, who has been watching this from behind his desk with a wary look. Fang has lost a little weight since Pascual first saw him, and he looks just a little bit less contented with his life. Pascual says, "These are the people you're dealing with, Dexter. If I were you I'd think twice before I got in bed with them again."

Dexter has the good grace to look embarrassed. He says to Carlson, "Mr. Rose was instrumental in getting my cousin to safety. I can testify to that. I think you should pay him what you said you would. At the very least, he deserves your heartfelt thanks. He certainly has mine."

Carlson nods and turns to Pascual with the mother of all insincere smiles. "Well, that I can certainly give you, Mr. Rose. You have the heartfelt thanks of the agency for your assistance."

"Nothing," says Pascual, rising to his feet. "Don't ask me for anything ever again." He turns to Fang. "Give Archie my regards and tell him for God's sake to watch his back."

▰▰▰▰

Pascual comes up out of the tunnel under the railroad tracks, crosses the promenade and goes a few steps out onto the beach. A few late-afternoon bathers are splashing in the tepid Mediterranean waves; others are lying on the sand, kicking a ball back and forth, sunning their paunches or gazing out to sea. He wanders toward the water's edge, feeling for an elusive sense of contentment he vaguely remembers. Heaven is where you are, Pascual thinks, but he has learned that hell can also be where you are, and he has yet to recover.

Pascual turns to see a woman emerging from the tunnel. Heaven is where you are, he revises, as long as Sara is there. He has to catch his breath, watching her come over the sand toward him, carrying her sandals. "You came back," she says.

"*Vida mía.*" The embrace lasts for a long time, and unlike the last clinch Pascual was in, this one is food, air, water, life itself. Sara pulls away at last, dark Gypsy eyes glistening and hair blowing in her face, and says, "Can you explain something to me?"

"What?"

"Can you explain why one million euros suddenly appeared in my bank account two days ago?"

Stunned, Pascual stands listening to laughter, the murmur of the waves, traffic on the boulevard, the cries of seagulls. "What?"

"The payer is something called *Pomona Corporate Services*, based in the United States. I went to the bank and checked. It's legitimate."

Pascual laughs at her bewilderment, pulling her to him. "It's legitimate. You are a wealthy woman."

"Where did it come from?"

Pascual wheels her away from the water and toward home. "From the ends of the earth, my love. From a man who honors his obligations. You will have to pay taxes on it, of course. But tonight you are buying me dinner."

## acknowledgments

The author wishes to thank a number of people who generously shared their knowledge of life in Singapore and Indonesia and cast a critical eye on the author's attempts to depict it. This novel absolutely could not have been written without their help. Jake Jacobs, Lance Frey, Kenneth Tiong, Siok Farber and Rick Ross patrolled the Singapore beat, and Heru Handika was kind enough to critique the parts of the novel set in Indonesia. It should go without saying that any mistakes or implausibilities remaining are solely the fault of the author.

**Dominic Martell** was born in the United States and has spent most of his life there, but he has lived and traveled extensively in Latin America, Europe and the Middle East. He has worked as a teacher and a translator. The first three novels featuring repentant ex-terrorist Pascual March appeared in the 1990s, chronicling Pascual's quest for atonement in the chaotic early years of the post–Cold War period. A quarter of a century later, in the transformed landscape of the even more chaotic post-9/11 digitally connected world, Martell began to wonder what had become of Pascual and decided to bring him out of retirement.

PHOTO: KEVIN VALENTINE